Bright lights flicker in the dark evenings of summer. Pinpoints of hope float against the black descent of night. The sweetest of small and innocent creatures find their way through the shadows. Fireflies seem to dance on sheer air, illuminating the space between heartbeats.

Children give off a similar brave glow, despite the challenges of their young lives, and the lessons of childhood are often painful, the shedding of fragile wings in the gloam of an uncertain future. The stories in THE FIREFLY DANCE see that reality; the authors know that childhood is sweetly sad and sadly sweet, profound and deceptively easy to categorize, yet poignant to remember.

Phyllis Schieber's Sonya, a child of Holocaust survivors, is confronted with the responsibilities of her legacy when she has a poignant encounter with a classmate, another child of survivors, and her mother, in a local shop in their 1970's New York neighborhood.

Kathryn Magendie's Petey deals wryly with her family's move from the cool blue mountains of North Carolina to the hot flatlands of Texas.

Augusta Trobaugh's stoic Georgia boy leads us through his surreal encounter with a mysterious backwoods toddler who turns out to be anything but ordinary.

Sarah Addison Allen's indomitable Louise invites us inside her wistful yet wisely observant life in a small Appalachian town, after her father dies.

These are not stories of sentimental childhood memories, of funny escapades and simple emotions. These are small jewels reflecting the essence of what it means to grow up dancing among the shadows of life, carrying a brave, small beacon because you know that even the brightest days always, *always*, end in darkness.

The Firefly Dance

by

Sarah Addison Allen
Augusta Trobaugh
Kathryn Magendie
Phyllis Schieber

Bell Bridge Books

Copyrights

Bell Bridge Books
PO BOX 300921
Memphis, TN 38130
ISBN: 978-0-9841258-6-9

Bell Bridge Books is an Imprint of BelleBooks, Inc.

We at BelleBooks enjoy hearing from readers.
Visit our websites – www.BelleBooks.com and www.BellBridgeBooks.com.

10 9 8 7 6 5 4 3 2

Cover design: Debra Dixon
Interior design: Hank Smith
Photo credits:
landscape (manipulated) © Christophe.rolland1 | Dreamstime.com

:Lftd:01:

Table of Contents

The Firefly Dance

The Firefly Dance

Jewel-like immortal
does not boast of its length of years
but of the scintillating point of its moment.

The child ever dwells in the mystery of ageless time
unobscured by the dust of history.

Fireflies, excerpt, Rabindranath Tagore, 1861-1941, India

Phyllis Schieber

The Stocking Store

I was seventeen the last time I went with my mother to the Stocking Store. I have more important concerns now than the simple errands of childhood. I am busy protesting the war in Vietnam and listening to rock music. Martin Luther King and Robert Kennedy have both been murdered within a few months of each other. I am devastated by these losses, but I am also in love for the very first time. When I tie my hair back with a scarf, he says I look like a gypsy. Still, I say yes when my mother asks me to accompany her to the Stocking Store. I think she is even more surprised than I am.

I still call it the Stocking Store because I do not know it by any other name. We call the store where we buy all our buttons the Button Store, and the small cave-like shop that both repairs and sells umbrellas the Umbrella Store. I still long for the red umbrella with the pink ruffle and the appliquéd poodle with its rhinestone collar. I often dream about that umbrella. I can see myself twirling it before a crowd of admirers.

These small shops are part of our daily lives. The Cheese Store, the Pocketbook Store, the Hat Store, and the Toy Store are places that need no other identification. But it is the Stocking Store that I love best. It is in the Stocking Store that I first come to know exactly what it is that makes me different from others.

The women who work in the Stocking Store take special care of their hands. Their skin is smooth and supple. Their nail polish is never chipped. My mother tells me that these women sleep with white cotton gloves. Each night they apply scented lotions to their hands and then cover them with clean white cotton gloves. "Like surgeons," my mother says, holding her hands aloft to show me. My mother, Giselle, paints her own nails, but only for a special occasion. She promises me a real manicure if I stop biting them, but even this is not enough to persuade me.

My mother always likes Edith to wait on us. Edith paints her lips the same bright red as her nails. Her blonde hair is very short and straight. I do not know how old she is, but I know she is older than I and younger than my mother. I know this because she is not yet married, but she has already finished school. Edith likes my mother. I can tell by the way she smiles whenever we walk into the shop. "Mrs. Applebaum," Edith says. "It's always such a pleasure to see you and Sonya. What can I help you with today?" My mother almost always buys the same six pairs of stockings unless she needs a special color for a new holiday suit. Then she buys a pair with seams. Those are my favorite.

The shop is very small. The window display never changes. There are many mannequin hands positioned on pedestals. Each hand is covered with a different shade of stocking. All the hands look the same, except some are left hands and some are right hands. One hand has a huge emerald on its middle finger. Of course, the ring is an imitation, but I love the way the stone sparkles through the sheer nylon. All the fingernails of the hands are painted pink. I would have chosen a different color. I like the salmon color my mother uses.

Edith is the only salesgirl who wears a ring. I think she might be the one who insists on the emerald ring on the hand in the window. Edith wears her high school ring. It has an amethyst stone set in the center. "My birthstone," she tells us without our even asking. Edith tells us a lot of things without our even asking. I like the way she turns the ring so the stone faces her palm before she shows my mother the shade of the stocking. Edith knows my mother's size without asking. "The usual?" Edith always says. "Seven-and-a-half in Barely Beige. Right?" My mother nods. Then Edith turns behind the counter and opens a drawer marked: BARELY BEIGE. Throughout the store there are built-in drawers. They are deep and wide because they have to hold countless stocking boxes. I watch as Edith removes a slim blue box. There are six pairs to a box. She tears the blue paper seal and gently, gently parts the white tissue paper to reveal the delicate contents. She checks to make certain the stone on her ring faces the inside and then slips her hand into the stocking. Edith's skin is so white, so flawless, that it could have been the hand of the mannequin in the window.

"O.K.?" she says. "Six pairs of Barely Beige?"

My mother looks to me for approval. It is a mere formality. I know that she will buy the stockings regardless of what I think. I am always tempted by the display samples on the counter. I would have picked Bit of Black or Blushing Pink. Edith always waits for my consent. Then she arranges the stiff tissue paper and returns the blue seal to its original position. If you buy six pairs, you get the box. If you buy less than six pairs, they are lifted from their cardboard nest still in the tissue paper. Next, they are folded and put in an unmarked brown paper bag. The blue boxes are the most prized. I used to collect them and play Stocking Store at home. It feels like a very long time ago.

There are never any men in the Stocking Store. It is a sanctuary for women. In some ways it is like the beauty salon, but really different. There is always a great deal of activity in the beauty salon. And noise. The beauty parlor rumbles with the countless conversations that go on at one time. The Stocking Store is quiet. The loudest noise is the rustle of the tissue paper. Everyone speaks softly. Perhaps it is because the merchandise is so fine, almost gossamer in texture. "Like spider webs," my mother would say. The comparison is fitting. My mother is so rarely poetic that I enjoy this description and ask her to repeat it often. "What do you always call the stockings?" I say. She always smiles when I ask. "Spider webs," she says. And we are both pleased.

Now I think that the Stocking Store is old-fashioned. I wear dark colored tights and work boots. I have no use for the garter belts and panty girdles that my mother still insists on wearing. She resists the new panty hose even though they sell them at the Stocking Store. I agree to go with my mother today only because I have my eye on a pair of dark green tights that I want her to buy for me. They will go well with my new black Capezio ballet slippers.

Edith is long gone together with all the stores that have disappeared, one by one. We buy our umbrellas from street vendors or on sale at the big department stores. The Button Man has died. No one wanted his store. We go to Woolworth's now to buy new zippers or lace trim, but it's hard to find any buttons equal to the selection in the Button Store. Many things have changed, but many things have stayed the same. In some ways, I think I already know that there will be very few more trips to the Stocking Store.

We do not even know the name of the woman who waits on us. She does not know my mother's size or remember to ask after my father or brother. This woman does not remark on how much I've grown or what a young lady I have become. It is even more silent than ever in this once revered haven, but now it is because there are few customers.

"What can I help you with today?" the woman says.

"Barely Beige," my mother says. "Size seven and a half."

The woman is rough with the blue paper seal. She tears at the tissue paper thoughtlessly. She does not slip her hand into the stocking and dramatically pause for just the right amount of time.

"How many?" she says.

"Six," my mother answers.

Even though I do not collect the slim blue boxes any more, I am disappointed when the woman lifts the six pairs and proceeds to place them in a paper bag.

"I'd like the box, please," my mother says.

"The box?" the woman says.

My mother nods, but she is distracted by a small disturbance at the front of the store. I follow her gaze. Toby Weiss is speaking with great tenderness to a short, slightly stooped woman. At first, I think she must be Toby's grandmother.

"C'mon, Mama," Toby says. "It's too much for one day. Let's go home."

Toby hangs out with the fast crowd at school. We are in the same grade. We have gym, history and French together. I always see her smoking in front of school in the morning. Now she looks towards me and nods imperceptibly. I have heard stories that her mother was a bit odd, but I have never seen her before. Toby's father attends all the school functions alone.

Toby's mother speaks in a heavily accented voice. I recognize that she must be from Poland. I am quite good at identifying accents. It is a game my brother and I often play.

"Sarale," Toby's mother says. "Pinch your cheeks before the morning selection. If you look able to work, they won't take you. Pinch your cheeks. Here. Let me show you."

Toby bends at the knee and leans in towards her mother, allowing her to touch her cheeks. I watch as Toby's mother extends a shaking hand and pinches Toby's cheek. Their movements are even. It is clear that they have done this many times before.

"Don't be afraid, Sarale. Mama will take care of you."

"Thank you, Mama," Toby says.

I am surprised at the sound of Toby's voice. It is so soft, so filled with sorrow. The Toby who sits in my classes is sullen and coarse. When she speaks, it is usually to call out something inappropriate.

"I told you, Sarale. It will be all right. Stay close to me, and it'll be all right."

Toby's mother smiles and pats Toby's cheek. Then I see the numbers on the inside of her thin white arm. The blue identification of the concentration camps is not an unfamiliar sight in the enclave of Holocaust survivors where I live in Washington Heights. I am more surprised to see people without numbers on their forearms than I am to see people with them. But the skin on Toby's mother's arm is as thin as parchment. I feel the need to look away from Toby and her mother. None of the people I know ever behave like Toby's mother. The people I know are lively and spirited. It often seems as if they have to make up for everything they lost. If they are sad, they keep it to themselves. They believe that in this way they are protecting their children from pain.

"What could I do?" Toby's mother says. "She insisted. 'Let me go with the transport, Mama. I am starving. There will be food there. Let me go.' What could I do? All the children went. I don't know any who came back. One woman hid her baby in a suitcase, but they found it. I could have saved my Sarale, but she didn't listen. What could I do?"

"You did the best you could, Mama," Toby says. "Come on now. Papa's waiting for us outside."

My mother steps forward as Toby leads her mother by the arm. Next to Toby's mother, my mother looks very young and very beautiful. She takes Toby's mother's face and looks into her eyes.

"*Siz nisto a shlecter mameh. Deigeh nisht. Azoi gait es,*" my mother says, reassuring her that there is no such thing as a bad mother. After all, my mother's gentle words comfortingly suggest, that's life, so what is there for one to do?

Toby's mother nods and begins to weep quietly, still nodding.

"*Azoi gait es,*" Toby's mother repeats.

Toby does not look at anyone. We watch as she leads her mother out the door and into her father's arms. Their car is double parked in front of the shop. Toby says something to her father and waits as her parents move with great effort towards the car. I wish she would leave with them, but she comes back into the shop to speak with us.

"She gets confused a lot," Toby says. "She was in a labor camp, Skarzysko. One of the *lucky* ones."

Toby laughs, but the sound is hard and bitter. Now she sounds like the Toby I know from school. *One of the lucky ones . . .* the phrase echoes in my head. My mother always tells my brother and me that *we* are the lucky ones.

"They took truckloads of children to Treblinka. Her daughter, my sister . . . well, half-sister, was on one of those trucks. Sarale. She was nine. My mother just can't get over it. She was all right when I was little. Sometimes she would call me Sarale by mistake, but that's pretty normal, I guess. Now I don't even think she knows who I am."

My mother reaches for Toby's hand, but she steps back.

"I'm all right," Toby says. "Really. It's just that no one talks about it. I mean, we're surrounded by it all the time, but we never talk about it." She turns to me. "*We* should really talk about it. About how it feels. About what it means, and how it makes us different."

Although my mother is witness to this entire exchange, she says nothing. Toby's father honks the horn, and she leaves without saying goodbye. My mother looks at me, and then looks away quickly. She pays for her stockings and thanks the nameless woman.

The Stocking Store closes the next month. My mother mentions this to me over breakfast one morning.

"No more Stocking Store," she says. "Gone. Forgotten."

She makes a whistling noise through her teeth.

"Ancient history," she says. "No one will remember that store twenty years from now. *Azoi gait es.*"

I know we are no longer talking about the Stocking Store. We have never talked about my responsibility before, and I am afraid. Yet, I know what to say, what will lessen my mother's concerns.

"*I'll* remember," I say.

She turns then, coffee pot poised in the air. This time she looks straight into my eyes and holds my gaze.

"Promise?" she says.

I nod solemnly and take the coffee pot from her hand.

"Sit," I tell her, and she listens. I pour her coffee. She takes her coffee black. I wait as she sips from her mug, drawing back sharply and causing me to start.

"Hot," she says.

"Careful," I warn her as I ease into my role as her protector.

"You, too," she says, almost reflexively.

I set the pot back on the stove. My mother is humming a familiar melody, something achingly poignant, something almost too painful to listen to one more time. Toby was right. We should really talk about it. We should give "it" a name and talk about what makes us different and whether or not we really are the lucky ones. I know we are the gatekeepers, but I don't think that's a matter of luck at all. I place my hand on my mother's shoulder. She looks up and smiles at me, but she keeps humming, and I smile back because to tell her that the melody breaks my heart would be more than she could bear. And, after all, it is also my job now to keep her safe, to tell her story, to remember the Stocking Store.

Kathryn Magendie

Petey

Chapter 1

Before Daddy and the other men lost their jobs at the textile mill, Petey Graham's parents had money for plenty of good groceries, every other year a beach vacation to the outer banks, and Momma went to the beauty parlor once a month. Sometimes Momma'd get Daddy to drive the whole family to Asheville, where Petey and her little brother would turn into an aching steaming whining heap of bore while Momma shopped for a dress, high-heels, and spiced perfume from J.C. Penney, or to Waechter's to find the perfect material to make her own dress. She'd buy Hill and Petey new clothes, even though they couldn't care less. Petey liked to wear her dungarees or pedal pushers and either Keds or flip flops. Hill said his fur was fine by him; he was always silly like that. The best part was when shopping was over and they'd stop to eat at S&W Cafeteria before driving back home to Haywood County.

When Momma worried about Daddy finding another job, Daddy said what he always said, "It'll all work out. I'll *make* it work out." Even though he said he was afraid more textile mills were on their last legs and he'd have to think what came next.

Momma answered as she always did, "I know you'll do what's right."

Meanwhile, he set out to do odd jobs painting houses and fixing porches, a temporary job at the local Esso filling station while Old Man Joe was out with pneumonia, at a diner washing dishes, and on Saturday evenings at a tourist shop pretending to be what the tourists thought was a Hillbilly. Those jobs didn't pay near what he'd been making, but he said it was better than nothing at all.

Petey had wondered what her parents would come up with for

their *Plan for the Future.* What they'd come up with was another baby on the way, and that didn't seem like much of a plan to Petey. She figured she was getting too old to be a good big sister to a new baby. Not like how it was being a big sister to Hill. Eleven and six were just-right ages for sister and brother to play together, and when she needed to, for her to boss him around. Momma said the baby coming was bad timing, but her words didn't fool Petey, for Momma had a sweet smile play on her lips, rubbing her stomach that held a tiny secret no one could see but Momma knew was there.

One day while Petey was lying in the hallway where it was cool and dark, pretending she was in a mysterious cave in a mysterious land, Petey overheard Daddy tell Momma some of the men were moving to Texas to work at a plant that was hiring lots of people.

Momma's voice squawked, "*Texas?*"

"I'm not saying that's what we'll have to do," Daddy said, "but we got a baby on the way, bills to pay. It's a good opportunity to learn a new trade and the money is decent."

"Just wait and see, Quinn. Things will work out here. Something will come up."

"Waiting and seeing doesn't work for a man with a family."

Petey jumped up and ran outside. She walked to the creek and sat with her back against a tulip poplar and thought about what she'd do when school was out and she had the whole summer to do whatever she wanted. She and her best-ever friend Angela were going to eat banana splits until they split and ride their bikes and go swimming. She decided to forget all about what Daddy said. She knew he'd never leave North Carolina.

There were more soup and beans for supper and not as much meat as before. Momma still baked because she *had* to—baking was a part of her, same as her arm or leg. Before they had to watch their nickels, she'd baked cakes, pies, cookies, yeasty sweet rolls with orange icing or regular icing, sweet and not-sweet cornbread, sourdough and rye and pumpernickel and white breads, cute petit fours, pastries with or without filling or nuts, tarts, and even pizza dough that she flipped into the air and twirled around. The neighbors loved Momma, for she gave away what her family couldn't eat (and they could eat a lot, Petey knew, a *whole* lot). Since Daddy'd lost his job, Momma still had to bake to stay happy, but not so much fancy and near to more practical.

Then it happened. The phone rang right after supper and Daddy rushed to answer it. After he'd talked a little while and then hung up, he called everyone into the living room.

He said, "I've taken a job and we're moving to Fort Worth, Texas."

"No, Quinn," Momma said, her hand flying to her mouth as though to stop more words from flying out.

"I'm sorry. I had to. There's nothing else to be done."

"But Daddy," Petey said, "we can't move. We just can't."

Hill let out a whimper, stood close to Petey, almost holding her hand but not quite.

"I don't like this, either. Don't make it harder on me than it already is." He then told Momma to start packing and he'd call the landlord to tell him they had to leave their house.

Momma shut herself in her bedroom so she could cry without anyone seeing her. She would not cry in front of people, especially her kids. She said a crying momma was scary to kids.

Daddy knocked on the door, calling to her, "Honey? Come on; it'll be okay. Beth?" Then he went outside and sat on the porch steps, his head in his hands.

Twenty-minutes later, Momma slipped out, washed her face in the bathroom, dialed up the phone, and said, "Let me speak to Mabel." She tapped her long rose-petal pink fingernail on the telephone table, then said, "I don't think I can stand it. We're moving away." She shook her head. "No, to Fort Worth . . . *Texas*." She sighed, then, "He has to do what he has to do, but still . . . I'm . . . I'm so upset! Leaving our home!" She nodded her head, said, "Okay. I will. I'll call you later," and hung up.

Momma had then put her hand on top of Petey's head. Where her hand lay felt warm and happy, even if the rest of Petey felt cold and sad. Then Momma went out to sit with Daddy on the steps. Petey watched as she leaned on Daddy and he put his arm around her. Petey turned away, ran out the back door, jumped on her bike, and pedaled as fast as she could, fast enough to let the wind push all her troubles away and out behind her.

Their Smoky Mountain valley was cool and misty when Daddy shoved the last box into the back of the station wagon. He gave the car a pat, as if it were a pet dog. Other than his kids and Momma, it was his most prided possession—the only car he'd ever bought brand spanking new. The night before they were to leave, he'd washed and waxed it, and told people who happened to walk by and stop to talk, even if they'd heard some story of it a million-gazillion times before, "Yup, a 1966 Ford Country Squire, only three years old and still looking like it did when I bought it new off the lot. It's the *premium* station wagon in the Ford line. Got a magic tailgate; see that?" Then he'd show how the tailgate opened out like a door instead of like his old station wagon with the two-piece thing where he'd have to raise up the window and lock it in.

Momma, Daddy, Petey, and Hill all climbed into the car, and without saying a word, Daddy backed out of the driveway. From the car window, Petey watched as they pulled out of their neighborhood, drove down Highway 19 past the farmhouse with the black barn and the horses nickering so sweet, as they left Haywood County and crossed over into Tennessee, and then as the mountains shrank smaller and smaller until they were out of her sight. She wondered if she'd ever see North Carolina again.

Her guts tied into knots and her bladder clinched tight so that she thought she needed to *go*. She asked Daddy to stop at a filling station, but when Petey went into the bathroom, all she really wanted to do was hide there.

There was a scratch at the door, as if a dog wanted her attention, then, "Hurry up, Puh-*toon*-ya!"

Petey didn't feel like a Petunia. But Momma had ideas about how she wanted things to be, like naming her kids after flowers and rocks and hills. Momma liked to name her kids after things from the earth. So far she had a Petunia and a Hill; she next wanted either a Violet or a Rock. Petey inspected the toilet seat to make sure it was clean; it wasn't too bad and it wasn't too good.

"*Peteeeeeeey*, Daddy said he's going to leave you here and you'll have to go home with another family. Daddy *said*."

She began layering toilet paper over the seat.

"You hear me, stink-breath? I *said* Daddy's *leaving* you."

"I heard you! I'll be there when I'm done, baggy-britches."

The sounds of her brother's feet thundered off on the gravel, and his voice shrieked loud, "Daaaadyyyy, Petey said she's coming. You better not leave her!" He then laughed big and loud.

She heard Daddy laugh, the station wagon door slammed, and the engine revved and slowed, revved and slowed, like he always did when he teased about leaving one of them behind. The sounds of the revving stopped, and Petey could picture Daddy sitting with his hands on the steering wheel while he waited. He'd check the time on Grandpa's old watch on a chain, then put his hands back on the steering wheel.

Petey eyed the toilet paper, wondering if it was enough to keep germs off her bare behind, but she wasn't quite ready to *go*. There was a dirty mirror in the bathroom. Petey made sure she did not even take a peek into it. Momma was always getting onto Petey for messy hair, smudges on her face, her clothes not buttoned right. But Petey couldn't, wouldn't, look. Without using the mirror, Petey pulled her hair out of the band, caught it up as smooth as she could, and redid her ponytail. She didn't need a mirror to do something she could do without looking since she was five years old. She didn't care about her hair the way Momma cared about hers, any ole way.

Momma said her own hair was meant to be on a palomino horse's tail and not on a woman's head. Petey thought Momma's hair was gorgeous and alive, and could imagine it trailing out behind her as she ran, like a horse's mane and tail trailed out so pretty as it galloped. Petey's hair was more like her daddy's, soft and shiny but plain ole brown. Petey pulled down her shorts and underpants, sat on the layers of toilet paper, and waited.

More scritching and scratching. "What are you *doing* in there?"

"Beat it, stupid-idiot."

"Are you teetle tee tee teeing?"

"None your beez wax."

"Teetle teetle, Petey's teetle tee tee teeing!"

"I'm going to jerk a knot in your tail if you don't get away from that door."

"Ha! You won't catch me. I'm swift and thunderous on my paws."

"*Get . . . a . . . way!*"

When she was sure he was gone, she tried to pee. All she squeezed out was a trickle. She fixed her shorts and flushed, but not all the toilet paper went into the bowl. Petey kicked at it, and most of it fell into the water. She flushed again and went to the sink. While washing up, she kept her eyes on her hands. She didn't want to see what was behind her in the mirror, watching her, waiting for its chance to rip her apart. Like in the scary movie a neighbor girl had watched when she stayed with Petey and Hill, while their parents visited Grandma in the hospital for her appendix surgery. The girl had told Petey to go to bed, but Petey had sneaked back to the living room door to watch the TV screen.

In the movie, there was a man who looked into a mirror and saw something behind him, but when he turned around nothing was there.

Later, he checked another mirror and he saw it even closer, and again when he turned around nothing was there. It kept happening in different places with different mirrors, until finally the man couldn't turn away. A horrid thing came closer and closer and closer and the man kept watching it in the mirror—closer closer closer—the man's mouth opened like he wanted to scream but couldn't. Finally, it was right behind him and set to tearing into him, ripping out his guts or maybe pulling off his face—actually Petey wasn't sure what it did to the man, since she'd closed her eyes tight and had only listened to the horrid screaming as she turned and ran back to her room and jumped under the covers.

Petey made herself forget about the screams in the movie, and looked around for something to dry her hands, and since there was nothing, she wiped her hands on her shorts. She flopped her shirt up and down, where water from the sink had splashed, and hummed while she read writing on the bathroom walls: *Tooties got a stinky butt and eats boogers; sandra likes girls and that means she's gonna go to H E Dubble L!; Mark + Jenny; I am not going to H E Double L, you are, you big fat liar who can't spell Double; I wanna to marry Ricky Malone and to have his babies; this bathroom stinks like chicken farts; Ricky Malone is MINE, not yours! He said so; if you rite on the bathroom wall that means you are a dum tenessee hick; Sally hates Marcy; Well, you just wrote on the wall and can't spell, so what does that make you?; Marcys gonna kick Sallys butt.*

Scratching scratching, then the rattling of the knob.

"Hold your horses, Hill."

"Momma said she has to get in there, Miss Priss Pot."

"All right. I *said* I'm coming."

"You've been in there for-*ever*. Like an hour."

"Have not."

"Well, you've been in there a long time and Momma says get out and I'm thirsty."

Petey opened the door and Hill pointed at her. "You got your britches and shirt wet. *Ha ha!* You are a stupid head with stupid wet on your stupid se-e-elf." He barked at her, gave a howl, and then ran to where the drinks and snacks were, jumping around like a jackrabbit with its little cotton tail on fire. Petey dug into her pocket for the money Daddy gave her.

"I'm as thirsty as a frog gone lost in the desert," Hill said.

Petey slid the change into the slots, wondering how long the snacks had been inside the machine, and if dust and bugs were on them. Maybe they'd be all right. Maybe they wouldn't be. Petey figured things could go either way; figured that was how the ole world would turn from then on.

Chapter 2

When Hill and Petey hopped back into the car with grape drinks, Nabs, and bags of chips—Petey liked Fritos and Hill liked BBQ potato chips—Daddy and Momma hushed up talking. She knew then they had been saying *serious stuff*. They never talked about *serious stuff* while Hill and Petey were in earshot. Back at home, she'd always sneaked to listen outside their bedroom to hear what was going on.

She'd heard them talk about leaving the mountains and even though boxes were filled with their things, and the big truck came with two men filling it with their things, and Daddy shook the landlord's hand and handed him the house keys, she'd wanted to believe he'd change his mind. She'd believed up until they'd climbed into the station wagon and sped off. She didn't understand about men and their work and doing things for their family. Wasn't staying where they were happy just as important as some ole job?

While she'd stood outside their door a few nights before they left, Daddy'd said, "It's a terrible thing for a man to lose his livelihood and have to make hard choices that involve his family."

"I'm tore up about it, too," Momma said.

"A man's got to be able to support his family. Or he isn't a man."

"You'll miss your mountains," Momma said. "And what about my momma? What will she do with me so far away? She'll miss her grandkids bad."

"I can't talk about this anymore. I just can't."

"All right, Quinn. I know you're doing your best. I trust you."

It was quiet for a bit, then Daddy'd said, "Beth! What are you doing?"

"The kids are outside . . ." Then Momma laughed, a funny-sounding laugh. It made Petey want to laugh, but then when she heard the bed squeak and Momma say, "Oh Quinn," Petey hightailed it out the front door, gagging and saying, "Eeeewww." She told her bike, which she used to pretend was her trusty steed until she grew out of it (mostly), "Romance is boring and gross." Her bike-steed always agreed with anything she said or thought. Petey would never be married unless maybe, just maybe when she was about thirty. Thirty was really old, so by then she'd have lived her life how she wanted to without anyone telling her what to do. And she'd not have babies slung around on her hip, all that crying and slobber all the live-long day and night. And she'd never have to move where she didn't want to.

"Petey? What're you thinking about?"

"Nothing."

"You can't think nothing, 'cause your brain is always thinking something."

"My brain is thinking you're a pain in my hind end."

Hill crunched chips with his mouth open, then said, where Petey could see all the mashed mess, "Nuh uh. You are, not me." He opened his mouth wider and stuck out his tongue to show her even more of the soggy half-eaten chips.

"Stop it; that's gross."

Hill laughed, took a swig of his drink. He drank with his mouth all the way around the bottle top, instead of pursing his lips and slurping it out like everyone else did. When he tipped back the bottle after drinking, bits of food floated inside.

Petey turned away and stared out of the car window at everything passing her by. Every so often, she'd notice Momma's palomino hair blowing in the wind. It blew longer than before, since Momma had been trimming her own hair instead of having it styled at the beauty parlor.

"Petey! Is my tongue purple-urple-super-duper-durple?" Hill stuck out his purplish tongue.

"A little bit."

Hill took a gulp of drink and then panted with his tongue dripping. He barked at her, once.

Petey rolled her eyes.

"When we get to *Fart* Worth will there be cowboys?"

"I dunno."

"How come you don't know?"

"I just don't. Now leave me be."

"Where we going to live? Will we live on a ranch and stuff?"

"No. We will not."

"Where then?"

"Do I look like a encyclopedia?"

"You sure are grouchy, Prissy Panties."

"You sure are ugly."

"Am not," Hill said. And he wasn't; Petey knew that. Her little brother had the cuteness disease and she didn't believe there was a cure for it. She wished she had the cuteness disease or even better the beautiful disease.

She wondered where they'd live, too. What their house would look like. What kinds of people Texas people were. What she would do with herself once there. How she'd do without her best-ever in the whole world friend.

She had ridden her bike to Angela's house to tell her they were moving. They'd held onto each other and cried, not even caring if they were big babies. Angela gave Petey a favorite fire-pink pen so she could write to her and think about Angela while doing so. When she'd ridden away from Angela, she kept turning around to wave, while Angela kept standing in her front yard waving back, until Petey turned a corner and couldn't see her anymore. The rest of the ride home felt like her body was one big toothache.

Up until the day they left, Petey woke at first light so she could visit all her secret places she went to be alone and think about things: the place she hunted for special rocks in the creek, at the switchback in the trail where she'd taken the empty hornet's nest and brought it home to hang in her room, under the locust tree where she watched the fawn and its momma tiptoe on their little hoofed feet to feed on the corn she threw about.

The day before they left, Grandma drove in from Watauga County. She pulled Petey into a hug and Petey smelled snuff, her grandma's sweet rose powder, and how her dress smelled like sunshine from hanging on the wire line Grandma stretched between two trees. Petey didn't cry. Hill cried, snuffling and whining like a puppy into Grandma's dress.

Grandma asked Momma and Daddy, "How you'uns going to stand it in all that heat and flat and with all those cowboys and bulls snorting and barbeque not even done the right way?" She couldn't figure on a place without mountains, and snow and quiet. She said, "That Texas will be loud as can be!" Not like how all they could hear from Grandma's house was birds, squirrels (she called them boomers), and the wind in the trees.

"Petey! Hey Petey! Petey! Watch this." Hill pulled his eyelids up, showing the red nasty inside.

"They're going to get stuck there."

"Nuh uh." He flipped them back down and blinked hard and fast.

"I saw a boy with his eyelids stuck like that forever, at school."

"Did not." Hill sat back as if he was tired of trying to get her attention.

Petey cracked her window and let the air blow in from outside. It didn't smell like home. She tore open and then licked the inside of the Frito's bag, hungry since she hadn't eaten breakfast. She'd tried, but her mean ole stomach had bucked up and made like it wanted to throw the food back.

Hill tore open his bag and did the same as she, except he lapped at his like a stray dog.

They ate the Nabs next, three each, the peanut butter and cracker sticking between their teeth all brown, orange, and nasty. Momma said to them. "We'll stop to eat at the next rest area."

Daddy said, "And everybody better do their pee-business while we're there. I don't want to stop any more'n I got to."

"If it were up to your daddy, kids, he'd drive all the way through without pause." Momma pushed Daddy on the shoulder, and Daddy said, "That I would, straight through, kazoom kazaam."

When it seemed they'd driven and driven and driven and Petey's stomach was whining with hunger, Momma pointed to a rest stop sign. "Don't forget to stop."

"Well, I *am* hungry for those sandwiches," Daddy said.

"What we got to eat?" asked Hill.

"Peanut butter and apple butter sandwiches." Momma had made the apple butter and the bread herself. Daddy said she'd have made the peanut butter if she had a mind to. Petey liked Jiff the best, creamy not crunchy. The only time she liked crunchy peanut butter was when Momma put it on apples—and Petey would only eat North Carolina apples, period period at the end of her sentence period.

Daddy parked, they found a nice picnic table, and from a grocery bag, Momma took out sandwiches wrapped in wax paper. There were still other things in the bag, like more bread, salt, pepper, tomatoes, and whatever else Momma had packed inside. The tomatoes Momma had picked from her garden before they left. She kept what she could and gave the rest to their neighbor, and the neighbor said they couldn't believe such a fine family had to go way down south in the flatland. Then they stood around talking about how Petey's family wasn't the only ones; there were others who had to move away, too.

Momma wrote a note about her garden to the people who were moving into their house, how the tomatoes grew, and the beans, and squash, and melons. She told them about the wild blackberries and the apple tree. She told them about the coon she fed, the funny white possum that came round, the hummingbirds that buzzed the feeder, and about the other birds—grosbeak, goldfinch, cardinal, nuthatch, titmouse (Hill always giggled over that bird name, his hand over his mouth), sparrows, and all the rest. She wrote them about taking in the feeders at night so the bears wouldn't get to them. And she wrote about how nice the neighborhood was, and how Haywood County was the best place to raise children.

Petey wanted to write the people moving into their house how much she hated them and why didn't they go back to where they belonged instead of living in *her* house. Even if it wasn't hers right out, Daddy had rented it since Hill was born—six years—and he had talked about buying it from the owners once he saved enough.

In between bite-and-swallows of sandwich, Daddy was telling Hill how Texas used to be Mexico's but people from the states wanted Texas for their own. There was a famous Battle of the Alamo where the Mexican army beat the United States Texan people, and that's why the Texans cry out "Remember the Alamo!" He went on to tell about other fighting and arguments and settlements. It was sort of interesting, and she was sure Texas people liked their history just fine. But Petey liked North Carolina history because it was her history of where she was born.

Petey knew Bath was the first town in North Carolina, and how Blackbeard the Pirate was killed at the North Carolina coast. She especially liked to read about girls in history. How Sarah Malinda Pritchard Blalock cut her hair and wore men's clothes so she could join the army and was the only girl soldier in the Civil War, far as anyone knew anyhow. There were first girl lawyers and doctors from North Carolina, and a first free slave girl to get a degree, and all kinds of things girls did that made Petey proud to be one herself.

Daddy was saying, ". . . and that Texas barbeque. And steaks and Texas-Mexican food. Texans love their beef and their Tex Mex. My new boss said there's a restaurant on near-bouts every corner that we can try."

"And pray tell what money you'll find for restaurants?" Soon as Momma said that, her face turned red and Petey knew she was sorry for her mouth speaking before she thought of the hurt it'd cause. She said, "I'm sorry, Quinn."

"It's okay," Daddy said, but he looked sad.

Momma had then leaned over and kissed Daddy's cheek. He stroked her hand, picked it up and kissed it. Petey turned her head away; it hurt too much to see how Daddy all of a sudden didn't look big and strong and Momma all of a sudden didn't look as if she could wrestle a problem down and make it behave right. Petey had squeezed shut her eyes and when she opened them, her parents were back to the way she wanted them to be, her regular parents.

Daddy then jumped up, scaring Petey out of her thoughts, hugged Petey tight, twirled her around, and pulled on her long ponytail, while she cried, "*Stop it,* Daddy." All the while, she secretly loved the way he teased and twirled her.

Hill ran off, peanut butter stuck to his face, his sneakers kicking up just-mown grass. He barked at dogs doing their business or sniffing around in the grass. If the dogs came too close, he growled at them. People stared and pointed at him. Momma called sharp to him to stop and he did. He always listened to Momma; he said she was the alpha dog.

When they piled back into the car, Daddy turned up the radio and tried to find a station that played his favorite music—Etta Baker, North Carolina Ramblers, or the fastest fingers in the whole world, Raymond Fairchild, or anyone else who played good traveling music. He instead had to tune to a country-western station. Petey hated all that singing about tears in beers and wives in another man's arms and trucks that were a fella's best friend, next to beer or Old Crow or Jack Daniels.

When it was dark and everyone was stone-tired of being stuck inside the car, Daddy stopped at a rickety motel in Arkansas with a sign that blinked on and off with some of the letters not blinking so it read ACAN Y instead of VACANCY. Daddy went inside to pay for the room, soon was back with a key, and drove around to room number 12.

Inside their room, Petey checked the sheets like Grandma had told her to. Grandma said if they weren't "white as cloud nine" then Petey should call the front desk and make someone come give everyone clean sheets pronto. Grandma told a story about how once she stayed in a hotel where the bedbugs had bitten all over her legs, and that was why she always said, "Good Night; sleep tight; don't let the bed bugs bite," with an extra *oomph* because she *knew*. Where Grandma lived in Watauga County wasn't very far from Petey, but it was way far from Arkansas, and a trip to the moon away from Fort

Worth, Texas.

The Arkansas sheets were nice and white, smelled like spring, and were softer and thicker than most sheets were. Momma fingered the top sheet. "I never did think a little motel like this would have such nice linens." She then set to making them a supper of tomato sandwiches with extra pepper, except for Hill, who said pepper made him feel too sneezy.

Daddy gave Petey and Hill the Fanta drinks he'd bought at the filling station down the road, along with two big pickles he broke in half.

Petey and Hill sat on their bed cross-legged to eat. Hill bared his teeth at Petey when she sat too close, and she rolled her eyes at him.

Momma and Daddy sat at a little table with two chairs and didn't talk much at all, and when they did, it was silly things like, "Just enough pepper on the tomatoes, Beth."

"Why thank you. Driving went well today, not much traffic;"

"Yup, lucked up so far and hope tomorrow is as lucky;"

"It was coming up a cloud earlier but looks like it passed us by;"

"Yes, yes, I know you hate riding in the rain, anymore."

Not so much like the easy laughing and talking about all kinds of things that went on at their supper table at home.

Daddy cut on the TV and up popped Mutual of Omaha's *Wild Kingdom*, one of Daddy's favorite shows. He still talked about the time Marlin Perkins wrestled the big snake in the water and near-abouts drowned and was near-abouts squeezed to death. During TV watching, Petey and Hill took turns brushing teeth. Momma had a suitcase with everyone's pajamas and a change of clothes, and Hill upended the whole thing searching for his underpants with puppies on them. He found them where they always had been since Momma packed them, rolled inside his pajamas. He hooted and held them up for Petey to see.

Daddy pointed to the rumpled clothes on the floor. "*Cri*-mon-ey, Hill! Look it what you done."

Momma only sighed and began folding all the things back in place.

"That boy is a *mess* in all sense of the word," Daddy said, then he laughed and ruffled Hill's hair.

After that, Petey had, just *had*, to give Hill a noogie on the head that their daddy had ruffled, to make him cry *uncle* for being a big pain in everyone's hind end. She grabbed him in a headlock and gave a polish to his head with her fist.

He growled and gnashed his teeth, and when she didn't stop, he cried, "I said *Uncle* in *dog*, stupid idiot. Can't you understand *dog*?"

"No I can't. Talk like a human why don't you?"

Hill barked at her.

Momma told them to settle it down or they'd be thrown out in the street. She sat on the bed and bounced on it, then rubbed her hands across her belly that grew bigger by the minute. Momma said, "Glad these beds are comfortable. I'm about wore out."

"I'm give out myself," Daddy said.

Petey grabbed a gown and clean white underpants, the underpants hidden in the gown so nobody could see them, and ran to the bathroom before Hill could.

Hill stomped to sit on the bed with Momma, his arms crossed over his chest. "You make me so mad, Petey! So mad!"

She only laughed at him and slammed the door, then set about checking the tub for bugs, and when there weren't any, filled the tub with warmish water. She was careful not to look anywhere near the mirror. Mirrors in strange places at night were the worst of all. In the movie, every time the man was in a strange place at night, everything was scarier.

While Petey washed, starting from her head and working to her toes, in the way Momma taught her, she thought about how Hill had told her she didn't need to be looking into mirrors anyhow. He said she had buggy fisheyes and fat fish lips. That's *exactly* how he said it, and his words still made her mad even though he laughed and poked her arm so his words wouldn't sting and be more like teasing.

I wish I was as lovely as a princess, Petey thought. She liked the word lovely even more than pretty or beautiful. Lovely was how a person acted along with how a person looked.

Petey scrubbed between her toes, a place Momma said everyone forgot about and they shouldn't, since dirt found its way there sure as anywhere else. Even though Petey didn't feel lovely, one time in the schoolyard Barry Burke had said she was "cute as a newborn kitten" and then he'd grabbed her and kissed her.

Right. On. The. Lips. She'd beat him up, even though secretly she liked the way his lips were soft against hers and how the kiss happened as short and light as a butterfly lighting and then flying away. She'd never see Barry Burke again, not that she cared any ole way. Not one bit. She stared down into the water, at how her legs seemed bent and funny. Everything felt strange.

After she dried off and put on her gown and clean underpants, Petey came out of the bathroom and Hill went in next, telling her, "Gosh-a-mighty, you take for-*ever* to do every littlest thing!" He was done with his bath faster than the Speedy Gonzales mouse—*He sort of looks like the Speedy Gonzales mouse*, Petey thought, giggling to herself.

All night Hill kicked his big sister. She knew he did it on purpose to get back at her for the noogie. She couldn't sleep anyway, so why did she care.

The next morning for breakfast, Momma handed them each an apple and a banana. Petey ate the fruit and asked her stomach to please keep it down there. It did, as a favor to her since she was so sad. Daddy turned in the key, and they set out again.

The land became flatter without hardly a bump to call a hill much less a mountain, and the wind was thick-hot compared to her cool mountain breezes. Petey tried not to look out the window but she couldn't help herself, curiosity took over her brain and made her watch everything as their 1966 Ford Country Squire flew down the highway to Texas.

Chapter 3

When Momma saw the house they were moving into, a two story with pimpled blue paint built by the side of scraggly woods with trees that hardly ought to be called trees at all, she put her hand on the side of her face and said, "Oh my word."

Daddy eased up under what must have been a carport before it turned into a house for birds and squirrels and rust and who knew what all else. "It's not that bad, is it?"

Momma didn't answer at first, then she took in a breath, let it out, and said, "At least it's a good-sized house."

Daddy turned off the engine, cleared his throat, said, "Only the top level is ours. The bottom level is rented out to someone else. But it has all the things a regular house has: a bathroom, kitchen, everything!" He said *everything!* as if it was the most wonderful thing in the big ole world, and maybe beyond to the Milky Way.

Momma sat quiet, hand flat on her belly, as if she was soothing the baby brother or sister who'd have to live in that house and not know how pretty the other one had been.

"It's temporary, until we catch up on things." He smoothed his fingers on the steering wheel. "The one who lives in the bottom part, Mr. Mendel said she's on vacation. Somewhere far away, he said, but couldn't recall." He turned to Momma. "Maybe you two will become friends."

Momma sat up tall and then turned to the backseat. "You kids stay outside until your daddy and I get things straight." They slipped out, walked across the yard, and up the iron steps. Petey could hear the steps rattle as they climbed.

Petey peeled her sweaty legs from the car seats (she thought some of her skin surely had been left behind), jumped out into a blazing furnace heat, said, "Whew," and let her tongue hang out as if she was a dying cow in a far away desert with camels. She humped her back and showed her teeth. Hill galloped, neighing and braying, then he sniffed the air. She laughed at him and he laughed back at her. His eyes near took up his whole face. She wondered if her eyes were wide as supper plates, too, like wild animals trapped and put in another place.

Hill ran across the yard, which had patches of dirt and not much grass, and Petey turned around in a circle to take it all in. She couldn't see any neighbors' houses, but they'd passed them set back from the road, along with a grocery, post office, and a run down playground with a chain across the gate. She walked by the lower level and tried to see into the window set in the door. She stepped closer, pretending to be minding her own beez-wax. The inside was dark, and just as Daddy said, it seemed no one was home. She sneaked up and peeked in, her face pressed to the window.

There was a kitchen and on top of the kitchen table was a big vase full of clear and colored marbles, with three feathers that stuck out at the top. The wall was painted a color that Petey couldn't quite make out, and there was a painting of the same vase and what was in it, except the painting wasn't very good. The refrigerator had bunches of magnets on the top part, the freezer part. When Petey pressed her face flatter against the glass, she could see where on the kitchen floor leading into another room stood a statue. Petey recognized it from a book; it was a Buddha. Petey had never seen a Buddha in a kitchen in her life.

Hill called out, "Petey, come see!"

She couldn't tear her eyes away, and wondered what else was inside, and who lived there, and why they'd have a Buddha on their kitchen floor.

"*Peeeeeteeey*! Hurry, come quick! Come see this here thing. I think it's a alien."

She ran over to where he was squatted, and squatted down with him. They both watched the ugliest bug she'd ever laid eyes on. It had a flat roundish body, and the tail curled up and over its back. She'd never seen a bug like that in the woods where they played back in North Carolina. When she explored for discoveries, she found things like bright orange salamanders, fat centipedes, bagworms hanging from their silk thread, webworms that Hill and Petey knocked a hole in so wasps could get in and eat the worms, and there were mean no-see-ums that ate up Petey's arms and legs, fireflies lighting up the night, but she'd seen nothing like the nasty thing Hill was excited over.

"What're you thinking, Petey?"

"I dunno." But she was thinking how that thing didn't look friendly one little bit; she knew that, sure as she knew lots of things. Like Fort Worth was too hot and too flat. Like once summer vacation was over, she'd be starting sixth grade at a school where she didn't know any kids at all. How her brother or sister would be born and not know what a mountain was. She asked him, "Where'd it come from?"

"I tumped over that rock, and he was under it."

"I wonder what kind it is."

"A alien." Hill picked up a twig to poke it. It turned towards him, curling its tail all jittery.

She picked up a twig and poked it, and it turned towards her.

Hill reached out towards it. She knocked away his hand. "It might bite, stupid idiot."

"Nuh uh. Can't bite me if I grab it by its tail, dumb head."

Hill reached out to pick it up by the tail, and next she knew, she was snatched back so hard, her teeth slammed together. Hill was flying backwards, too. Daddy stared down at the both of them.

"Are you two addled?" Daddy ran his hand through his hair, sending it up into spikes. "Scorpion's stingers are in their tail and got enough poison to kill a hundred kids. They zap you and in five seconds you're gone. Poof!" He meant business. "Stay away from scorpions and other things you don't know about, you hear?"

They both yes-sirred.

Daddy searched for the scorpion, kicking at the dirt and dried up leaves, flipping over rocks. When he didn't see it again, he turned back to where Hill and Petey were still sitting on the ground. "You kids be careful, you know how your momma gets to worrying." That meant he was worrying, too.

They nodded, and Daddy went back to unloading the car.

"Is a scorpion a alien?"

"It's a bug, Hill."

"I still think it looks like a alien."

"Do what Daddy said, so it won't sting you dead."

Hill ran off to explore more, letting out yips and barks. Petey didn't know what to do with herself, but she sure was glad to be alive and not dead and full of scorpion poison.

The moving truck rumbled up and two men jumped out talking and laughing, their big bellies blobbing around. Daddy laughed with them, and soon they were clapping each other on the back. Momma joined them, pointed to the truck, then to the house, put her hands on her hips and cocked her head. Daddy said something to Momma. The men looked from one to the other, then at each other and shrugged. Momma said something to Daddy, and then turned to go back up the stairs and into the house; she wasn't happy. Daddy hung his head for half a tiny bit of a second, then turned to help the men unload the truck.

Petey was itching to see what the house looked like inside, and wondered if she'd have a room like at home where she could gaze out the window at the mountains, except there weren't any mountains in Fort Worth. She lay on her back under a puny tree and imagined she was lying under the tulip poplar by the creek at home, listening to the water run by and the wind making the leaves wave so that peeks of sky winked at her. She pretended she was going to walk the trail to search for hawk feathers, or buckeyes to put in her pocket for luck, or for the wild turkeys that hid up to the last minute before they half-ran, half-flew up high into the full mountain woods.

Petey pulled up from the ground and went under the rusted iron stairs, peeked into the downstairs window again. She felt bad for being a snooper, and thought how embarrassing it'd be if the person really was home and caught her. As if that happened, she jerked back from the window and stood out in the dirt, kicking at it to send little dust storms into the hot air. Even the wind felt as if it blew out of an oven door.

"*Peeeteeeey*! Come play with me."

Because she was bored, and for no other reason *at all*, she ran to catch up with her little brother. They chased each other until the sweat ran into their eyes. He fell on all fours and howled like a wolf, running around her legs and sniffing her ankles.

"You are such a fool. Get up."

"Awoooooo!" He sniffed her leg, stuck out his tongue and touched it to the top of her foot.

"Yuck! What're you doing?"

"I was tasting you to see if you're tasty." He grinned, then said, "I'm a hungry wolf looking for something to eat. Maybe I should gobble your leg!" He grabbed her leg and pulled it to his gaping mouth.

Petey pulled away her leg and ran, laughing in fun-terror.

Hill was right at her heels, calling out, "Come back here. I won't eat but a bite of your leg and you can keep the rest."

When they tired of that, they sat with their backs each against a scrawny tree. Hill said wolves got hungry the same as people, and they can't help it if they eat a farmer's cow or goat. He said, "I'm so hungry I could eat a cow or goat, even the guts. I'd slurp up the guts like spah-guh-etti."

"That's nasty."

He jumped up and tried to climb the tree that wasn't even a good climbing tree at all.

Petey sat there, a lump of boring and sad.

When Momma called them in to eat supper, they raced up the stairs, feet clanging the iron, trying to see who could reach the top first. When Hill won, Petey said, "Well, I made the most noise."

Hill haw hawed; he knew he'd won fair and square.

Inside the door was the kitchen, just like downstairs. The kitchen wasn't dirty, but it sure looked wore out. The yellow paint was faded, and the curtains on the window were uglier than a baboon's behind, with pictures of fruit and vegetables all over them.

Petey peeked into the room next to the kitchen. It was the living room, painted yellow and with Venetian blinds pulled open. Their furniture stuck out like a bruise on a baby. She then washed her hands in the kitchen sink, and Hill copied her, even though at home Momma had told them not to do that.

Momma stirred canned chicken noodle soup in a pot and from the oven drifted the smell of something sweet. She already had sandwiches, cut in triangles, on the table. She pointed to the chairs, "Sit down, kids." She checked the oven, then next spooned out soup into two bowls and set the bowls in front of them. "When you're done, I'll show you both to your room."

"Room?" Petey asked.

Hill had a tomato sandwich halfway to his opened mouth, asked, "Room?" just as his sister had.

Momma huffed out her breath, then said, "Eat, you two." She went down the hall.

Petey thought she'd never tire of tomato sandwiches or tomato on her meat sandwiches. Momma's garden at home gave them plenty. From the looks of the dirt outside, she wasn't sure Momma could grow anything much.

They ate fast, slurping up the soup even though it was too hot for soup, stuffing the sandwiches into their mouths until their cheeks puffed out, red juice dribbling down their chins.

Petey said, "You look gross."

Hill answered, "You do, ugly beast."

"You are a worm's hind end."

"You're the stuff that comes out of it, out the . . . out the a-nus."

"That's disgusting."

Hill looked prideful at Petey, pleased as sweet iced punch to be disgusting.

They put their dishes into the sink, shoved each other enough to make their point, and then trudged off to find Momma.

Down the hall to the right was Momma and Daddy's bedroom, painted blueberry blue, with the baby cradle on what Petey knew would be Momma's side. A few more steps to the left was an ugly bathroom in the nastiest shade of green Petey had ever seen, even the ceiling was green. She said, "Yuck, it looks like a ugly sour pickle."

Hill stood in the doorway. "We got to pee and get baths in there?"

"Where else, you fool?"

Next door to the bathroom was a closet, and across from it to the right was another blue bedroom. They stepped inside. Momma had their beds already made up, with Petey's orange and white bedspread that Petey was so tired of she could yawn and vomit at the same time, and Hill's bedspread with scampering dogs all over it that he never was tired of. Her bed was to the right and Hill's to the left. Just as with the other rooms, furniture was crowded in. From the opened windows, Petey heard one of the movers say something, and then Daddy's rumbling voice answer, then the other mover said something, and Daddy answered him.

Momma stood on a chair, tacking a sheet to the ceiling to cut the room in two. She had that look that said no kids had better start their whining, even though Petey was getting ready to start up anyway. Momma said, "This will make it more private. Later I'll fix it better," and her voice sounded so thick with the about-to-cries, Petey shut her mouth and let it be. Momma stepped down from the chair, gave a little "Oh!," and held onto her stomach.

Petey ran to her, tried to help her sit. "Momma? Are you hurt?"

"I'm okay. Just wore to a frazzle, I guess." She eased down into the chair. "Maybe I better take a soak in the tub."

"I'll run you a tub," Petey said.

"Thank you, sweetie." Then she said to Hill, who looked from Petey to Momma and back again. "Go help your daddy."

"Oh-kay, doe-kay." He galloped off, shaking his head and neighing.

Petey hurried to the bathroom, said, "Ugh, it's ugly," and ran a tub for Momma. She searched through the box with BATHROOM written in black letters, and found Momma's lilac bubble bath. She poured a bit under the running water, sat on the toilet lid until the tub filled halfway, and then tested the water to make sure it wasn't too hot. When the tub was almost full enough, she went back for Momma, who sat on the chair holding her stomach, a far and away gaze settled in her eyes. Petey said, "Your tub's near-abouts ready."

"Thank you. I'll be there in a minute."

"I can help you walk."

"No, no. I'm fine." But she didn't get up. "Get the cobbler out of the oven for me, will you, please?"

Petey went back to the bathroom and turned off the water, tested it again to make sure it was okay, pulled the bubbles into high peaks and blew them up and around. The little rainbows were pretty and the lilac smell made Petey feel better. She left the bathroom, and in the kitchen took out the peach cobbler to cool, then went to the living room to stare out of the window. Daddy and Hill worked to get the last of the two boxes into the house. The truck was gone. From the way she could see it, some of their furniture hadn't made it into the house and she guessed the men were taking it. Maybe Daddy sold it to them. Whatever had happened, she hated not having all that was theirs.

She hated how it was all so final. She hated how they were stuck there.

She thought sure she heard Momma crying. Once she'd heard Momma tell Mabel something about being naked in the tub could set off crying more than any other time. Petey's own eyes burned and her throat and chest felt hot. Her whole body turned itchy and on fire.

She ran outside, down the steps, and tore off to the scraggly woods. Behind her she heard Hill calling out to her to come back, where was she going, wait for him, don't run away. If she could have, she'd have run all the way back to Haywood County. If she could have.

Chapter 4

Momma hurt so bad. Everyone wanted to hurry to the car, but Daddy had to help Momma and she couldn't move fast. Momma walked easy, as if walking normal would cause something awful to happen, and her face was bound up into a knot of worry. Daddy at first asked Petey to stay home with Hill and when she threw such a hissy fit, Daddy said she could come. Once they were all in the car, they rushed to the hospital, the whole car gone quiet.

Ever since moving day Momma had been feeling poor, and at first Petey thought it was because she felt like Petey did, missing home. Then one night, Petey heard Momma cry out to Daddy and Daddy hurry to their bedroom.

Petey sneaked out of her room and stood in the hallway.

Daddy asked, "Is this normal?"

Momma answered, "Not so I can figure."

"Should we go to the hospital?"

"I hate to worry over the money. Let me rest a spell and see."

"This worries me something fierce," Daddy said.

"If it gets worse or if I'm not feeling better by morning, we best go then."

When they were quiet, she peeked around the doorjamb. Momma and Daddy lay together in bed, the top of Momma's head tucked into the crook of Daddy's arm, her face into his chest. It had made Petey's heart feel funny.

After that, Momma had felt better for a while. Then Momma felt worse than ever.

At the hospital, they took Momma back to where Hill and Petey couldn't go, and all they could do was sit and sip orange drinks and wait. After a time, Daddy came out to them, hugged them hard, and then backed away, his arms down at his sides, his eyes like shined marbles.

Hill said, "What we got? A brother I hope. He can be in my wolf clan. Awooooooo!"

Petey stared at her daddy, waiting. She touched his sleeve.

"Daddy?"

Daddy took their hands and led them down the hall. Petey's ornery stomach was hollering at her again. Hill let out a sharp whine.

When they stepped into the room it was cold.

The nurse held the baby, said, "You kids aren't allowed in here, but I made an exception." She sniffed.

Daddy took the tiny baby from the nurse and cradled it. He said, "Poor little Rock."

"Momma?" Petey's skin tightened all around her face. Momma had died. She couldn't stand it. She couldn't. Her heart beat so hard it hurt her chest. Her veins bubbled up hot blood. Her brain exploded in a headache like she never had before. Petey reached out to touch her. Her skin was warm, and then Petey saw a tear slide down into Momma's ear. Petey was so relieved Momma was alive, she had to lean on the bed so she'd not fall to the floor.

Daddy touched Rock's tiny fingers and toes. "Oh, little fella. My little boy."

Momma held out her arms, reaching for Rock. Daddy gave him over and then he sat on the bed, put his hand over little Rock's head, his palm so big on that little head that it near disappeared under Daddy's touch.

The nurse said, "He's with God, poor little thing."

Momma held Rock close, and sang, "Sadly we sing and with tremulous breath, as we stand by the mystical stream; in the valley and by the dark river of death, and yet 'tis no more than a dream; only a dream, only a dream, of glory beyond the dark stream; how peaceful the slumber, how happy the waking, where death is only a dream."

It likened to tore Daddy to pieces so he stood and turned to the wall. Even the cranky nurse wiped her eyes and left the room.

Hill kept asking, "What's wrong with my little brother? Huh, Petey? What happened? Why's he not crying? Why's he blue like that? What's going on?" Until Petey told him to hush.

Daddy gave Petey nickels and dimes and told her to find the candy-bar machine. He whispered in her ear how she was to explain to Hill that Rock had gone to Jesus. She wasn't sure what she thought about God and Jesus herself, anymore. They both sure didn't seem to be around when people needed them most of all. Petey never said that aloud since it made people look funny and be upset.

Hill gobbled down his Hershey's bar. Petey took tiny bites of her Zero; her stomach kept giving little shivers and rolls. She watched the doctors and nurses come and go, with their stethoscopes around their necks, trays of medicine, their shoes squeaking on the shiny floors. One doctor stood talking to a man, and put his hand on the man's shoulder. The man shook his head *no* fast then slow, and the doctor stared down at his shoes. The man began to cry. Petey looked away and handed her Zero to Hill.

After Hill wolfed down the rest of her Zero bar, Petey told him that Rock had died.

"How can a little baby be died when it hasn't even lived any yet?"

"I dunno."

"My little ole brother didn't get no chance to do nothing I get to do."

Petey couldn't think of a thing to say, so she said what Daddy said, "He's gone to Jesus."

"What's Jesus want with my little brother, Petey?"

She shrugged, because she didn't know.

"I thought I'd have a little brother to play with."

"Me, too," Petey said.

"Don't seem right and I can't figure on it."

Petey couldn't either.

When Petey didn't think she could stand sitting there doing nothing one more second, Daddy finally came to get them. He brought Petey and Hill back home. Momma had to stay in the hospital. The house was quiet and sad. Daddy took the cradle and brought it downstairs. Petey watched out the window as he went around back towards the caterwompee storage shed where all the yard stuff was. When he came back in, he then packed up the baby's things in a box and brought the box out there. Daddy's shoulders were rounded in and his face took on age.

Later, when Petey had to go to the bathroom, she was even more afraid to look into the mirror, in the case the little baby brother was behind her, sad that it was dead while she was still alive. It would call out to her, begging her to come with him so he wouldn't be by himself. Petey had to stop thinking about it, hard hard hard. She put her mind on running creeks and cool breezes and the way the mists made blankets over the valley.

That night, Hill didn't want the sheet kept down and kept sniffling and snuffling tears until she said it was okay if he caught the sheet on the hook to keep it open between them. She secretly didn't mind, since she didn't want to feel alone, either.

Early the next morning before the sun hardly was up, Petey woke and saw that Hill had climbed into her bed sometime in the night. He hadn't done that since he was four and had a bad dream. She didn't say even half a word, didn't push him out and say, "Gross, Hill." She let him stay, and until the sun rose all the way, she lay there thinking about Momma holding little Rock.

When Momma came home everything felt strange like on a science fiction show. Little Rock had to be buried and Momma jumped out of her slow-motion trance to pull a conniption fit until Daddy said of course there was no question they'd go home to bury Rock. She didn't listen to Daddy saying "of course." She kept saying she'd not have her baby buried in a strange place. She said his spirit should come to rest in Haywood or Watauga counties; she'd accept either. And on she went with Daddy trying to calm her down. He said he'd arrange for everything, the funeral, talking to his new boss about being gone a few days, and for Momma not to worry, they'd bury Rock in Haywood County.

Petey couldn't figure if it made it worse to go again and know they had no home there or if it was worse never to see the mountains at all. When they drove back, Petey felt as if she held her breath until the station wagon curved round a bend and there her mountains rose up before her. Her throat found a big lump, and her stomach felt pushed in. Her heart thumped fast. She couldn't take away her eyes.

While there, they stayed at Uncle Zack's in Asheville. He lived by himself and didn't seem upset about it. He liked to tease Petey about boys and other silly things, but not in a mean way. When she was little, he'd swung her round and round until the whole world turned one big blur.

Angela wouldn't be going to the funeral since she was at a summer camp, so she'd not see her best-ever friend. Petey's grandma came to Haywood County and cried so much over Rock and her poor daughter who lost her baby that Daddy was afraid she'd have a heart attack and go to join Grandpa. Daddy's parents had long since passed on, but Daddy's other brothers and sister came from where they lived in Georgia, West Virginia, and Tennessee, and stood close by Daddy and Momma. Momma didn't have any brothers or sisters of her own.

The night before the burying, Petey slept on a pallet on one end of Uncle Zack's screened-in porch, with Hill at the other end. Uncle Zack's house was almost as small as Grandma's little ole shack. In Uncle Zack's bathroom, there was a long wide mirror and Petey had a hard time not seeing herself. She covered it with a towel when she had to go in there.

The next day, when the preacher said the service was over and Rock was to be lowered down, Momma fell on her knees and then pressed her face to the ground. It took Daddy and Uncle Zack to pull her up and away. Petey wanted to vomit all her breakfast. Hill stood so close to Petey, he kept knocking her sideways. He whimpered and grabbed her hand. She let him, that once. When they were back to Uncle Zack's where people were squeezed inside and spilled to outside, Daddy had to call Dr. Timothy from Asheville to give Momma something to help her calm down.

When it was time to drive back to Fort Worth, Petey ran behind her uncle's house, scooped up a handful of dirt and pebbles, and put them into a bag to carry home with her. The dirt and pebbles held the sparkles she'd always pretended were special magic dust.

She then again had to watch the mountains fade away, fade away, fade far far off and away.

Chapter 5

When Momma ate, she picked at her food, looked at it, touched her tongue to it and made a face as if she was trying to figure things out. She didn't want to bake; she didn't want to eat; she didn't want her long bubble baths even though her favorite thing after baking up a cloud of flour storm was soaking in a tub.

Daddy said, "Honey bunch, you got to eat better. Please?"

"I don't feel it's right to eat, Quinn; pretend like everything's normal. I'm alive to eat and sleep and feel the air on my face. My Rock is under the ground where it's dark and cold. I can't stand it." She pressed her hands to her eyes.

Daddy stood and went to her, rubbed her neck, kissed her cheek, took away her hands from her face. "You know that isn't Rock. It's not him. He's not there. Our baby is with Jesus, sitting on his lap."

"How do you know he's with Jesus? How do we know where we go when we die?"

Hill began whimpering and Petey reached over and patted his arm, even though she was scared of where she'd go when she died, too.

"This is sad talk, bad talk, grieving talk is all this is." Daddy stroked her hair, said to Petey and Hill, "We go to heaven when we die, kids. We see Jesus. What they put in the ground is only a shell. Rock's an angel now and he's helping Jesus. Jesus needs him."

"I need him more'n Jesus does! No momma ever should have to put her young-un in the earth." Momma turned up her face to the ceiling. "You hear me, Jesus? You got no right. No right taking my tiny little boy." She turned to Daddy, took a breath that sounded as if it was hot and ragged going down her throat, then told him, "And he looked up at me, before he couldn't get his breath again. He looked up at me and wanted me to help him and I couldn't. I tried to help him and I couldn't. The doctors and nurses just shook their heads. I should've gone to the hospital right away that night. I should've."

"No, honey, that's not real thinking. You got to quit this. The doc said there was nothing nobody could do. Not them and not you. And little Rock didn't suffer. He felt our love before he left. I know he did."

Daddy hugged on her, whispered in her ear, stroked her hair. Momma shook her head, shook her head. Daddy stilled it with his palms.

Petey wished she had some magical words to say to her momma. She missed Momma's smile, and the way she tried to get Petey to help her bake and Petey would say, "I just want to eat it!" She missed how Momma high-stepped it into the kitchen and tied on her apron and that meant the house was going to fill up with sweet. Missed Momma's hands covered in dough and flour, streaks of white on her cheek. Missed the way Momma's pies and cakes and cookies cooled on the table and how she let Petey lick the cake icing when she baked her world's most famous chocolate cake.

Daddy picked up Momma's fork and pushed potatoes onto it. He said, "Here, take just a bite, come on now."

Momma turned her head.

Daddy said, "Oh my beautiful one. I wish you'd eat."

Petey took up the plates to carry to the kitchen sink, said, "Hill, you go on outside now and play a while," just as Momma would say, if she were saying anything. Hill didn't act a stupid idiot about it, and instead ran out the door, slamming the screen. She heard howls, long low pitiful ones.

She washed all the dishes without being asked. While she was wiping off the table, Daddy led Momma to the bathroom, and as Petey finished cleaning up, she heard the water splashing and Daddy telling Momma everything would be all right. All right. All right. All right.

As the days passed and Momma still didn't act all right, Daddy's face dragged down even more, and Hill took to running even wilder in the woods, climbing trees and hiding behind bushes, growling at Daddy and Petey when they tried to get him to come inside. Daddy threatened to whup him, something he or Momma had never done before. Making Hill behave had always been Momma's job and Daddy wasn't so good at it. When Daddy said he'd get him a switch and meant business, Hill would finally stomp out from the woods. Petey knew Daddy wouldn't ever use that switch, but it still made her legs itch to think about it. Hill figured it out, too, because next chance he had, he'd bared his teeth and howled off to his hiding places.

Sometimes on a whim and whimsy, Daddy laughed at him, shaking his head and telling Momma, "Our son, the wild beast. He's a *mess*."

Momma would smile, a tiny bit, and that smile was as if her lips were frozen and hard to move.

Petey woke with her face stuck with sweat to her pillow and felt scared-weird from her too-long nap and from her dream. Her brain felt as if it was wrapped in toilet paper, at least two wrappings, and her mouth was dry, her tongue dry, her eyes gritty from Texas dirt flying in the windows.

She sat up, then swung her legs over the side of the bed, pushed her feet into her flip flops, rose, and left her room to find Momma. She found her at the kitchen table looking through her photo album, tear tracks down her cheeks. Momma wiped her face when Petey slipped up to stand by her.

"I hadda bad dream." She'd dreamed she was stung by scorpions over and over, until she had so many scorpion bites, she was full of poison, enough to kill a million kids. She was trying not to cry, in her dream, so Momma wouldn't worry. Then Momma sidled out and saw her there, puffed up like an egg casserole, and instead of helping her, she said, "Now what will I do with you? Getting bit up like that? Now I'll have two dead children! What am I to do with two dead children? Jesus will have two of my kids. Isn't that a fine kettle of stinking fish?" Then Petey woke up.

Momma turned a page in the album.

"I got bit by lots of scorpions and was about to die." Soon as Petey said the word "die," she clamped her lips shut and felt horrid, stupid, selfish.

Momma reached over, stroked Petey's back from shoulders to waist, and turned another page. Petey leaned back into Momma's hand and looked down to a picture of Momma when Momma was young. Her hair was long over her shoulders, and she stood strong-legged, laughing into the camera. She used to tell the story of how she worked at a bakery and her boss said she was the best baker of all he'd ever seen. He said her bread rose up just so, her cherry pies weren't too tart or too sweet, her cookies never burnt at the edges or bottom, her sweet rolls at the center heart of the roll moist and that good-kind-of-chewy. Momma said one day she wanted to have her own bakery. What happened instead was Daddy bopped in to buy a cake for his girlfriend, and when he saw Momma behind the counter with her sweet-sugar-scented palomino hair and her hazel eyes, and how her hands kneaded the dough and her cheeks flushed with flour, he said he forgot all about his girlfriend and only had eyes for Momma.

Daddy had a dark mustache then and he worked as a filling station man. Petey didn't want to think that her and Hill being born and Rock dying before he had a chance to do any living made her parents lose their shine. She imagined what her parents would be doing if their kids hadn't come along. Petey pictured Daddy and Momma going to Egypt or Africa, or to New York or New Orleans, drinking fancy drinks with cherries in them. But they'd always come home to the mountains, no matter where they roamed. They wouldn't need as much money, because it would be just them two. Momma would work in her bakery and Daddy would be a filling station man. Daddy's shoulders would be wide and thrown back, and Momma wouldn't walk in slow motion, picking at her cuticles until they bled.

Momma then turned a page to baby Petey, and said, "Look at that girl."

"That's me, Momma."

Momma nodded, then rose from the table and made her a sweet tea with lots of ice. She sat down and sipped it, staring out of the kitchen window. Momma was living off of sweet tea, it seemed to Petey.

When she didn't say anything else, Petey eased out of the kitchen door and went outside. The air was close and hot and the crickets and cicadas screamed loud, then softer, loud, then softer. Oh how she wanted home. Everything was weird to her in Fort Worth.

She thought how Texans were proud to be Texans and how North Carolinians were proud to be North Carolinians. Petey wondered could the two mix up and be proud somewhere that wasn't home? Petey didn't think it could happen. The two places were too different. There were no mountains in Fort Worth and instead Petey could see for miles and miles and miles without hardly a break, unless it was houses or squatty trees. Petey read in the encyclopedia how the mountains of North Carolina had more kinds of trees than all the trees in the north part of Europe. Daddy had said Texas wouldn't have seasons like home, either. He said in Texas it was more like summer and then winter, with fall and spring only being suggestions.

When Daddy came home from his work, he was so tired he plopped right on the couch and told her, "Little bit, I sure could use a glass of tea." He liked his tea with the ice only halfway up the glass instead of all the way like Momma.

When she handed him his tea, he took a long swallow, his adam's apple bobbing up and down up and down. He then smiled at her and said what he always said, "Ahhhh, that hits the spot." That time he added, "Feels like I'm back on the mountain and a cool breeze just flew down from the ridgetop."

Petey went to the kitchen and made herself some tea so she'd feel that way. She sat beside her daddy, leaning into him, waiting for the cool breeze feeling to come down over her. It didn't work. All she felt was a cold ghost of sad pass by. She pretended different when Daddy asked her if she felt how he did. She said, "Uh huh." She figured sometimes a lie was worth telling if it made someone she loved feel better.

Daddy ruffled Petey's head, stood from the couch, and left to go to Momma.

Petey stared out of the living room window, making up things, thinking about things, remembering things, then pretended she had magic powers to make her and Hill and Momma and Daddy fly up and away back home to North Carolina. When they were there, they'd chase out the family who moved into their house. She hated that family so much it felt as if the hate was a hard ball heavy in her belly, one that didn't fill her up and only made her hungrier. Petey could eat a million pies and two million cookies and five million slices of cake.

There was a movement and Petey saw a piece of a shadow before she saw what made the shadow. A lady came walking down the driveway with her suitcase, and disappeared where Petey couldn't see her. Petey ran to the kitchen door, stood still and listened as she heard the door of the downstairs place open and then close. Petey heard rustling around, then everything was quiet, except for Hill's howling out in the woods. She put her ear on the floor and listened to see if she could hear what her neighbor was up to. There was a scraping sound, and then quiet again.

Petey hurried outside and stood on the iron steps. Night was coming on and Petey wondered if the bats would be back. She didn't hate them, but she didn't like them, either. She was afraid they'd fly into her hair, or bite her neck, even though Hill said that was stupid idiot talk. Just then, her brother flew out of the woods, yipping and carrying on like a stone-fool. She laughed, though. He was so comical with his face dirtied and his hair stuck on end from sweating. When he ran up the steps she put her finger to her lips.

"What is it, Petey? Why're you shushing me?"

She said, real quiet, "The lady down there is back."

"She is? Where? Did you talk to her? What's she look like?"

"Shhhh! Be quiet. I'm trying to listen. See what she's up to."

He listened for about two seconds, then was bored. "Who cares what some lady's doing?" Hill ran into the house. Petey went down the steps and strolled around. Maybe if she acted mysterious, the lady would be curious and come out and tell her who she was and why she had a Buddha in her kitchen. She didn't come out and as dark fell on top of Petey, it was time for baths and teethbrushing.

In her cotton gown, body and teeth clean, Petey did what she never did unless her Grandma made her and her Grandma always made her; she closed her eyes and prayed and prayed and prayed. And if God wouldn't hear her, she'd ask Grandpa to help. Sometimes he came to her in her dreams and said he was watching over his family. He'd been the best Grandpa ever until his heart gave out. He smoked a pipe and always smelled like spice, and grew tobacco, and said his own daddy had owned a still that made the finest moonshine ever. The moonshine was so clear, he said, it didn't seem like there was anything in the jar at all until the jar was opened and the person took a drink, and then it burned fire all the way down and caused people to lose their mind if they drank too much.

He'd said, "Onest a man drunk the whole jar, even though my pap told him best not to, and that man ripped off all his clothes, ran into the forest far up into the mountains, and never could be found again." He'd eyed Petey and Hill, "They hear him every so often," Grandpa said, "laughing his fool head off, his brain gone to mush."

Grandma always harrumphed, so Petey didn't know if it was true or if Grandpa was making it up. It didn't matter to her, she loved his stories.

Sometimes he told about the Cherokee, how they were forced to leave their land, most of their things, and walk all the way to Oklahoma, and that many of them had died along the way, in that Trail of Tears. He said Hill and Petey had some Cherokee blood in them and they should be proud of it. Petey figured Grandpa knew so many things and so many people, that he surely would go to God, or maybe Jesus, and talk one of them into doing something sweet, like letting them go home, or if that was too greedy-guts, then having Momma back like she used to be before Rock died.

When Hill came into the bedroom, Petey was already in bed, having finished all she had to say in her prayers and thoughts to Grandpa. Before he could get to his side, Petey saw there was still dirt on his feet. "You didn't get a bath."

"Mind your own."

Petey heard rustling and knew he was sticking his feet under the covers so Momma wouldn't know he was filthy.

She slipped out of bed and pulled aside the sheet divider. "I'm going to tell on you."

"No you won't. You never tell on me."

That was true. She sure thought about it sometimes, though.

Hill said, "I'm still hungry."

"What you want me to do about it?"

"You could sneak something."

"You know we aren't supposed to eat in the bedroom. Momma said."

"Why not?"

"'Cause it gets crumbs in the beds and makes a mess."

"But I'm hungry. I won't leave any crumbles."

"We'll see, okay?" She dropped the sheet and jumped back into her bed.

Her brother sighed, then said, "It's weird here."

Petey nodded, even though he couldn't see her. Outside, it was dark. Petey had early on figured out it was a different dark from home, and the sounds were different, too. There wasn't a creek, and there wasn't good wind in the trees. She could hear cars go by over and over on the highway not far away. At home, there weren't many people living in their little town to make much traffic. The air in Texas was hot and dusty, not clean and fresh like the mountain air. Daddy told her to stop comparing the two over and over. He said she was making things worse by not accepting. He said the two couldn't be compared since it was like the thing about apples and oranges, both were good even if they were very different things. Petey thought home was the sweet crunchy apple, not the sticky runny orange.

Hill let out a little soft howl and then he was quiet.

Daddy came in and tucked the covers around Petey, even though it was hot. He sat on the side of her bed. It had always been Momma who sang to them; Daddy had taken her place. He wasn't as good a singer and he forgot words and had to hum them. When he sang, *Single girl, Married girl*, most of it was humming, nodding his head, tapping his fingers on his leg in time. Then he kissed her cheek, said, "Sleep and dream good."

While he'd been singing, Petey kept her lips pressed together so she wouldn't laugh at Daddy's bad singing and the words he had to make up, like how he messed up how the single girl goes to the store to buy all kinds of pretty things and the married girl doesn't; Daddy had it backwards. She said, "Night, Daddy."

Daddy then went to Hill's side of the bed. "You didn't get in the tub a lick, did you, boy?"

She heard Hill admit, "Nossir."

"Well, we'll let it go this once." Then Daddy sang to Hill, "Oh, that ole ugly Boll weevil told that farmer, well you better treat me right, *mmmm*; he said, I'll eat up all your cotton and bed down in your grain bed, *mmmmm-mmmm*!; that ole boll weevil told the farmer; you'll need no . . . no . . . you'll need no 1966 Ford Country Squire machine!; I'll eat up all your cotton and you won't *mmmmm-mmmm* some gas-*ooooo-*line."

Hill hadn't done like Petey, he was laughing. Then he said, "That's not the words, Daddy."

"Ah well." There was a rustle, where Petey knew Daddy kissed Hill's cheek, then, "Night son. Sleep and dream good."

"Night," Hill said.

At the door, Daddy said, "Your momma will be in after-while to kiss you goodnight."

She did come in, a little while after Daddy. She didn't talk about things or sing (and she always knew the words), or ask them what she could bake up for their big ole sweet tooths. Instead, she kissed Petey on the forehead, pushed back her hair, and Petey figured she did the same to Hill, then Momma left the room.

Petey didn't fall asleep for a long time. She heard them when Momma and Daddy went to bed, and then everything was quiet except for night insects and cars. Once Petey thought she heard the lady bump around, but she wasn't sure if it was her.

Petey then sneaked out of bed and went to the pantry, took out a sleeve of crackers. She put her ear to the floor and could hear violin music playing, soft and sweet. She listened a while, and almost fell asleep right there on the floor. She sneaked the crackers back to their bedroom, hiding them in her chester-drawers under her cotton undershirts, for later, in case Hill woke up still hungry, even though crackers made the worst crumbs of all. As she laid her head on her pillow, she thought about the lady downstairs.

Her eyelids fell down and she couldn't open them again. Everything was so soft and sweet. Little furry puppies ran to her, their tongues flapping in the wind. She laughed and called out to them. When they were almost to her, their eyes glowed mean and their little baby puppy teeth turned pointy-sharp. They snarled and white foamed out of their mouths. Petey ran away, faster faster faster, and behind her there was snapping and snarling—she woke and sat up in bed to a bright early morning that was already hotter than the hottest summer they'd ever had in North Carolina.

In the kitchen, Momma was making toast. Her arms were bony, and the outline of her body in her gown was thinner than ever. Petey said, "Morning, Momma." She didn't tell her about her dream.

Without turning, Momma said, "Morning."

Daddy came in and kissed Momma on top of her head, then kissed Petey on top of her head. He poured himself a cup of coffee and sat at the table. Momma served him his breakfast first. There were eggs and toast and marmalade.

Petey said, "Momma, you haven't made biscuits in forever."

She shrugged, a tiny shrug, so tiny it could have been something that wasn't a shrug at all.

Daddy said, "I do miss your biscuits."

Momma handed Petey her breakfast. She said, "It's too hot here." And that was that. Petey could tell by the way Momma set her mouth she didn't want to talk about it.

Hill came in yawning, hands down the back of his pajamas, scratching his behind.

Momma told him to go wash his hands.

After breakfast, Petey and Hill went outside and Daddy left for work. Daddy never talked about the men joking around like he'd talked about at home. He'd been friends with the men at the textile mill for a long while, and even though a few of them had also moved to Texas, he didn't get to see them much, for it was a big ole plant, full of people bustling around, Daddy said. Petey wanted to tell him to give it more time and he'd make friends, just as he told Petey she would once school started.

Petey went quiet as an egg thief and sneaked up to the lady's window. When she saw the lady was turned in a way where she couldn't see Petey, she watched her eat her breakfast. Petey was interested in the way the lady set down her fork after each bite and chewed slow and easy. Momma's manners were always perfect, too. She'd get onto them for eating too fast or talking with their mouth open or their elbows on the table. Most times, they all tried to have polite manners, except for the times she and Hill forgot or were having too much fun with Daddy talking and joking and telling stories. Not so much, anymore. She backed away from the door before the lady caught her, pulled her bike out of the shed, and rode it in circles in the dirt.

Chapter 6

It was a hotter-than-the-blued-blazes day while Petey was looking for interesting rocks that she saw the lady come out of her house and grab a little red wagon with a rope tied on the handle so she didn't have to bend over. The lady set off down towards the road pulling it behind her.

Petey was surprised at how young the lady was, younger than Petey had thought. She wore a pair of black cigarette pants and a white top that she'd tied into a knot at the waistband of the pants, and on her feet were black slip-on shoes. Her hair was piled on top of her head and held with chopsticks, and was messy in a way that was pretty and interesting. On her wrists flashed slim silver bracelets, about ten of them it looked to Petey. Petey had never seen someone who seemed so foreign even while being so American. She was like a movie star, except her face didn't have the I'm-better-than-you-since-I'm-famous look that lots of Hollywood people had.

Petey hid behind a clump of bushes and waited for the slow count of five before she followed the lady. She followed her down the road, keeping far enough behind her, hiding behind bushes when she needed to, creeping along—she tried to think how a brave warrior Indian girl would walk quiet through the woods to hunt for food, or spy on the enemy, or spy to see what some boy she liked was doing.

The lady walked all the way to the grocery, and when the doors closed around her, Petey counted to ten and then went inside. She pretended she was shopping so she could watch what the lady put into her wagon. The lady picked up packs of cookies and cake mixes (Petey's momma had always had a fit if anyone bought cake mixes), olives in black and green, a jar of salsa, two cans of tuna fish, oysters in a can (nasty ole oysters looked like snot to Petey), two loaves of soft white bread that Petey knew wouldn't have much taste, not like Momma's bread. The lady spent a lot of time at the meat counter and finally put a roast into her wagon, then some potatoes and salad fixings. The lady stared into her wagon, then let out a sigh.

While she paid for her food, Petey went outside to wait. When the lady came out of the grocery pulling her wagon with the grocery bags in it, Petey pretended to be milling around, slipping along with the breeze, not a care in the world, like nobody's beez-wax was hers and she was nobody's beez-wax.

"Are you going to talk to me or just keep following me around and humming?"

Petey's head shot up where she'd been looking at the ground.

The lady gave a pretty laugh, and her face was bright with a smile.

Petey's face burned.

"I'm Anna. Who are you?"

The lady, Anna's, voice was pretty, all light and soft, but strong at the same time.

"What's the matter, cat got your tongue?"

"No, ma'am." Petey kicked at the dirt, then said, "I'm Petey."

"Well, I'm much too young to be a ma'am." She held out her hand. "It's nice to meet you, Petey."

Petey shook her hand. Her hand was soft as a newborn puppy.

"You live upstairs from me."

Petey figured she'd seen her spying and the thought made shame and embarrassment slip into her blood all the way to her marrow. She said, "Yeah, me and my brother and my parents live upstairs from you."

"That's so nice." She pulled the wagon closer to her. "Shall we?" She pointed to the road towards home.

Petey walked beside her, trying to be as sophisticated as Anna. It was hard to be sophisticated, since Petey was wearing raggedy cut-off shorts with holes in them, a stained t-shirt, and her floppiediest flip flops that kept her feet and ankles dirty. After a bit, she couldn't stand her curious thoughts anymore, so she asked Anna, "Where did you go on your vacation? Daddy said the landlord said you had a vacation somewhere's far away."

"I was in Japan. Last year I went to Italy, and next year I want to go to Greece."

Japan, Greece, Italy. Petey was astounded. She'd never been anywhere other than North Carolina, and Texas, and the states they'd passed in between.

As if Petey had said something, Anna said, "I know, I know. How come I live in a half-house when I can afford to travel like that?" That tinkling laugh again, then, "That is precisely *why* I live in a half-house, so I *can* afford to travel all over."

Petey nodded, then said, "Oh," in case Anna didn't see her nod.

"My parents left me some money. I'd rather have my parents alive, though." She looked sad, then, "Yes, well, life is strange sometimes." She jerked the wagon from where the wheel stuck in a hole.

"You're a orphan?" Petey had never met an orphan before.

"I guess I am." Anna seemed surprised at that notion.

Petey didn't know what to say about being an orphan.

Anna shrugged with one little shoulder. "It's okay. Really."

"Our brother died soon after he was out, um . . . was out of Momma's wombal area."

"I am so sorry. My dear people, so awful to lose loved ones."

They walked along and Anna talked about how she was born in Dallas and ended up in Fort Worth after her friend moved out of the half-house and she was able to move in after her—a bargain, she said. She then said, "I bought things to make a dinner. I'm not much of a cook, I'm afraid. There's this guy." Pink flamed on her cheeks. "He has dark hair and dark eyes and is so quiet, but strong, too. You know?"

Petey didn't really know, except her daddy was quiet but strong so she could relate to that. Then she remembered Barry Burke had dark hair and eyes and wondered if when he kissed her she had that same look come across her as Anna did, at least before Petey beat him up. She wondered what it would be like to cook for a beloved with dark hair and dark eyes who was quiet but strong, then decided she'd rather someone cook for her.

When they were on the gravel driveway back to the half-houses, Petey hoped Anna would invite her in. She asked her, "Do you need help with your groceries?"

"Well, you can help me take them in, and after that you can keep me company while I put them away."

Petey's heart set to thumping and she couldn't help but grin. Off in the scraggly puny woods, she heard Hill give a couple of sharp barks.

Anna laughed, then said, "That brother of yours is the cutest thing. I watch him sometimes from my window." She opened her door. "You're lucky; I was an only child."

Petey couldn't believe it. Anna an orphan and no brother or sister. She said, "My momma was a only child, too."

"Well, seems we have things in common, don't we?"

When they walked into the kitchen and Anna turned on the light, Petey's mouth near dropped all the way open where Anna could see the flappy thing hanging there. She set down her bag of groceries on the counter and tried not to gawk. The kitchen was painted red, and the cabinets were black. On the walls were pictures that must have come from Japan, and Italy, and wherever else Anna had been; Petey hadn't ever seen things like that in America. She hadn't been much of anywhere to see much of anything like Anna's things. On the floor were colorful rugs. And the magnets were from all over creation. Some of the magnets were shaped like states or countries, some like animals or birds, fish, or flowers, or square with writing on them.

Anna went back outside for the third bag while Petey stood, moving only her eyes around so she wouldn't be seen as too nosey. When Anna came back in, she began putting up the groceries, and told Petey she taught dance to girls, and sometimes even to couples who wanted to be romantic again. She said she'd never be a professional dancer herself because she wasn't good enough. She didn't seem upset about it, Petey didn't think.

Anna's kitchen was beautiful and strange, like Anna herself. Their half-house was ugly and sad, sort of like how they'd become, especially Momma. She felt shame for how their half-house looked. She didn't want to feel that way about Momma, her house, her whole stupid idiot life. But she did.

Anna stretched up to put away the tuna. "I love tuna sandwiches," she said. "With pickles, onions, mustard and mayonnaise."

Petey remembered when her parents had talked about fixing up the place, and how she could paint her half of her room any color she wanted, and Hill could paint his any color. She had decided on a lightest lilac, like Momma's bubble bath, and she wanted a bedspread she'd seen in a Sears catalogue, white with flowers embroidered on it, and a soft rug in the shape of a flower. Hill wanted his half painted with zebra stripes.

Anna went to the refrigerator and put away the rest of her groceries. "In this heat, I should've put away the cold things first." She shook her head.

Nothing had been fixed in Petey's half-house. The yellow was still yellow and the green still green and the kitchen curtains still baboon-behind ugly. Petey stared at the Buddha where it sat as if another person, its hands face up and in its lap. It looked wise enough to give her answers to all her questions, if it could talk.

"That posture of the Buddha is meditation. I used to meditate a lot, but lately I seem just too distracted." She did seem discombobulated as she folded the grocery sacks and put them away. "This dinner," she sighed, then, "Why did I pick roast? I have never cooked a roast! And I told him I'd bake a cake. I hope that mix is okay. Everyone likes chocolate, right?"

"They sure do." She didn't tell her how Momma would shake her head and toss that cake mix in the garbage, pronto presto chango.

"Well now, would you like to see the rest of the house?"

Petey almost shouted, "Would I!" but instead said very politely, "Yes, thank you kindly."

"Let me wash my hands of all the grocery grime."

While Petey waited patient on the outside and impatient on the inside, she heard a bump from above and had the sudden wonder if Anna had to listen to them stomping around all the time, especially Hill. She promised herself to be quieter and to talk to Hill about it, too.

Anna led her past the Buddha and into the living room. The living room was painted a sandy color, and there were red pillows and throws on chairs, and a footstool that looked like some kind of animal but wasn't real animal when Petey touched it. The dark brown couch slung low and seemed to float above the floor, and on it were more pillows, while over the back was thrown a soft furry throw in the same dark brown as the couch. There was a woven, thick-roped cotton chair that hung from the ceiling and Petey was dying to sit in it. There were more pictures that seemed foreign to her, and another statue, except the living room statue was of three naked women huddled together.

Anna said, "That's the Graces." She stood next to Petey and pointed to each woman. "Aglaia is splendor, Euphrosyne is festivity, and Thalia is rejoicing. Do you know your mythology?"

Petey shook her head, then said, "Well, maybe a little from school."

"Do you know who Zeus is?"

"Yeah! He's a big scary god with lightning bolts."

Anna laughed.

Petey wanted to find more ways to make her laugh, just to hear it.

"Zeus and Eurynome are the Graces' parents, although some say Zeus and Hera are. And there's some quibble over what the Graces represent." She touched the statue. "They are lovely, whatever the mythology." Anna turned and smiled at Petey (and Petey thought, *No, you are lovely*), then Anna said, "Now, on with the tour, although as you know it will be a rather short tour." She glanced back at Petey following behind her. "And remind me to give you a book on mythology. You can return it when you're done."

On the hallway wall hung what looked sort of like a blanket, except it was smaller and had a stick through it so it could hang from the hooks. On it were two beautiful birds and lots of flowers. Petey touched it with the very tip of her pointing finger. It was soft.

"Those birds are bird of paradise, aren't they pretty?" Anna touched it with her finger as Petey had, except she ran her finger across the bird as if petting it. "This tapestry came from Sicily, where my old boyfriend lived for a time. It's patterned after the ancient mosaics. He gave it to me, right before he married someone else because I wouldn't marry him." She turned from the tapestry and said to Petey, "They met in a yoga class, my boyfriend and his wife to be, that is—she *was* my best friend." She smiled, as if glad for how it had turned out, after all, then said, "She wanted the tapestry, but I kept it. He told me I could, that it was a gift to me." Her brows came together. "Some people are just greedy!" She stepped away from the tapestry. "Well, such is life; let's finish the tour."

Petey's eyes were wide and her brain ran round trying to imagine all the things Anna knew about or had happen to her. She'd never heard or seen such ever in her life. Grown woman things. Boy and girl things. Far away things. It was all wondrous.

Of course Anna's was no ugly pickle bathroom and instead was painted the same sandy color and there were thick towels in a dark brown. The rug was woven of something like wheat or straw, but was soft under Petey's flip-flopped feet. Down the hall were the other rooms, just as with Petey's half-house. In Anna's, one bedroom wasn't a bedroom at all. Instead it held a sewing machine, material, thread, and paint, canvas, along with some pictures leaned on the wall.

Anna said, "Too bad the Ancients aren't my muses. I took a painting class. That's where I met Stephen." The pinked cheeks again. "That's the guy I told you about. He's a gifted painter and a wonderful teacher, but one of his students . . ." she pointed to herself and then to the paintings, "isn't so good."

"I like those over there." Petey pointed to the ones with all the color. "I like them 'cause they're so bright and beautiful." And that was a truth. They were full of reds and browns and yellows and oranges and purples, and here and there sparkling silver or gold would surprise Petey, and the paintings all glowed in the light coming in through the windows.

"Thank you, Petey. You're kind for saying so."

The last room was Anna's bedroom and Petey's knees knocked in, for it was that pretty. Anna's bed was a dark mahogany, and draped over the bed was pretty netting that floated around and over the bed. The bedspread was a deep purple, and there were colorful pillows and throws, some with sparkles. The rug was white and furry and soft as a baby's behind when Petey slipped her right foot out of her flip flop and ran her bare foot over the rug. On the wall on either side of the bed were candles inside glass and metal holders. The whole room smelled spicy: cinnamon, cloves, and other spices she couldn't say what they were but made her want to flop on the bed and daydream about far away places.

Anna asked, "So, what do you think?"

"It's beautiful." Petey right then wished Anna were her sister.

"Well, time to make some tea, right from Japan. First though . . ." She crossed the room, went to a low bookshelf, said, "Let's see. Here it is," and pulled out a book that looked old as Grandma. "This is the book I was telling you about." She handed it to Petey. "It was my dad's so take good care of it."

Petey felt the most special person on earth. She followed Anna back to the kitchen, ran her hands over the book, and couldn't wait to see what was inside. She'd take the best ever care of it.

In the kitchen, Anna took the vase with the sparkled balls and feathers from the table and set it on the counter. "Isn't this a sight? Sometimes I have ideas that don't quite make it right from my brain to reality." She put on water to boil. "Do you like hot tea?"

Petey nodded, even though she'd never had hot tea. She wondered who'd drink hot tea on a hot day, but she was willing to try it. Just as Petey sat at the kitchen table, she heard Hill calling to her. She wanted to tell him to shush it up. He called again, "*Peeeeteeey*, time to eeeaaat!*"

"Your brother is calling you to lunch."

"It's okay. I'm not hungry."

Hill was closer, and hollering louder. "Petey! Momma said now, come *now*. Time to eat. Now!"

"I don't want your mom to be mad at me. Come back and have tea another time."

Petey stood. "Thank you."

"For what?"

She held up the book. She didn't know how to say *thank you for showing me things I've never seen before in my life* without sounding stupid.

"Hold on. One more thing." She reached into the pantry, moved things around, tipped her head to the right then to the left, and finally pulled out a box. "This tea will help your mom to feel better. Tell her to brew it and then relax where she likes to relax the most as she sips it."

Petey didn't have the heart to say Momma didn't relax in her bubbles any more. She said, "I'll tell her. Thank you." She took the box of tea and headed out the door, out into the hot, and smack into Hill.

"What were you doing in there? Who is she? What's she like? Is she a witch? Is she ugly with a wart? She's not 'cause I saw her and she's puh-puh-puh-ret-ty. How'd you get in there? What's that book? And what's that there?"

"Can you just shush it, Pus-picker?"

"I can't help it I'm curiouser than a cat." He meowed, then licked his hand like it was a paw, and that paw was something dirty.

"Eeewww. Quit doing that. You'll get worms."

"Come on; let's eat. Momma made—"

"Let me guess. Soup and saltines."

"How'd you know?"

"'Cause that's all she makes hardly ever now, anymore."

Hill clanged up the stairs, said, "Beat you again." Even though Petey wasn't even in the mood to race and hadn't even tried one bit so it didn't count.

When she walked into the kitchen, the ugliness of it hit her across the face. The whole half-house hit her across the face. She sat at the table and ate her tomato soup with saltines, drank her milk. Daddy wasn't much of a food shopper and bought weird kinds of soup brands, and crackers that sometimes were stale. Momma knew how to stretch a dollar better, except she hadn't been out of the house since they'd come back from Rock's funeral. Petey felt a little nit of a bug enter her brain that burrowed in and told her she hated Rock, maybe a little. Hated him for dying. And that little nit of a bug made her feel like a mean ole fool. She couldn't help it. She wanted things back like they were.

After she ate she went outside, but she didn't see Anna again. She wandered around the yard and thought about school starting soon. She gave a little shudder. New school, new kids. And what if they found out about Momma never leaving the house and being so skinny? What if they thought Momma was crazy? That was a fate worse than most things. She'd known about a girl where everyone said her momma was crazy, that she'd shoot anyone who tried to come up to her shack in the woods, and how she let her girl run wild all over the mountain. They whispered about her and sneered their lips and other awful things Petey didn't want to have happen to her.

That night Petey pressed her ear to the floor and listened for Anna. She heard the soft violin again and imagined Anna listening to her music while drinking her tea in the tub, or while trying out dance steps with her little feet on her soft rug. She remembered then she hadn't given Momma the tea, and ran to do so before Momma went to bed.

Momma held the box of tea. "What's this?"

"It's a special tea from Japan. Anna said to drink it while relaxing in the tub and it'll help you feel better. You drink it hot, Momma."

Momma opened the box and a flowery-green smell drifted out. She put her nose to it, took in a soft sniff. "There's chamomile, lemon balm, lavender, and some I can't quite figure out." She closed the box. "So, you've met the downstairs neighbor then?"

"Yes, Ma'am. She's real nice, and she's pretty. And her half-house is so beautiful. It has things from all over! She's been to all kinds of places and has statues and all kinds of pillows . . ." Petey took a deep breath to stop herself from babbling, but more blew out, ". . . and she's a orphan, and teaches dancing, and she has a boyfriend named Stephen, and he's a painter but she almost married another boy but her greedy friend stole him away . . ." Petey had so much to tell Momma, like she used to, only she wasn't sure if Momma still listened.

Words were all over the room, on the floor, in hers and Momma's hair, on the counters. Everywhere. Some floated up and bounced around, some lay heavy, some rose back up so Petey swallowed them again to use later.

Momma cradled the box and finally said, "I guess a little tea won't hurt."

"You got to do like she says or it won't work."

"That's foolishness."

"No, Momma. She *said*. Anna said you got to drink it while relaxing so you'll feel better."

Momma stroked the box but didn't say if she would.

"Momma. Guess what?" After Momma said, "What?" Petey said, "She uses cake mixes and cornbread and biscuit mixes. And she's going to cook for her date but doesn't really know how. *Mixes*, Momma!" She waited for her to tell her how awful that was.

Momma turned to set the tea on the counter, and some of Petey's words were swished away by Momma's movements. "Time for you to get back to bed. Is Hill in there, or is he running wild? That boy better be in bed."

"He's in there, Momma." Petey went off to bed, thinking how if telling Momma about the mixes hadn't worked, then nothing would. Not even special tea from far away Japan.

Chapter 7

Petey and Hill rode the hot bus that smelled like bologna. The bus driver had a mustache that was so long it drooped down to his chin and he most days wore a t-shirt that read, "God Bless Texas." It wasn't the same t-shirt, but differing ones, in red, black, gray, and white. He sang songs about yellow roses or someone having a cheating heart. When he told jokes, the whole bus laughed. Like, "Why did the chicken cross the road?" and they'd all ask, "Why, Bus-Driver Bill?" and he'd say, "To get away from this bus afore I run over it to tenderize it for my supper!" And even though it wasn't all that funny, the squinty-eyed look he gave and the way he said it made it funny.

School wasn't as much fun. Petey didn't know what Hill did in class, but on the playground he ran around barking and growling and snuffling the bushes, and that caused a lot of the kids to call him a weirdo. Petey almost had to beat up three boys and a girl. The boys backed off and said they wouldn't fight a girl, even though Petey said she could fight like a boy just fine. And the girl cried and whined before Petey could even hardly lift up her fist. Petey tried to tell Hill to pretend he was a human being while at school. Her little brother forgot or didn't care. Then out of the blue-with-chances-of-showers sky Hill made a friend, a skinny little blonde boy with big green eyes and a runny nose.

Petey did her work and mostly kept to herself. There was one girl who tried to be Petey's friend. Petey wasn't ready. She thought about it, though, for if she made friends with Mary, maybe like Angela, Mary would tell Petey when her buttons were buttoned wrong, or her ponytail was messed up, or if there was a stain on her blouse. She could whisper to her new friend about mirrors and she would understand, like Angela did. But what if Mary didn't understand? What if she laughed at her and told the whole school and they thought she was a weirdo or even worse crazy?

At least school gave Petey something different to do, since being at the half-house all summer, and in those scraggly woods, and all that dirt, could be quite boring after a time. She couldn't always have tea with Anna. And Petey needed something to keep her mind away from their too-quiet half-house. How long did it take for a momma to stop missing a baby who'd only been on earth less than an hour? How long did it take for a momma to see her real live kids needed her more than the dead one? Petey felt like slapping herself when she thought things like that. The thoughts slithered in anyway.

After school every day, Petey jumped back on the bus, and just as in the mornings, Bus-Driver Bill sang loud songs and told silly jokes and they laughed; and even though the afternoon bus smelled of sour milk and sweaty boys, Petey didn't mind. At home, Petey would do her homework and then wander around. She didn't let on to Hill that she kind of sort of almost missed him; since he had a friend to pal around with he wasn't under her feet so much.

On a Saturday morning, Petey woke up and stretched. She rose out of bed and saw Hill was already up and gone. When she went to the bathroom, she stopped and sniffed. Was that lilacs? She wasn't sure. She cleaned herself up, not looking into the mirror. Then she had a sudden thought. If she couldn't change herself being afraid to look into mirrors, how could she expect Momma to change herself from being sad? The thought bounced around in her skull, making vibrations that went through her whole body until her skin hummed and her teeth wiggled in her gums.

Petey took a deep breath, let it out slow, then again, deep breath, out slow. She raised her eyes to the mirror, her heart thundering. She first gazed only into her own eyes, and then she took in the reflection of the pickle bathroom behind her. Then just as fast, she tore away her eyes. So far, so good, though her heart was about to burst out of her chest to fall onto the floor beating out all her blood. She hurried out of the bathroom.

In the kitchen, Daddy was finishing up his coffee. Momma was still in their bedroom.

"Hi, little bit. Sleep well?" Daddy asked.

"I guess so." She went to him and leaned on his strong body. Put her head on his big wide shoulder.

"Made friends at school yet?" Daddy smiled at her.

She shrugged, then asked, "Do you like your work, Daddy?"

He tipped up his cup, slurped out the rest of the coffee, then said, "It's not a man's way to think about whether he likes a job or doesn't like a job. It's a job. He does it for his family."

Petey figured that meant he still didn't like it all that much, or it meant what it meant; she wasn't sure. Daddy didn't make much of a Texan, she didn't figure, since he'd been born in Haywood County. Momma was born in Watauga County, but she'd lived in Asheville right out of high school, and when she met Daddy, she moved to Haywood.

Then Daddy said, "Some of the men are okay." He shook his head, "Those Texans said I need a belt buckle big as my head, some cowboy boots, and a big Stetson, so I can come ride their bulls they keep out in their back yard. I figure they're teasing me, like when I had to act all hicked up for the tourists at that tourist shop." He chuckled, and Petey was hopeful at that chuckle. Daddy said, "There's a letter from your grandma on the counter. I have to go into work for a while, then I think I'll do some chores around the house."

"What kind of chores?"

"Oh, this and that. I've let it go too long."

Petey held her breath for two counts of two. Maybe they would finally make their half-house look better. Maybe if it did, she could ask Mary over. Maybe.

Daddy stood, stretched up to near the ceiling and then swooped down to grab Petey up. She laughed, and didn't even tell him she was too old. He said, "You're going to be too big one day, so best get in all my hugs and kisses now." He planted a big wet nasty slobber kiss on her cheek.

"Stop it! That's nasty, Daddy."

He let her go, laughed. Then he called out, "Beth! I'm off."

He waited until she came out of their room. When she entered the kitchen, Petey was surprised to see Momma was already dressed. She'd been in her robe and gown most all the time and when she did change into her regular clothes, it wasn't until after noon. And before Rock, Momma had loved dressing in her clothes. She said clothes were more than covering up nakedness. Petey had always shrugged at that.

Daddy kissed Momma, grabbed his keys from the peg, and headed out the door.

Momma asked what Petey'd like for breakfast.

"Homemade biscuits."

"How about some peanut butter toast?"

"Okay, Momma, but I can do that." Petey took out the bread. Store-bought. It wasn't like they never had store bought, it was only they'd never had it all the time before. She put two slices in the toaster and then went to the pantry for the peanut butter. There wasn't even any homemade jam or jelly. Texas had good fruit, and at the grocery she'd seen some huge berries. Perfect for jam or jelly. Mary had told her that Texans were proud and could brag the bark off a tree in one big long strip over how Texas had everything bigger and better. She said it as if she was proud even of the bragging, like it was all a part of what being Texans was all about.

One day at school one of the older boys had hollered, "Everything's bigger in Texas!" then had pointed between his legs—There! At his *Thing*! His friends laughed, slapping their thighs.

A girl said, "How *vulgar*." She tossed her dark curls back, giggled, and licked her lips to make them shine, like she didn't think it was vulgar at all but cute as can be.

Petey had hurried away from them, her face flaming hot as the Texas wind.

While the toast toasted, Petey remembered Grandma's letter, took it, and stuck it into her pocket to read later. She knew there'd be a dollar or two for her, and news about the mountains. Sometimes Grandma sent pictures. One time she sent Petey Grandpa's very own jackknife. Petey kept it wrapped in the tissue nestled in the box it came in and put it in her chester-drawers.

Grandma had told her to take good care of Grandpa's jackknife, that he'd whittled things with it from the time he was a kid, so Petey knew it was really really really old. Every so often, she took it out and tried to whittle with it, but she'd never be as good at it as Grandpa had been. He could do anything. He was bigger than Texas. She missed him something fierce. The wrong people left the ole world, is what Petey thought. They left whether old or young or even teeny tiny before they were able to live. Just didn't seem right for people who were loved and loved back to have to leave.

Petey spread peanut butter on the toast, thick, just as she liked it.

Momma sipped coffee and as always stared out the window. She then turned to Petey and said, "That toast smells good. I can't think of the last time I had peanut butter toast."

"I can make you some, Momma." Petey tried to act casual about it, but inside her heart did a skippity-do-dah-day. She bit into her toast and the peanut butter stuck where she had to rub her tongue against the roof of her mouth to get at it.

"Maybe later," Momma said, after just a bit of a hesitate, like she had thought about it a little.

Petey let out a big ole sigh, but quiet inside herself. The tea Anna had given Momma was on the counter, and she opened it. She couldn't tell if any was gone, but there was a mug beside the tea. Petey had that hope rise up once again. While she finished off her toast, Petey popped another piece of bread into the toaster to make Momma a peanut butter toast. Just in case. When it was ready, she said, "Here Momma."

Momma smiled at her, stuck her finger into the peanut butter, licked it away, then said, "Thank you for making it."

Petey washed her plate, taking her time so she could see if Momma would eat the toast. When she turned, three bites were gone; the plate was pushed away.

Petey told herself to go stare into the mirror a second time. And she did. She dashed into the bathroom, looked at herself for the count of one-two-three (one for each bite of the toast), said, "Ha!" then ran out into the hall and into her bedroom.

It was still hot outside, even in the coming fall, so Petey decided to read *The Incredible Journey*. She loved Luath the brave loyal Labrador, Tao the proud fearless Siamese cat, and old Bodger the faithful sweet bull terrier. When she was to the part about Luath having porcupine quills all in his muzzle, poor Luath, she smelled something cooking. Not exactly cooking. Burning. She tossed down her book and ran into the kitchen. Momma stood in the middle of the kitchen, sniffing the air.

"What's that burning, Momma?"

"It must be coming from downstairs."

"Anna said she was going to cook for her beloved. To make him love her, I guess." She then said to Momma all in a rush, "Like how Daddy found you at the bakery, and you said how you baked sweets and when he ate them it made him even sweeter, and how that made him fall in love with you and you with him, and how you put your whole heart in everything you baked and that made Daddy fall harder, and if you cook with love, the food gives back love."

A funny look sprung into Momma's eyes. "Yes, I did say that, didn't I?"

"Yeah. And remember how you helped out Mrs. Patterson that time? She was sick and wouldn't eat nothing hardly (*like you*, Petey almost said), and you baked her that big huge coconut cake, her favorite? She said after that how her zest for food was back; she said it just like that, zest for food. She said you have magic in you that comes out in your food."

"It's love," Momma said so quietly Petey wasn't sure she heard it at first. Momma sniffed the air again. "Burning and something else. Cake-mix cake. I know it when I smell it."

"I told you; she cooks with *mixes*. Imagine that, Momma. Mixes!"

Then Momma seemed to be tired of talking about it. "Well, she has to learn by her mistakes, I guess." She sat at the table.

Petey felt the anger rise up out of her, full and fuller. She was so mad her breath scorched her lips as she heaved out the words at Momma. "You aren't *ever* going to be like you were before! All cause of Rock being dead. Well, me and Hill aren't dead! I'm alive, see?" She pinched herself on the arm hard, harder, then harder still.

Momma stood. "What are you doing? Stop that!"

Petey pinched more, her raggedy nails dug into her skin, her fingers pinching, pinching, pinching. The pain spread up her arm as if she'd been stung by ten stinging nettles.

"Petey!" Momma grabbed at her. Petey jerked and turned away, still pinching. Momma came around, trying to pull at her hand. "Stop it, I said!"

She kept pinching, harder, deeper, tears burned out of her eyes.

Momma pulled at Petey's fingers; she was crying right in front of Petey, saying, "Please, Petey! Please stop!"

Petey at last let go and faced down Momma. "I wish little Rock wasn't dead, but that don't mean I got to feel sad all the rest of my life, do I?" Petey's face was hot; her whole insides were boiling up and her arm throbbed. "I'm tired of feeling bad. I been looking in mirrors. I been trying." She stomped her foot. "You tried nothing! Nothing!"

Momma turned away from Petey, laid her hands on the counter and leaned there. "You can't understand. You're a child."

"I understand lots of things. I'm not a baby anymore."

"Petunia. Please."

Petey went to the door. "I'm going to go help Anna get her beloved. I'm going to help her all I can." Petey stomped out the door and rattled down the stairs.

Hill had an old stuffed toy rabbit in this mouth and was growling. When he saw Petey, he spit it out and said, "What's wrong? What's all that yelling? Why's your face so red? What happened to you? Why're you bleeding?"

"I'm mad mad mad mad!"

"Me, too," Hill said. "I'm mad as a mad bull." He charged towards Petey, "Grrrrr, grrrr, I'm a mad bull, grrrrr!"

Petey pushed him away.

"Are you mad at *me*, Petey?" Hill's lip trembled.

Petey felt horrid; he was so small, and cute as a butter bug, and he was her only brother. "I'm not mad at you, 'kay?"

He grinned, picked up the stuffed toy with his teeth, and shot off on all fours. Petey couldn't figure how he did that so fast.

At Anna's opened door, Petey smelled the burning even more. She peeked inside, unsure if she should let herself in. Momma'd taught her kids good manners about going where they weren't invited. She said, "Anna? It's Petey," and stepped one step in.

Anna sat at the table, her head in her hands. Smoke lifted out of a pot on the stove.

"I've come to help you cook for your beloved."

When Anna looked up, her face was red and wet and her eyes swollen. "I ruined it! I burnt the roast and the potatoes, too. And the cake is crooked and awful."

Petey stepped all the way into the kitchen. She opened the lid on the pot and inside was what used to be the roast, but what turned into a hard chunk of char. On the counter was a cake that leaned crooked to the side, and the icing had melted in nasty oozes. Petey knew Anna'd frosted it before it cooled; she knew this from watching Momma.

"My mom wasn't too great of a cook, but we were going to take classes together. We were so excited." Anna slid her eyes to the Buddha. "That's all we talked about for weeks. Dad teased Mom about it, how he'd finally save money on restaurants, and how he couldn't wait to taste our cooking. Mom turned to Dad and said, 'Well, don't think I'm waiting on you hand and foot!' Dad looked at her with his eyes all rounded, and then they teased each other. They were so happy. I was, too." Anna sniffled and wiped her nose with a tissue. "I was still in high school. A policeman came to get me out of class. Some drunk slammed into my parents. They were there to kiss me goodbye that morning, and then they weren't there to ever do that again." She blew her nose. "That Buddha used to be in Mom's garden. She said it made her feel happy and calm and peaceful. She liked to garden," she looked up at Petey, "like you told me your mom does."

Even if Petey's parents were acting weird, they were still alive and they kissed her most every day, sometimes more than once. Her stomach reared up and told her it was feeling nasty. She didn't want to think about her parents being dead. Then she wondered if how she felt thinking about her parents dead, the feeling as if her heart was squeezed and her stomach was twisted raw, was how Momma felt since Rock left. She shouldn't ought to have yelled at Momma.

"I'm sorry for all that sad story. I seem to be telling you things about me as if you were my age instead of . . . how old are you?"

"I'm almost twelve." Petey stood tall; she wasn't a little kid anymore.

"Well, then you understand how it is to be a woman."

Petey nodded, though she didn't really all that much understand.

"What a sight I must be." She then said, "Oh! What happened to your arm?"

Petey turned to the counter and tried to fix Anna's cake, though it was a lost cause as it slid around, the icing melted, the edges of the cake hard. She went to the roast and tried to scrape the burnt off of it, but it was hard and useless. Petey felt useless herself. She wanted to help Anna, but wasn't sure where to start.

Anna stood, left the kitchen, and when she returned she held a white tin box with a red cross and First Aid written on it. She washed her hands, and from the box took a cotton bandage, tape, a piece of cloth, alcohol, and some cream. "I'm going to have to call off the date. I don't know why I bragged how I could cook." Anna poured a bit of alcohol on the cloth, took Petey's arm and wiped the pinched places with the alcohol-dampened cloth.

Petey sucked in air when the alcohol touched the raw places.

Anna next spread the cream. "And why do I have to prove I cook? Why do I have to prove anything to a man?" She gently placed the cotton bandage over Petey's hurts. "It's just . . . it makes me think of my parents, you know? Silly, I guess." She smoothed the tape at the edges of the cotton. "It's why I travel, I suppose. They were going to travel when they retired. They shouldn't have waited." She put away the things into the tin box. "When my parents died, I pulled my hair so hard some came out by the roots. It felt better to feel that pain than the other pain." She then looked right into Petey's eyes.

Petey looked down at her arm, then back to Anna.

Anna went to the sink and washed her hands. "I never did take those cooking classes. But I've been traveling to the places they wanted to go."

Petey said, "Momma says we cook for love. To show someone we love them."

Anna set the tin box on the counter, then picked up her tissue and blew her nose.

Petey stared again at the roast. Maybe if she cut off all the burnt parts something good would be in the middle of it.

From behind her she heard, "You had the temperature too high on that roast . . ."

Petey swung around so fast, her head near-abouts fell off her shoulders.

". . . and you can't bake a good cake from a mix. It'll never taste right even if it looks pretty, which that one certainly does not." Momma stood in Anna's kitchen, her apron tied around her. Her apron. Her clean white apron.

Petey's heart filled with a great big love that exploded right out of her skin and made the room glow bright.

Momma went to the roast pot and stuck it in the sink, roast and all, and poured water over it. She poked at the cake, shook her head. "That won't do. That won't do a'tall." She took a pad from her apron pocket and wrote onto it.

Anna stood next to Petey. They were quiet, watching as if hypnotized by Momma.

Momma reached Petey the list and some money. "Go to the grocery and get me what I wrote down. Make Hill go with you, and quickly. No dawdling, you hear?"

Petey still stood there, as if she was cut out of stone like one of the Graces. All three of them could be a Grace, the way they stood together, waiting for what wonderful thing would come next. Momma leaning on the sink; Anna with her eyes rounded and wide and hopeful; Petey with her hand to her lips as if trying to hold onto any words that would slip out and give them to Momma, instead of the mean words she'd said earlier.

"Petey? Can you do that?"

She lifted away her hand, reached out to take the list and money from Momma, and said, "Yes, Ma'am!" Petey looked at Momma's blocked letters and read some of the ingredients: potatoes, flour, eggs, a chicken, buttermilk (would she be making her fried chicken? The one Daddy said won first place at a fair?), baking chocolate, cream cheese.

Momma said, "Hurry it up so we can get started. Anna and I will clean up this mess while we're waiting. Right Anna?" Momma gave up a trembled smile.

Anna ran to Momma and hugged her. "Oh, thank you thank you thank you! I know it's silly, but I want this to be so perfect."

Momma let Anna hug her, her arms straight down at her sides.

Then something came over her, Petey reckoned, because Momma lifted her arms and hugged Anna back. Petey hurried out before she did something embarrassing, like crybaby stuff. She yelled for Hill, gave a sharp whistle, and he bounded out of the woods. She told him about Momma wanting things from the store, and about how she wore her apron again.

Hill said, "Well I'll be a monkey's Uncle Monk."

"You're the monkey himself, bologna breath."

Hill made monkey noises, one arm dragging the ground. Petey laughed, grabbed her little brother by the t-shirt, took hold of Anna's wagon rope, and down towards the road to the grocery they went. In her daze and wonder at it all, Petey didn't even realize she was singing aloud until Hill joined her, "Went out to milk; and I didn't know how; I milked the goat; instead of the cow; a monkey sittin'; on a pile of straw; a winkin' at his mother-in-law; oh! turkey in the straw, turkey in the hay; roll 'em up and twist 'em up a high tuckahaw; and twist 'em up a tune called turkey in the straw . . ." And even though the mountaintop was far away, Petey could pretend, a little, that she was home. Momma's apron had made her feel that way.

In the grocery store, Hill did *The Point* when he found something, just like those pointer dogs, and Petey would put it in the wagon. He sneaked in a bag of candy and Petey put it back. He sneaked it back in and Petey put it back on the shelf again.

When Petey and Hill were back from the grocery and to Anna's half-house, they took a grocery bag each from the wagon and went inside. The kitchen and dishes had all been cleaned and put away. Anna and Momma weren't there. Petey called for Momma, and from upstairs she heard, "Up here!"

Petey and her little brother climbed easy up the steps, each carrying their bag; Hill having to hug his to him so he wouldn't drop it. Petey made sure she had the bag that held the eggs with her. They set the bags on the counter and stood watching Momma and Anna looking through recipe books. Momma's palomino hair close to Anna's darker hair.

Momma said, "Put away those groceries, kids. We got lots to do."

Petey began taking things out of her bag. There at the bottom was the candy. She said to Hill, "You stinker. How'd you do that?"

Hill haw haw'd.

"Hill? Help Petey put away the groceries, okay?"

"Oh-kay doe-kay."

While Hill and Petey put up groceries, Momma wrote on a sheet of paper, every so often putting the pencil to her lips.

Anna said, "A real chocolate cake. I can't believe it. It has real chocolate in it."

"What did you think was in chocolate cake?" Momma raised an eyebrow.

"I don't know. I mean, I always had mix cakes."

Momma shook her head with her for shame-for-shame look. Petey loved to see that.

When the groceries were put away, Petey asked, "Can I help?"

"Yes, you *may* help." Momma turned to Hill. "What about you?"

"I don't wanna cook the food. I like to tear it up with my teeth, grrrrrr! Then I swallow it and it goes in my stomach and then to my in-test-TINES! And then—"

"That's enough, Hill." Momma said.

Hill pawed the ground with his foot.

Petey had always said the same thing as Hill said about only wanting to eat what Momma made, but Petey thought of Anna and her own momma, how they were going to cook together and never had the chance. Petey had a chance so she would take it.

"You can make some coffee first, Petey. Okay?"

"Okay, Momma."

"Hill, open up all the windows; turn on the fans. Let's get some air circulating."

Hill charged round the house to shove up windows, turn on fans.

Petey cut on the fire to start the water to boil for coffee. The sound of cookbook pages turning as Anna called out things that sounded interesting to her, Momma's apron, Momma setting out ingredients on the counter, smell of the coffee as it began to brew, Hill yipping with excitement, a breeze whirled through—all of it, everything—made Petey feel so full of hope and joy, she could have danced around the room in full swing.

She ran into the bathroom and gazed into the mirror for the count of ten. Only she and the pickle bathroom looked back at her. The smell of lilacs and spice were there. Maybe Anna's tea had magic like Momma's baking. Maybe Anna put her heart into picking out her teas and that was helping Momma. Or maybe it was Momma saving and helping Anna. Thoughts swirled all around Petey's head and she realized she was still staring into the mirror and nothing scary was in the mirror with her. She ran back to the kitchen so she wouldn't miss anything.

Momma and Anna stood shoulder to shoulder as Momma showed her how to wash the chicken to prepare to cut it up. Anna watched as Momma patted the chicken to dry it off, then as she took her sharp knife and cut off one of the legs and then cut between the thigh and drumstick. She handed the knife to Anna. "Now you try it."

Anna's tongue stuck out a little as she cut into the leg.

"Be careful. That's a sharp knife. Just sort of wiggle the leg a bit if it gets stubborn. Don't lean so hard into it; let the knife and your hand work together. Your body should be more relaxed."

When Anna cut the leg and then the thigh and drumstick, she let out a "Whoop!"

Momma laughed.

Momma laughed . . . laughed. She *laughed*.

Petey poured Momma and Anna a cup of coffee, then asked, "What can I do?" More than anything she wanted to be a part of it all.

"Pour flour into that pan," Momma pointed to the square pan, "and then into that other pan," she pointed to the round pan, "pour the milk I've measured out, add that egg, then whip them together." She said to Petey, "All right?"

"Yes Ma'am. I've seen you do it before. I can do it."

"I know you can." Momma turned back to the chicken. She and Anna finished cutting it into pieces and started on the other chicken. Then Momma put the pieces into a big bowl. "Now, I'm going to cover these chicken parts in buttermilk. You bought buttermilk, didn't you, Petey?"

Petey ran to the refrigerator. "It's right here." She held the buttermilk as if it were filled with gold nuggets.

Momma nodded. Then to Anna, "First we'll salt and pepper." Momma let Anna salt and pepper the chicken. Momma then said, "And we'll add a little paprika." She massaged the chicken. "Okay, Anna, pour the buttermilk to cover the chicken." Anna poured.

Meanwhile, Petey had finished her job of putting the flour into the square pan, and the milk and egg into the round pan. She had whisked the milk and egg together. She waited for her next job.

"It's important to keep your hands washed and wipe everything off with soap and water when handling meats," Momma said as they washed. She then showed Anna how to season the flour mixture with salt, pepper, garlic and onion powder. She put a dash of hot sauce in the milk and egg, and told Anna, "Little touches make a big difference.

You don't want to over do any one spice, or have too many, simple in some things is best."

Anna wrote notes in a pad, face turned serious.

While the chicken sat in the buttermilk, Momma took out the frozen green beans since there were no fresh, and then peeled potatoes. Anna peeled beside her. Anna had a potato peeler; Momma used a paring knife. Her peelings were as thin, or maybe even thinner, than Anna's. As they peeled and cut the potatoes, they put the chunks into a pot of water to be boiled.

"Momma, what can I do?" Petey asked. She was near-abouts to have a fit just standing there.

"Clip my chocolate cake recipe to the holder." Momma said to Anna, "That recipe has been in my family for . . . well, for so long, no one knows where it first made itself appear."

Anna could only say, "Wow."

"And Petey, I think you can gather the ingredients for the cake. Start measuring them out?"

Momma had *never* let her do that. She nodded her silly idiot head, as if a cat got her tongue for sure and carried it off to Timbuktu.

"Remember, when baking we have to be particular. We can be more free and loose with some cooking, but not with baking if we want it to turn out just right. So measure careful and exact."

Anna scribbled more notes. Petey gathered ingredients.

"And it's best to measure out *all* your ingredients first. I once was going to bake a cake for my daddy's birthday and got my dry ingredients sifted, and then found out I didn't have any chocolate bar and only one egg!" Momma shook her head. "I likened to have thrown a fit I was so mad at myself. Couldn't get to the store, we lived a piece from it." Shaking that head again. "I learnt my lesson."

Petey wanted to hear more stories. She'd never thought of Momma as having stories. She'd never seen Momma as a *person* before, but right then she was like a real person.

Anna wrote more notes, and then gazed at Momma as if Momma held all the stars in heaven on her head. Petey bet if she went to the mirror right then she'd have that look, too.

Momma showed them how much oil to put into the iron pot, and how to make sure the oil was hot enough by sticking the end of the wooden spoon into the oil and when it bubbled just so that meant the oil was ready. When it was time to fry the chicken in the hot oil, Momma showed Anna and Petey how to dredge a few pieces of chicken at a time and explained to fry only a few pieces at a time so the oil wouldn't cool down. Momma put in the first piece of chicken, a thigh first, and then Anna put in a thigh. Momma let Petey put in a drumstick, only after making sure she knew to be careful so she'd not be splattered by hot grease.

The air filled with sounds of frying and the smells of chicken cooking. Petey inhaled all the way to the bottom of her lungs, and then some. Hill sniffed the air and panted like a hungry dog. Petey had almost forgotten he was there and couldn't believe how quiet he'd been. She turned to him, grinning, and he grinned back, his teeth stuck full of the candy he was eating.

Momma held out her hand to Hill. "Give it."

Hill whined.

"*Now.* You'll ruint your supper."

Hill handed Momma the candy bag and she put it on a high shelf. "You can have a little at a time, later."

When all the chicken was near-abouts fried, it was time for mashing the potatoes. Momma showed Petey and Anna the secret of putting the pot back on the fire to make sure all the water was out of the potatoes so they wouldn't be mooshy. Anna then added lots of butter, salt and pepper, and the cream Momma had measured out for her.

Hill said, "Can I mash up those taters?"

Momma said, "Wash up first."

"I already washed."

"When?"

Hill shrugged.

"Wash your hands good, always, before you get to cooking. That's a Rule you can't ever break in *my* kitchen."

Hill ran to wash his hands, and then came back to mash away. Afterwards, Momma would cover the chickens to keep them warm.

"Anna," Momma said, "one of those chickens is for you and your fellow. Everything else we're making is for our supper. You'll be staying for supper."

Anna said, "Yes Ma'am," then smiled over at Petey.

Petey could have danced on her toes all the way to Egypt.

"And you can do all this I've showed you on your own, can't you?"

"I think so," Anna answered. "But if I need you, can I come get you?"

"Of course you can," Momma said. "And that chicken, if you warm it up, be careful you don't let it dry out."

Anna nodded, scribbled something in her pad.

In a bit, as Anna sifted cake flour for the cake, Daddy walked through the door. He stood in the kitchen doorway with his mouth hanging open and his eyes popped wide. Hill ran to hug onto his legs.

"What in the world . . .?"

Petey said to him, "We're cooking, Daddy. We're helping Anna so she can cook for her date."

"What in the world . . .?" Daddy said again.

Momma talked as if things had never changed. As if she hadn't spent all those months fading away. "Go wash up. We're having fried chicken, mashed potatoes, green beans—oh! I forgot the biscuits!" She tightened her apron. "And if you're really hungry, I'll bake an extra cake once I show Anna here how to do one proper."

Daddy went straight to Momma in two long strides across the kitchen. He plopped a big kiss right on her lips, leaning her backwards, not even caring that we all were there to see it.

Anna laughed her laugh.

Hill barked two happy barks, then said, "Look at Daddy!"

Petey's toe dance went past Egypt and all the way to Saturn's rings where she went round and round, dizzy round.

Daddy turned, still holding onto Momma, and said, "So, this is Anna from downstairs."

Anna said, that pinky blush on her cheeks, "Nice to meet you properly."

"It's surely nice to meet you, too." Daddy let loose of Momma and went to the back. Petey heard the water running, and whistling. The sounds of water running, whistling, the kitchen sounds, made Petey hiccup with happy. Normal sounds. Good ole normal smells and normal sounds.

While Anna's cake baked (and Petey's mouth watered so much she thought she'd drool on her chin), they all sat down to eat: Momma, Daddy, Hill, Petey, and Anna. There wasn't much talking, but a whole lot of chewing and *mmm mmm this is good*. Even Momma managed to eat more than she had been.

Momma tapped her lips with her napkin, then asked Anna, "Now, are you going to call that young man back and re-set that date?"

"Yes. I will." Anna then said, "I'd like him to meet you, Miss Beth." She looked around the table. "I'd like him to meet all y'all."

"Well," Momma said, "We'll have him to dinner . . . later, not until after your date."

Right then, it felt as if Anna *was* her sister, that they were all a big family.

When supper was over, and the cake cooled, Momma showed Anna how to frost it so crumbs didn't mash in with the frosting. "Now, first you brush off all the crumbs on your cooled cake." Momma brushed the crumbs away with a pastry brush. "Next put a thin layer of frosting on." She layered on a thin layer of frosting. "We'll let that make a seal in the ice-box, then when we frost it the rest of the way, there won't be crumbs mixing in."

Anna said, "I never thought of that!"

Petey felt proud of Momma. She stepped close, touched her on the hip, and Momma turned and smiled at her as she used to, with her eyes lit up and her cheeks puffed so cute with a dimple showing. In the heat of the kitchen, pieces of her palomino hair curled from its kerchief and sprung around her face.

When the kitchen was cleaned up and Anna's cake iced, Momma wrapped up the fried chicken for Anna. She said, "You make those potatoes like I showed you, and along with the cake—Petey you carry down the cake for Anna—your man will flip. I'll send down a piece of the next cake for you to taste after-while."

"Thank you, Miss Beth." Anna put her head into Momma's shoulder.

Momma stroked Anna's shiny hair. "There there, now. It's okay."

Petey stayed quiet as she could be. She was glad Hill and Daddy were outside and it was just the girls again.

Momma said, "Well, now. Time to get busy on that other cake. You two go on down, then."

Anna picked up her chicken, and Petey picked up the chocolate cake. The cake was heavy, the way she remembered, except Petey knew it was moist and light in taste. As she headed out the door behind Anna, Momma was already measuring ingredients for their cake for dessert.

Downstairs in Anna's kitchen, Petey put down the cake. Anna put the chicken in the refrigerator. She said, "I can't believe your mom did all that for me."

"That's just Momma. It's her way." She didn't say, *that's how Momma used to be and now she is again and it's cause of you, Anna.*

Hill called out, "*Peeeeeeteeeeeey!* Daddy says come here. Petey! Hurry up! Daddy says."

Petey told Anna she'd see her later, and, "I hope you have a good date."

"I hope so, too." She shrugged. "But, if not, at least we'll eat well." She laughed her lovely laugh.

When Petey ran out to Hill and Daddy, Daddy was jingling his keys to his 1966 Ford Country Squire. "Come on, you two. Your momma needs some more things at the store."

"We already got stuff from the store," Hill said.

"She needs some other things. Quit bellyaching and come on." Daddy's words sounded like he was fussing, but his face and smile said he was glad about things.

Petey noticed in the back of the station wagon there were bags from the hardware store. She wondered what all Daddy'd bought and what all he'd be doing with the half-house.

Petey let Hill have the front seat and Petey took the back, and then they'd switch up on the way home. Daddy shot off for the grocery store. Once there, Petey and Hill helped Daddy find what all he had trouble with and soon their basket was filled. While waiting in line, Daddy jangled the change and keys in this pocket, and then sang, "Black Jack Davey came riding through the woods; and he sang so loud *mmm-mmm*!; made the hills round him . . . hills round him . . . *mmmm-mmmm*; and he charmed the heart of a lady; *ohhhhhhh*! He charmed the heart of that *laaa*-dy . . ."

When their groceries were loaded into the station wagon, Daddy sped home with all the windows open to the Texas night and bugs splatting the windshield.

Momma had on a clean apron, and there were things lined up on the counters, and their chocolate cake was in the oven. They all put up groceries, and then Momma said, "Now, I need all of you to skedaddle. Out. Fly away little birds. Leave me be for a while."

Hill said, "How come? What're you going to do? Why you want us to skee-dee-daddle?"

Petey wanted to ask the same thing. She thought she could help.

"Let your momma have some time, kids." Daddy steered Petey and Hill to their room. "Won't hurt you to stay in here a while. Read a book, or whatever you do."

Momma called out, "Daddy'll bring you some cake in a bit, but I don't want to find crumbs everywhere and especially on the beds."

Later, after they'd had their cake while sitting on the floor of their room, Hill climbed out of the window and onto the scraggly tree limb, shimmied down the tree, and without a sound ran around the yard flapping his arms—Petey knew because she watched him until she was bored.

Petey took *The Incredible Journey* from her nightstand, opened it at the page she'd put a bubble gum wrapper to hold her place. She was almost finished. The dogs and cat were almost home. Petey thought hard about the dogs and cat. How even though those animals had been far from their family, somehow they were finding their way to where they belonged. Their *family* was their *home*. She thought on that a long while. Chewed on it. Tasted it. Swallowed it. Let her stomach have at it. Let it get in her veins and fly around with her corpuscles (she loved the sound of that word, and the way it made her mouth move funny, *cor-pus-cles*).

After she and Hill had their baths and teethbrushing, she settled in with Anna's mythology book, opening it as careful as she could. She read about Athena first. She liked how Athena was a girl warrior god, and had wisdom and justice. It was weird how Zeus swallowed Athena's momma while she was pregnant with Athena, and Athena came right out the top of Zeus's head. And how Athena never was even a baby, but was born grown with her armor on, ready to do battle.

When Petey woke late into the night, the book on her nightstand and the light off—Momma or Daddy must have come in to check on her—she lifted the room divider sheet to see Hill was asleep, his fist caught up under his chin and his covers tangled. The house was quiet and the air in the room smelled like Texas, dark and something sweet that wasn't flowers. She put her ear to the floor. When she didn't hear any violin music, she pictured Anna sleeping with a smile touching her lips. She tiptoed to the bathroom, but didn't want to look into the mirror at night. After letting loose her bladder and then washing her hands, she forced herself to look up into the mirror once anyway, real quick, to be brave. It wasn't too bad.

Petey sneaked down the hall. Her parents' door was closed, and all was still. When she went into the kitchen, her eyes bugged out and she whispered what Daddy had said, "What in the world . . .?"

On the counter and on the table were Momma's goodies. There was another chocolate cake not counting the leftovers of the one they'd had for dessert, a carrot cake, and a lemon cake. There was an apple pie, cherry pie, and blackberry pie. There was a peach cobbler.

The whole kitchen smelled of Momma's sweets. Petey gawked, stuck her finger into one of the pies to make sure it was real, sucked the cherry juice from her finger. It was real. Dreams didn't taste so good.

Petey went back to bed, and was soon drifting away. Anna and Momma had baked so many pies they were wading through them, looking for Hill, who was howling and yelling, "I'm lost in all these pies! I can't eat my way out! Help! Help!" They were laughing and laughing. Laughing and laughing. Laughing. Petey awoke to someone laughing.

She shot out of bed and ran down the hall. Daddy stood laughing in the kitchen, while Momma brewed coffee. Momma had a little grin at the corners of her mouth.

Daddy said, "I knew you were up half the night, but . . . Beth? My lord!"

That started off Momma. She baked most every day. She gave Anna pies and cakes until Anna begged her not to give her anymore. Anna took some to the dance studio, even though she said half her students wouldn't eat a sweet if it hopped up and slapped them silly. Daddy took goodies to work, and came home telling Momma how everyone asked for more. Momma had Daddy carry pies and cakes down to the church supper on Wednesday, even though they never went to the church supper. She baked for the nursing home. She baked for Petey and Hill's school teachers and principal and Bus-Driver Bill. She baked for the policemen at the police station and for the firemen at the fire station.

And during all that baking and sweets and pure-D madness, Anna had had her date. She'd had to re-fry another chicken and bake another cake (with Momma's help) since her date turned out to be a week after Momma had shown her how to cook. Momma told Hill and Petey if they so much as stuck one nostril in Anna's business, she'd punish them for a month. Petey about jittered a fit she wanted to spy so bad. All she had was a peek at a dark-haired head as he stepped from his little car with the top down and into Anna's house. Anna ran up the stairs twice and asked Momma for advice. Petey'd danced from one foot to the other, but Momma had given her a look that said to keep her mouth closed.

Finally, when Petey couldn't hardly stand it anymore, Anna brought Stephen up to supper. The whole time Stephen kept his sweet eyes to Anna as if she were something he wanted to put in his pocket and keep forever. What Petey liked the best was how Anna was the same, whether Stephen was there or not she didn't act silly like some of the girls Petey saw at school when they were around boys. Anna stayed Anna. Petey was proud of that.

And still Momma kept baking. Petey ate so much sweet, her pants began to tighten. Daddy said he'd had to move a belt hole over. Hill stayed as skinny as always.

One day Daddy came home from work with a big grin and said, "Wrap up two of those chocolate cakes, and can you bake a cherry pie and a lemon meringue?"

Momma said, "There's chocolate pie over there already made."

Daddy pulled money out of his pocket. "No, you don't understand." He reached out the money to Momma. "This money is yours. They want to *buy* them. They said no more taking your bakeries for free."

Momma stared at the cash, reached out and touched it. Then she washed her hands, tightened her apron, and set to work.

Daddy put the money into a jar and made a label for it that read, "Momma's Sweet Jar."

That week, Momma had orders for three more cakes, two pies, and three-dozen cookies. When Daddy was back from taking a cake to the church supper on Wednesday, he told Momma the pastor wanted to buy some of her cakes, pies, and cookies for a bake sale to raise money for the church. He said, "He'll pay for the ingredients, plus pay you for your labor."

"I can't take money from the church."

"He insists. Says the church will make plenty money and he wants things to be fair."

Momma tied up her palomino hair and put on a clean apron.

Petey helped her more and more, learning more things about baking than she ever thought she could learn. She'd been helping cook suppers, too—biscuits and gravy, stewed chicken, meatloaf and potatoes, beans and cornbread.

Soon, Momma asked Anna if she wanted to help, for pay. Anna said, "Yes! I think I'm getting pretty good at it."

Momma said, "You're a natural. You just needed a chance."

Anna lit up like a Christmas tree that had finally been found by the perfect family and taken home.

Momma said to Petey, "And I'll start paying you a wage, too, Petey."

Petey about split her lips she smiled so wide.

The orders were coming in faster. Momma never complained, just kept going, sometimes late into the night to where Petey would wake up and smell the baking and hear Momma's whisk whisking or the oven door squeaking or the mixer whirring.

Sometimes while they worked together (Petey after school, Anna after dance classes), Momma and Anna told stories. Momma would tell how she used to gather frogs when she was a little girl, and put toilet paper diapers on them, naming them silly names like Peanuckle or Boomdidledee or Skeedaddledah. That made Petey laugh. Momma said she had to make up a lot of games to play alone, since she was an only child. She told how one Christmas when she was little, they'd not had much under the tree, but she hadn't cared. She said Grandma always made Christmas happy somehow, no matter if they had any money or not.

Anna told stories about her parents, and how she'd been an only child, too, so she had similar stories of playing games by her lonesome. Sometimes she talked about Stephen, and Petey didn't mind hearing that so much since Anna didn't act all gooey-eyed and romantical. Like how he'd taken her to the movies, or out to eat at restaurants, or how she'd cook something for him using the notes and lessons Momma gave her. She said she was even teaching Stephen to cook, so if they were ever married, not that she wanted to be married mind you, she said (and Petey smiled), he could do some of the cooking himself while she put up her feet.

Once Petey woke to go to the bathroom and walked in on Momma lying in a sea of bubbles, a cup of tea steaming on the side of the tub. Petey said, "Oh, sorry Momma."

"That's okay, sweetie. I'm just relaxing. Anna's tea is wonderful . . . wonderful."

Petey thought maybe she'd like to try some of that tea. She went back to bed and soon she was leaning back against a tulip poplar, her feet dangling in the cold creek, while the mountains rose up all around her and the air smelled fresh and new. She woke startled, with an ache in her chest that she'd not felt for a time. Until that dream, she'd almost let herself forget how she missed North Carolina. Everything had been so exciting. But with the dream came the toothache in her body feeling. She turned over and covered her head with her pillow. It was a long time before she felt her eyelids dropping down down.

Chapter 8

Petey flopped home from exploring in the woods to find Daddy painting the kitchen. The ugly as a baboon's behind curtains were down and the glass gleamed. Momma stepped in with a bucket and big sponge, eyed Petey, and said, "The faster we get this place cleaned, the faster you can have that lilac wall you've been wanting."

Petey hated cleaning more than goose grease on the sidewalk but she grabbed a sponge and set to work. Soon as Hill panted in from the scraggly woods, he was put to work, too, even though he howled about it.

While Petey cleaned, she wondered why she felt more cranky than happy. She thought about her best-ever friend Angela, who wrote letters that weren't as long as they used to be, but felt longer with all the things she didn't say and Petey only imagined. There was the letter where Angela said Barry Burke had been holding hands with Sarah, and how Angela went to the movies with Serena and Anita. Petey didn't understand the hard knot the letters caused in her stomach, so hard that sometimes she couldn't hardly swallow her supper. Her stomach acted as if it was mad at her. That night, she asked Momma if she could use her soap bubbles and have some of her special tea.

Momma looked her over, as if expecting to see something on her skin that told of her inside hurts. "What's wrong?"

Petey shrugged.

"You sick?"

She shook her head.

"Can you tell me at all?"

"I miss home, that's all." Petey kicked at the kitchen table chair. "I mean, Angela's making new friends. And I miss playing in the creek." She took a breath, let it out, her cheeks flaming. "And Barry Burke was holding hands with Sarah." She quick-added, "But I don't care about him any-ole-way. Don't know why I even said it." She kicked the chair harder.

Momma put on the kettle to boil. Petey followed her when she went to the bathroom and ran a tub of lilac bubbles. "Get in the tub.

I'll make you some tea."

As Petey sipped the tea and lay in the bubbles, she thought about things. Thought about how people couldn't have everything they wanted all the time. How she should be happy enough with Momma gaining weight and smiling and baking. With Daddy making new friends at his work. With Hill finding a friend and him maybe not quite so wild, even if he still acted like an animal covered in fur. She should feel happy enough, still . . . still.

She thought of how when she saw her daddy painting, instead of feeling happy she'd had a cramp through her body. She knew then that seeing that paint meant they were staying in the half-house and not going back to North Carolina. Didn't it?

She finished the tea, rinsed off, and didn't feel anything different one bit, couldn't feel any answers to all her questions. She felt like one big question mark.

Then before she knew it, Petey came home from school to a whole different half-house. Even though her parents had been doing something every day, she'd not had the full force of it all until most everything was done. She'd seen the catalogues open and things circled like curtains, towels, and all that. She'd seen the paint card samples with names that came from the earth like ocean, sand, sage, eggshell. She walked around the house, looking, touching. But that day as she came home from school, *slam bam* it hit her—their half-house was fixed up nice.

The kitchen was painted a soft green like a lamb's ear plant, and the cabinets cream like the milk come straight from the cow's udder. At the window there was a darker green cloth pull shade (Petey thought, *maybe colored like herb from the garden green*) that was pulled most the way up to let in a cooled breeze. In the living room was also the lamb's ear green with the baseboards painted the same cow udder cream as the cabinets, and there was a flower-printed rug under their coffee table at the front of their leather couch. On the windows were nice blinds and thin cotton see-through curtains that swept to the floor and swayed in that breeze that passed through the opened blinds.

There was no more pickle bathroom, and instead was half green painted wall on top and on the paneled bottom was the cream. On the floor were dark green bathrugs. Petey thought they must have had a sale on the lamb's ear green and from-the-cow-udder cream. She had to admit it made the half-house seem bigger having the same colors go from room to room.

Her parents' bedroom was all cream, with a colorful quilt that Petey recognized was one her grandma made; it had been put away before. She stepped into her room. Hill had his way and there were zebra stripes, but only in a zebra painted over fresh cream-painted wall. The sheet between their beds wasn't there and instead there was a heavier white (milk from the store white) curtain. Daddy said he had another idea he was going to try later. Petey's side of the room was lilac and she had her bedspread with the wild flowers, and her rug shaped like a flower bloomed.

Petey wandered outside and walked around their yard. Momma had put in a garden and Daddy was still trying things to make grass grow better.

It all was as if they were never leaving.

Petey ploddered back into the house. Momma had left a note that she was at the grocery with Anna. It seemed strange not having Momma at home all the time. Petey was glad, but that glad mixed with lonely. She was a stupid idiot girl who was never satisfied.

Daddy at work. Hill was at the playground with his friend. Petey was alone.

She lay on her bed and felt the cool from outside. At least the weather wasn't as hot. There'd been no snow or promise of snow. They'd had a few cold nights, and one freeze where the trees were heavy and glittering with ice. The weather couldn't seem to make up its mind whether it was winter or summer, back and forth back and forth the cold and hot went. Petey picked up *To Kill a Mockingbird* and decided she needed to escape. That was the best thing ever about reading books; how she could go anywhere she wanted just by following the person she was reading about.

She was so into the story, at the part where Scout was rubbing Walter Cunningham's nose in the dirt (oh, Petey loved it!), she hadn't noticed that Anna and Momma were back. When she rose and went down the hall and into the kitchen, they were rolling out pie crust. Anna was talking about a trip to Greece and how maybe Stephen would be going with her. Momma said she'd love to see Italy or Scotland.

Then Momma said, "Do you think you could teach me to dance a little? I've always wanted to know how to rumba or that dance they do when the man has a rose in his mouth. It's such a romantic dance."

Petey about fainted dead away; she had no idea Momma wanted to do those romantical kinds of things with dancing and roses in the mouth.

Anna said, "I'd love to teach you to dance. That would be so much fun."

Petey felt as if she were a stranger in the house. Everyone seemed to be doing fine. Everyone was going on and finding new things. Hill had a friend. Daddy had his projects around the house and sometimes had some of the men from work over for barbeque. Momma was filling and re-filling her Sweet Jar from all her baking, and she was talking about dancing around with flowers. Anna was like a part of the family—like a sister—just as Petey had wanted. All Petey had done was look into mirrors like a stupid idiot.

Momma turned to her. "Hi, sweetie. Did we wake you from a nap?"

Petey shook her head no.

"How was school?" Anna smiled at her.

Petey shrugged.

"Your mom wants to take some dance lessons. What about you?"

Petey shook her head no.

Momma stepped to her, put her lips on Petey's forehead, as she always did to check for fever. She stepped back. "I hope you aren't getting sick."

Anna looked at Petey and Petey stared down at the floor.

"Miss Beth, can you excuse Petey and me a minute?"

"Sure. I'll get the cherry filling started."

Anna said, "Petey, come on." She headed outside.

Petey followed Anna down to Anna's half-house. Once inside, Anna sat at her table and pointed to the chair across from her. Petey sat.

"Petey?"

Then it all gushed out as if Petey had vomited. She told Anna how long she'd wanted their house to be nice, and that had come true. How she wanted Momma to be herself again, and now she was and even more so. She told how she wanted to hear her daddy whistle as he worked around the yard or house, and he was doing that. How she wanted Hill to have a friend and not feel bad for being so different, and he had a friend and couldn't care less if anyone thought he was different. And how she was never happy no matter what.

"And I tried the tea while soaking in Momma's bubbles and I didn't feel a thing different. I'm a lost cause," Petey said.

"You can't use your mom's tea! Everyone is unique, and every unique person has to have their own unique tea." She stood, went to her pantry. "I need to think about this. What kind of tea is especially for you and you alone? And when you drink it, you must be where you like to relax. You can't copy what someone else does, you see?"

Petey shrugged again, but it felt rude, so she said, "I guess so."

Anna pulled out teas, opened them and sniffed, put them back. Pulled out more, sniffed, put back. Once again, sniff-put back. At last, she held a tea and said, "Aha! This is *your* tea. It has hibiscus flower, and rosemary, and other secret herbs and spices." She came back to the table. "I bought this tea at a strange little shop. There was this beautiful woman there and she said, 'Take this tea.' And I asked, 'What is it for?' and she smiled and said, 'You'll find out when it's needed.'" Anna stroked the tea box, "The entire time I was in that shop I knew it was special and magical and all the teas in it were, too. I saved this tea even though I didn't know what I was saving it for, or for whom. Now I do. Just as she said." She slid the tea to Petey.

Petey thought it was the most beautiful tea box she'd ever seen. It was a reddish brown wood with colorful carvings of birds and flowers that seemed so real that she thought she could smell the blooms and hear the birds sing. She reached out and touched the box, then opened the lid. Spice, herb, and sweet flew up into her nose. She put the lid back on the tea and picked up the box, held it to her chest. "Thank you, Anna." Then in a rush. "I wish you were my sister for real."

"But I am, Petey. Don't you know that? Your family is like my family, so that makes you my for-real sister, right?"

Petey smiled, smoothed her fingers on the box, rubbed the carvings.

"Now, let's go help your mom get those pies done. I'm making her take a night off tomorrow so she can come to dance class."

That night, Petey couldn't stop opening the tea box and taking in the smell. She couldn't wait to try it. She only had to figure out where she could drink it. Maybe in the garden, where it was always quiet and something always grew, even in winter.

Chapter 9

Petey held on to her booksack as the bus popped to a stop. Bus-Driver Bill said, "Get along little doggies!" Hill wasn't on the bus, so she was the only doggie. The little blonde-haired kid's momma had picked up him and Hill straight from school to take them for ice cream.

As Petey stepped off the last step of the bus, she felt someone close behind her. With her feet on the grass, she looked up at Mary stepping off behind her. Mary was grinning, her eyes bright as if she had lights lit up inside her brain.

"My mom said I could come to your house!"

Petey said, "Oh," and didn't know what else to say. She didn't want to be rude but she'd not invited Mary to her house.

"I can't wait to see where you live, maybe you can come to my house next; I live about, let's see, twenty or thirty minutes from here; I watch you get off the bus every day and think how I should just get off the bus with you and then one day I thought well why not and then I asked my mom and she said let me think about it and then she thought about it and said it was okay as long as she could come get me after two hours at the most and I said two hours only? and she said I shouldn't overstay my welcome and she asked if I could get your mom to make her a blueberry pie and a carrot cake and she'd pay her and even gave me some money . . ."

Petey walked faster to get away from all the words swirling around her face like gnats, but Mary only walked faster, too, swinging her arms, hitting Petey's arm every so often. Then she linked her arm around Petey's arm. Petey didn't know what to think about that. It made her walk funny, trying to keep in step with Mary until finally she pretended to see a rock she wanted and bent to pick it up. Mary let go her arm then and watched her as she put the rock into her pocket.

"Oh! You like rocks! I will find you rocks then. All kinds. Whenever I go somewhere I'll look at a rock and think; would Petey like this rock? And if I think you will, I'll pick it up and give it to you."

Mary's shoes slapped on the road and as they turned into the driveway, Petey felt weird. What if Mary thought her half-house was ugly, even with all the repairs and paint and other new things? Daddy had painted the whole house on the outside the same blue with white trim and it looked so much better. He'd fixed the carport best he could, and cleaned off the rust on the stairs and painted the stairs black, to boot. Daddy fixed the yard better, and Momma's garden would make vegetables and herbs and flowers and fruit. Petey never would have thought Momma could make things grow in that dirt yard, but she had and would.

". . . and just think summer vacation is almost here and I can't wait to go swimming; hey you want to go swimming with me?; we go to the community swimming pool and they have hot dogs and cotton candy and Cokes and all kinds of things . . ."

Petey couldn't believe they'd been in Fort Worth almost a year. The day they'd left North Carolina, Petey had thought somehow they'd find their way back way before a year had passed, and it looked like more than a year would pass again. She'd been drinking Anna's tea. Her relaxing spot, as she'd thought it'd be, was in Momma's butterfly garden, with the bench Momma had put there to sit on and look at her flowers and the butterflies and bees and birds that flittered about. The tea did help Petey. Some.

". . . and that dog slipped up and nipped me right on my leg and we thought he was mean until it turns out I had peanut butter on my leg and the dog was trying to get to the peanut butter; have you ever heard such a thing as that . . .hey! we're at y'all's house!"

"Yep. This is where I live."

"This is a *huge* house; my house isn't near this big and I thought I did have a big house, but Mom says she won't clean a bigger house she has enough to do with five kids and two dogs and a cat and a hamster and two mouses and two guinea pigs and I want a pig but Mom says there is *no way*! but this house isn't too too big don't get me wrong and *I love it!*"

"Well, it's not all my house. We live in the upstairs half and Anna lives in the downstairs half."

"Wow! That's really something. I've never been inside houses that are cut in two houses; what an idea, I am *intrigued*." Mary was practically skimming the air as they walked up to the half-houses. "And look at the pretty flower garden! And look at that! Is that tomatoes? Oh! I love fresh tomatoes! You live in the best place ever! You are so lucky to be back here and not all crowded up with other people; Dad says he could fart and the neighbors hear him and that's gross but I wonder if it's true, but y'all don't have to worry about that!"

Petey began to see things through Mary's eyes. And things were even better than they were before.

"Where's your brother? You have the cutest brother, I don't care what people say, they are just mean and don't know better."

"He's with his friend having ice cream."

"Oh! Did you know that blonde-haired kid was left on a church doorstep?"

"What? . . . He what?"

"Yeah. His parents didn't want him, I guess, or couldn't take care of him. Mom said he was scrawny and sick from not being fed right or whatever. They left a note and said to find him a good home. So the church took the baby in and then he went to an orphanage for a while but not long and the Tylers adopted him, but he sure seems happy about it."

"Left on a doorstep." Petey shook her head.

"No, it's good. He's happy as a little ocean clam, always grinning his fool head off and running around and all. The Tylers take good care of him and Mom said he's healthy and happy. And now he's got a good friend." Mary said to Petey, "Good friends are hard to find and best to keep."

Petey said, "Come on and I'll show you my room."

They clanged up the steps, and Petey could smell the sweet before they reached the door. The sweet was always there, even when Momma wasn't cooking. The sugar and sweet had seeped into the floors, into the cracks and corners, into the paint, into the curtains, into the chairs' upholstery, into their clothes, their hair. Everyone and everything smelled like sugar and sweet.

Mary said, as if reading Petey's mind, "The house smells like you, like vanilla and sugar. Ummm!" She ogled the pies and cakes and sweet rolls on the counter. "Oh, here's my mom's note for your mom. Where is she? How did she learn to cook stuff like she does? Everybody talks about it. They think she's some kind of wonder of the world or something."

"She's probably taking a dance lesson with Anna."

"Dance lessons! Wow! She dances, too? Oh! Your mom is in-*tree*-ging. And who's Anna? You said something about her earlier."

Petey explained about Anna. How she was a part of their family. How Momma and Daddy went dancing sometimes after Anna had taught them some fancy dance steps. She didn't tell Mary about when she had caught her parents dancing slow to the record player in the living room, and how seeing them dance like that, as if there was no one else in the entire universe but them two, made Petey's heart squeeze with love.

Mary said, "I like your house. It's pretty on the inside, too. I am *so* glad you invited me." Of course, Petey didn't tell her she hadn't invited her. They made their way to Petey's room, and Mary said, "Oh! Look at this! And look at the Zebra! And is this part your room? *I love it!* So *intriguing.*"

Daddy had fashioned a kind of wall between the two rooms, one that slid on rollers so they could open or close it. Petey kept it closed most all the time, unless Hill had a bad dream or they wanted to play together. She still had to walk through the door and then turn right to go into her part of the room. When anyone first walked through the door, they could see Hill's part and her part all at once and had to turn right or left according to which room they were going in.

Daddy had said he couldn't build a real wall because it wasn't their house. He said the landlord gave them a break on rent for all the other work he'd done, though. Then Daddy had said, "Besides, it's not like we're staying here forever."

Petey didn't ask where they'd go.

Mary asked, "Petey? I asked you where you got that bed? *I love it!*" Every time Mary said, "I love it!" she threw up her hands in a way that made Petey want to laugh.

"I got that for my birthday. I like it, too." She touched the white iron bed. Her twelfth birthday had been fun, but she right then thought how it would have been much more fun with Mary there jumping up on her toes and saying "*I love it!*"

Mary ran to the white-framed mirror that hung over the dresser. "Look at me; a complete disaster area on two legs; I swear if I could only be gorgeous I'd have the world in the palm of my hands, that's what my big sister always says; she is ob-*sessed* with being gorgeous and always goes on diets and loses and gains and loses and gains; not me; I eat what I want to eat when I want it."

Petey stood beside her. It was the first time someone had joined her in the mirror. It was the first time since so long ago that she even had a mirror in her room. And still, she was rumpled up and messy. Seems having a mirror didn't always mean Petey fixed herself up as she should. And she didn't think Mary was too much a mess, though she wasn't as perfect as Angela always had been.

They sat on Petey's bed and Mary talked and talked and talked. Momma came home, telling Anna the story about how Daddy'd once been caught in a snow storm and had to spend the night in the car, and how she'd worried and fretted, and how she had been pregnant with Hill. She'd gone outside over and over and searched and searched for Daddy's lights coming up the drive. She'd called the police, but they were doing all they could to help people. Momma said she didn't sleep all night and all night Hill kicked and kicked inside her, pushing against her, wanting out out out and how she prayed and prayed that Hill would wait, and lucky for them both, he did. She said she'd never forget that night.

They stepped into Petey's room and Petey introduced Anna and Momma to Mary. Mary jumped up and said, "How do you do I'm Mary but Petey already said that I just *love* your house and the garden and *everything* and my mom wants you to bake and she gave me some money to give you but wasn't sure how much and she'll be here in a little while to get me so you can talk to her because she's been wanting to meet you she bought some of your cookies and a pie at the church bake sale . . ."

Anna and Momma stared at Mary with their mouths partly opened.

Finally, when Mary stopped talking, Anna said, "I have a special tea for that."

And Momma laughed.

Petey went to bed that night and after Momma came in and sang to them (even though Petey thought she was getting too old for that, she secretly loved it) and thought about Mary. She had fun with her, and even with her mouth going on and on, Petey had laughed and felt happy. It was sort of the same as it had been with Angela, except different. It made things confusing, since going home to North Carolina was still her dream, but there were things in Texas that had turned out good. She was split right in two pieces, even if they weren't even pieces. Her North Carolina piece would always be bigger.

She couldn't sleep, rose, and walked silent to go to the kitchen for a glass of water. Hearing her parents' quiet voices, Petey stopped in the hallway outside the kitchen and listened.

". . . fellas want to have a barbeque."

"That sounds good."

"Have you looked at that building yet?"

Momma sighed, then said, "Yes, but I'm still undecided. I've definitely outgrown this kitchen, and Anna's kitchen. If we rent that building, can we afford another house? I know we've talked about moving to another place."

"If you rent the building, we'll soon make enough money for us to afford something else. But I'll be no kept man! I'm up for a raise. Maybe a promotion if things keep going as they're going."

Petey held her breath to the count of five, then let it out slow.

"We need a Plan for the Future, but a different one than we had before."

"Yes, I suppose so. Things have worked in ways I never imagined."

"Quinn?"

"Yes?"

"I know you miss the mountains."

"I just don't know. I'm tore up about it. Seems since we moved here things went from as awful as I could ever imagine to . . . well, to how it is now. Look at you." There was a pause and Petey imagined Daddy brushing Momma's palomino hair back, taking her hand. "You're smiling again and doing what you always wanted to do."

"And I could do it anywhere."

"You know things aren't that simple."

I miss the mountains, too, Daddy, Petey wanted to say.

"We could plan a vacation there . . . back . . . back home. Oh, I do miss home, too."

"Let's plan it then," Daddy said. "I'll check with my boss, see when I can take off."

Petey sneaked back to her room. She checked to make sure Hill was in his bed and he wasn't. She peeked out his window. He sat on his tree limb, looking out at the stars. Petey called out, "Hill . . . come to bed."

Hill hoo hoo'd, hoo hoo'd.

"Come on, stupid breath, before you fall and break your fool neck."

Hill grinned and his teeth glowed in the moonlight. He scrabbled down the limb and into his window.

Petey went back to her bed.

Hill went around the partition and said, "Good night, anus breath."

"Night, frog licker."

Petey was so sleepy, sleepy. They were all baking pies and cakes and more pies and cakes and some looked like weird shapes and some rose up to the ceiling and some pushed out through the screen door. Mary talked to Angela and Angela turned to Petey and said, "Does she ever shut up?" and Petey shook her head no. Angela shrugged and put on lipgloss and then said, "Got to go! See ya!" and she disappeared. Daddy appeared and said, "Everything's bigger in Texas," and he pointed to a mountain that was pushing up out of the ground, right under their house, up up up they went, so it was like they were in, and on, the mountains, but it was Texas, too.

Petey woke that morning wishing her dream was real, that she could be in both places. She didn't know which was worse, when she'd hated living in Texas and thought it horrid and hot and flat, or, when she knew the good things in it and it made her feel funny in her stomach to think of leaving them behind—like Mary and Anna.

One thing Petey knew for sure: life was always weird. Nobody ever seemed to get exactly what they wanted at exactly the time they needed it. There was always want.

Chapter 10

Petey closed her suitcase, grabbed the handle, and brought the suitcase out to the car. Daddy was already inside, hands on the steering wheel, ready to go. Hill was in the backseat, his head out the window, tongue hanging out. Momma watered her garden, one last time before they left for their vacation to North Carolina. They were staying in a little log cabin by a creek, off Soco Road. Uncle Zack was doing a furniture job in Georgia and besides, Momma said she hated to crowd him up. She didn't want to crowd up Grandma, either, and instead Grandma was coming to visit them later in the week.

Petey put her suitcase in the back, and then climbed in beside Hill. Her stomach fluttered and flinched. She was excited, and also worried. What if when they were there, back home, it wasn't like home at all? They'd be like all the tourists they used to watch. Back then, she'd felt so lucky to live there and the tourists were the ones who had to stay a little while and then leave.

Momma climbed up the iron stairs, went inside, came out with a box, and shut and locked the door. She went down the steps, knocked on Anna's door, and soon Anna stepped out with her suitcase, which she put in the back. Anna slid in with Hill and Petey, and Momma sat in her seat in the front. Petey had been so happy when she found out Anna was coming. Momma had said, "Of course she is," as if there was never any thought or question about it.

Anna said, "I am so excited! In all my travels, I've never been to North Carolina."

Momma said, "You'll love it. It's so beautiful."

"There's no place anywhere like the mountains," Daddy said.

Petey put her hands in her lap. She didn't feel like talking. She'd written to Angela to let her know she was coming, and Angela had written back to say she couldn't wait. From pictures Angela had sent Petey worried, for Angela had grown tall, and wore clothes that were fashionable and her hair was cut so it belonged on a grown woman and not a girl. She wore a bra, too. She'd told Petey all about it. Petey looked down at her chest: nothing.

They did as they'd done before, except when they stopped in Arkansas, they were able to get two rooms; one for the girls and one for the boys. They also were able to eat at a restaurant. The next day, Petey glued her attention to the window, watching and waiting for the mountains, knowing that right around a curve they'd suddenly be there, big and sweet as grandfathers. And sure enough, there, around the curve, up up up they rose. Petey caught up her breath. She thought sure Daddy caught up his.

Anna said, "My goodness."

Hill let out an excited whimper.

Momma said, "Oh." As if she'd forgotten how lovely it was. The last time they'd been there having been for poor Rock's funeral.

Petey knew Momma would go see her baby boy. See how the grass had grown over him. She worried Momma would go back to being sad again.

The whole car was quiet as they made their way into Haywood County, onto Soco Road, then turning at Moody Farm. They swept around, then up, and followed the creek round to the little log cabin next to the creek, on a road that didn't have hardly any other houses. Through her open window, Petey had heard two dogs bark at them as they drove by, and after that, other than the creek and the birds, all else was quiet.

They pulled into the driveway and everyone poured out of the car.

Daddy inhaled the air, deep and long, and said, "Ahhhhh."

Hill ran around sniffing everything.

Momma set herself to being busy taking things into the house; Anna helped her.

Petey stood by her daddy. He put his hand on her shoulder and held it there. It felt to Petey as if right then they were both the same person. But it was more like they were trees. Both their feet pushing down into the North Carolina earth, their faces lifted to the cool breeze, their ears listening to the creek rush rush rush, the birds singing, the air so sweet and clean—as sweet as sugar—the mountain ridges rising up around them. It was their home and that was that.

Scarcely one week. That's all they had there. Petey and her daddy stood rooted to the spot, and Petey just knew Daddy had to be thinking the same thing.

They spent the first three days showing Anna around. Daddy drove onto the Blue Ridge Parkway and he explained how it was 469 miles from starting in North Carolina to finishing in Virginia. They hopped on I-40 to Asheville to eat and walk downtown with all the locals and tourists. On a drive out to a secret picnic place that hardly anyone knew about, Daddy had a high-ole-time laughing at Anna's wide-eyes when on the skinny curvy road going up up, Daddy passed a car so close he could have reached out and flicked the other driver's ear. Anna had her hand to her mouth, then over her eyes, saying "Oh! Oh dear." In pretty little Maggie Valley they walked around the tourist shops, ate at Joey's Pancakes, visited Ghost Town in the Sky. Finally to sweet Main Street Waynesville, with its shops and food and people waving and saying hello.

On the fourth day, Petey met Angela at the ice cream shop. Everyone else was going to walk around and look at touristy things for Anna, things they used to laugh about, and still sometimes did.

Petey didn't hardly recognize her friend, for the pictures hadn't shown how much Angela really had changed, not only in how she looked. Angela knew the differences between them, too. She stood a head taller than Petey, dressed in bell-bottomed jeans and a top that showed a bit of her belly, white sandals, and her hair just so, and to top it off, Angela wore not only lipgloss but also makeup. Petey wore plaid shorts and a cotton shirt, flip flops, and no make up, no lipgloss, her boring hair pulled back with a silver and turquoise barrette that Anna had given her. She'd been so proud of the barrette and had planned to tell Angela how it came from New Mexico and was handmade. She wasn't so sure she'd tell her, not after seeing how Angela was so womanly and Petey was so girlingly.

Angela hugged Petey, then they went to the counter to order. Petey ordered a banana split so she could eat until she split, just as they'd talked about doing before she knew she had to move away. But Angela said, "I think I'll just have a small single cone."

Petey felt like a greedy gut when she was handed her banana split and Angela her tiny cone.

They sat down with their treats and at first they had nothing to say, then Angela began talking about people Petey didn't know. Petey listened, eating her banana split, everything Angela said bouncing around the ice cream shop and landing with a thud. None of it made any sense because it wasn't familiar to her. It was as if she were in her dream, where North Carolina and Texas were the same place, different yet combined.

Angela stopped to lick her ice cream, tapped her lips with her napkin, then she reached across to wipe Petey's face and suddenly they were both laughing. Angela said, "Well, old habits die hard, I guess."

Petey thought how Angela even talked like a grown up. She asked her, very mysterious, "Do you have a mirror?"

Angela cocked her eyebrow, said, "Yeah," handed her cone to Petey to hold, pulled a mirror from her purse (Petey didn't have a cute little purse; she kept her money in her pocket), and handed it to Petey.

Petey gave back Angela's cone, held the mirror up to her face and looked at her reflection, hummed like she was *la tee dahing*. Dabbed the rest of the ice cream from her face that Angela hadn't wiped off, then handed the mirror back to Angela.

Angela smiled at her, said, "Well, I'll be!," and put the mirror back into her purse. She opened her mouth to say something else, when someone from across the room called, "Angela!" and she turned, then waved, said to Petey, "I'll be right back," and jumped up to hurry to a table full of giggling girls.

Petey finished off her banana split and tried to seem as if she didn't mind that Angela hadn't introduced her or asked her to go over there, or that she threw away her cone before she even finished it. Petey looked down at her shirt where she'd dripped chocolate syrup and when she tried to wipe it off, it smeared even worse until it was a brown blob. Finally when Angela was back, she said, "Sorry. I had to catch up on some gossip."

Even so, Angela glanced back at her friends every so often to see what they were doing until finally Petey said, "I guess I better get back to my parents."

"Are you sure?"

"Yeah. Grandma's coming this evening. And I promised Momma and Anna I'd help cook."

"Anna. That's the neighbor downstairs, right?"

"She's a part of our family now. Like adopted kinda sorta."

"Oh, right. Okay." Angela smiled, then took lipstick from her purse and fixed her lips, smacked them together.

Petey stood; Angela stood. Petey said, "Well, guess I'll get going."

In a sudden rush, Angela grabbed Petey in a hug, squeezed her, and kissed her on the cheek with her sticky lip-sticky lips. She said, "I am *so* glad to see you again. I missed you. We were always such good friends. We still are, aren't we?" She cocked her head at Petey.

Petey's eyes stung. She nodded at Angela, said, "We sure are," then left the ice cream shop, turning once to see Angela sitting with her friends. Angela looked up, waved at Petey and mouthed, "See you later!" as if she really would see her later. That "See you later!" made Petey feel even better. It made her feel as if the world wasn't quite so unbalanced, as if she'd step and the world wouldn't crumble away like everything was built on loose dirt and weird dreams.

Grandma came, and Momma, Anna, and Petey cooked like crazy-go-to-meeting. Grandma for once put up her feet on the porch. There was roast (Anna did the roast herself) with garlic, salt, pepper, and onion. Potatoes and carrots, green salad, Momma's scratch-made special biscuits, white beans, and for dessert, strawberry shortcake. Anna made the whipped cream homemade. Petey was proud since she made the shortbread cakes all by herself.

After supper, Hill went exploring in the creek while Daddy and Momma showed Grandma their new dance moves. Daddy then danced with Petey, and then with Anna, and then with Grandma. Then Momma danced with everyone. They all about busted open their guts laughing. When Petey was tired of dancing, she went exploring before it was too dark. She hoped to soon see the fireflies and hear the frogs and night bugs come calling. She walked up the road and at the curve she slipped through to the woods where the creek flowed down, down, and farther down into the bigger creek below. It was cool inside the woods, and Petey took off her flip flops and stuck her feet into the cold water. She searched for interesting stones, and when she saw one, she plucked it up and put it in her pocket. After a time, she made her way farther up and her pockets filled with pretty rocks.

Off in the distance she heard howling and figured it surely must be Hill calling for his wolf clan. Petey found a log to sit on where she could listen to all the different sounds of the mountains. There was always movement and noise, but different movement and noise than from the city. The cities' movements and noises were from people and where they were going or what they needed or how they lived. The mountain forests' noises were from rushing water and animals scurrying and birds singing and wind in the trees. In the forest kind of quiet, Petey could hear some of the bird's wings as they rushed by her.

She heard a branch crack and turned to see Daddy heading towards her. He sat beside her and they were quiet for a time.

Then he said, "I know what you're feeling. Or at least I know how this pulls at your innards, being here, knowing we have to leave."

Petey nodded.

"It's strange being here like a tourist, isn't it?"

She nodded again, reached down and plucked a rock from the

ground, turned it over in her hands.

"These mountains are some of the oldest mountains in the world; did I tell you that?"

Petey nodded a third time.

"They've been worn down by time and wind and rain. That's why the mountains in the west are higher and rockier and all; they've not been here as long as our mountains."

She liked how he said "our mountains," as if the mountains were still theirs. And maybe they were.

Daddy plucked his own rock, shaped like a heart, wiped it on his pant leg, eyed it, and put it in his pocket. "I don't know what'll happen. But I want you to know that one day we all will come home."

A squirrel jittered down a tree and stared at them, a seed in its mouth.

"No matter what your momma and me do, you'll grow up and do what you have to do, or want to do. You see that? If you pine for these mountains, you'll find your way back to them."

"But don't you pine for them, Daddy?"

Daddy looked around the woods, up towards the ridgetops. "Yes."

"Then you'll find your way back to them, right?"

"It's not always that simple when you're a man with a family."

"Why not?"

"There's responsibilities and bills and . . . all that kind of thing. There's obligations."

Petey felt bad for being an obligation that kept her daddy from where he wanted to be.

"I know that look." Daddy pushed a strand of her hair back that had come undone from her barrette. "What me and your momma do we do for love. We had our family because we wanted a family together. I don't want you going off thinking it's your fault, like you're the reason, you hear? Us being away from home, living in Texas, has to do with a lot of things. You'll understand more as you get older."

"I guess so." Petey stretched out her legs, studied her dirtied toes. "So, you think we'll all come home one day?"

Daddy smiled, said, "Yes. I do. I feel it in my bones. Your momma and me talk about it all the time, after you and Hill go to bed." He looked at Petey with a light in his eyes. "And I know Hill isn't always in bed when he should be; that boy is strange-wild."

Petey didn't tell on him, but she didn't say otherwise, either.

"Keep an eye on your little brother when you can, hear?"

"Yessir." She watched the water tumble and bubble over the rocks. She had that good ole hope rise up in her. Hope hope. Hope.

They sat for a while, listening to the sounds of their home. Petey was again in two pieces. North Carolina piece. Texas piece. She never thought she'd admit to herself how Texas had some good sides to it, and how her half-house was a pretty little house, and how Mary turned into a good friend, almost as good as Angela had been, and in some ways better, just different better. But Petey knew that even if she moved to North Carolina right that very day, she and Angela wouldn't anymore be the kind of friends they'd been before. Things changed because that's the way of the ole world.

That night, everyone hunkered down for sleep. Petey and Hill were on pallets. Hill was so tired from running all over the woods, he didn't even try to sneak out. His hands and legs jerked every so often, as if he were having a wolf-dream. Petey sneaked to the porch and sat on the rocking chair. Through a break in the trees she saw all the stars, more stars there than she could ever see in Texas. But the moon was just as bright as anywhere. She watched the moon, shining down on her with its cold light that made her feel warm all the same. She stayed there a while, hearing the rustling of nighttime animals, the creek that never stopped. When she couldn't see the moon anymore, she went back to her pallet.

The next morning, the day before they were to go back to Texas, Momma said it was time to visit Rock. Petey's stomach grumbled at her and wouldn't let her eat breakfast. She'd prayed and prayed to Jesus, or Grandpa, or God, or the Angels, that Momma wouldn't slip back into the way she was before. Hill held onto Petey's hand on the way over to the cemetery. Everyone was quiet. Momma had her box with her, held in her lap.

They visited Daddy's parents first. He knelt there a while, then he put the pretty rock he'd found by the creek between their two gravestones, turned, and nodded at Grandma. Everyone followed Grandma as she went to Grandpa's grave, and everyone stood back as she talked to him. Then she turned and said, "That'll do it."

Momma walked slow to Rock's grave, a bunch of wildflowers picked from the mountain held tight in her right hand, the box in the other. They all followed behind, except Daddy, he went to Momma's side, put his arm around her. At the grave, Momma put the flowers there, then sat on the grass. Everyone else stood.

Momma opened the box and took out chimes with a little angel at the top. She said, "Sweet one, I surely miss you. I hope you're behaving up there and helping Jesus." She soothed her hand over the grass, as if smoothing a baby blanket. "My little one." She then brushed away pieces of dirt, leaves, and twigs from the ground and the gravestone, kissed the ground, then stood, face turned up to the sky with her eyes closed. She then went to the tree with branches leaning over Rock's grave and tied the chimes to the tree. The wind blew and the chimes sang their sweet tune. Momma sang, so soft and low Petey hardly heard her, "Don't you hear the bells now ringing; don't you hear the angels singing; 'tis the glory hallelujah Jubilee; in that far off sweet forever; just beyond the shining river; when they ring the golden bells for you and me."

Grandma had sung the last part with her and then said, "Amen."

Momma said, "I'm ready." Glancing back once at the grave, she then turned back to everyone, and said, "I know Rock isn't here. He's here," she pointed to her heart. "And there," she pointed to my heart, and then to Daddy, Hill's, and Grandma's heart. "And now, Anna." She pointed to Anna's heart. Then she smiled.

Petey went to Momma and hugged her, and Momma stroked her hair, then said, "Let's go now."

The chimes sang and sang as they made their way back to the car. The sun was warm as a loving hand on Petey's head, and at first she thought it really was Daddy's or Momma's hand. Maybe it was Jesus' hand. She didn't know if she'd ever know. She didn't know if she'd ever see Rock or Grandpa, or Daddy's parents she'd never known, in heaven one day, but Momma was right, they all weren't in that ground; they were all up inside people's hearts and memories.

The grownups spent the rest of the day sitting on the porch talking, or eating, baking, cooking, and eating again. Petey and Hill spent as much of their time in the woods and creek as they were allowed. The next morning, Grandma left first. She hugged Petey so hard it knocked her breath out. Before she climbed into her car, Grandma whispered to Petey, "I know you'll come back home." She sounded like Daddy even though she was Momma's momma.

When they were packed and ready to leave, Hill was nowhere to be found. They called and called and called some more. Daddy went off into the woods in one direction, Momma in another, and Petey in another still. Anna stayed behind in case he came back. Petey heard Daddy whistle his sharp calling home whistle. She whistled hers. Surely that would get Hill's attention. She heard Daddy's calls and whistles fade as he went farther into the woods.

Petey called and called to Hill, her stomach fussed and grumbled and growled at her. She screamed out, "Hill, you stupid idiot! You stupid stupid fool idiot!" Stomping through the woods, over the creek, standing on top of rocks, she yelled for her little brother to stop being a big ole brat and come on so they could go back to Texas.

She went back to the cabin to see if he'd been found. Momma stood on the porch with her dress dirtied and torn in places—she must have gone through stickers and bushes. Daddy wasn't back. Anna told Petey what she already knew from Momma's look, "Not yet," then she rubbed Momma's back. Momma said, "He knew we were leaving. I told him not to go running off far. That boy is too wild."

Petey ran back into the woods. She tried to think where he'd go. What kind of animal he'd be. Other thoughts scratched her brain: what if a bear had him? What if he fell and hit his head on a rock? What if he was lost in the woods and no one could find him and he couldn't find his way back?

At a fork in the creek to the left and up on a bit of an incline, Petey saw rocks that huddled together making a tiny cave. She ran up to it. And sure enough, there inside was Hill, curled up like an animal would when hibernating. Petey hoped he was only asleep. She didn't want to touch him, in case he was cold and hard, but she had to. She reached in and touched him and he was warm. She pushed against him, hard, "You stupid idiot!"

He stirred and looked at her, feral-eyed, then brother-eyed. "What's wrong? Why you look so funny? How come your eyes are red? Is it time to go home yet? I just got tired."

Petey wanted to hug him and wring his neck all at the same time. "We've been hollering and hollering for you. Momma's upset and Daddy's about to call the sheriff!"

He scrabbled out. He had the look of *oh no, now I'm in trouble.*

"Hurry, let's go." She grabbed his hand and pulled him fast as she could back to the log cabin. When Momma saw him, she ran faster than Petey'd ever seen her, grabbed him up and smacked his face with her lips over and over, while Hill kept saying, "Aw Momma, stop it. I'm sorry. I didn't mean it."

Anna gave Petey a big ole smile. She said, "Your dad's still looking."

Petey ran back into the woods, in the direction her daddy had gone, and hollered, whistled, hollered-whistled until she heard him holler and whistle back. They met halfway and she told him Hill was a stupid idiot and had fallen asleep like a wild animal in the woods. Her daddy threw back his head and laughed. Petey laughed, too.

"He must have been some wore out not to hear all our ruckus," Daddy said.

"I guess that's for true," Petey answered.

Daddy and Petey went back to the cabin, and there Daddy swept Hill up on his shoulders, calling him a wild little heathen. Hill laughed, happy as a lost-then-found lamb that he wasn't in trouble. Petey saw how little Hill still was, as if he'd never grow much more than he already was, but then Petey noticed how his pants and shirts were smaller, as if he'd grown since they'd come back to North Carolina like tourists and not-like-tourists all at the same time.

As the 1966 Ford Country Squire with its magic tailgate sped back to Fort Worth, Petey thought of when she was first leaving home, when the mountains disappeared. Back then, she'd not known what her life would be like, where she'd live, how she could stand it. Those things weren't mysterious anymore. It didn't make the toothache in her body go all the way away, but her bones didn't feel out of joint and her head didn't hurt, and her stomach didn't fuss at her so much. When the land grew flat again, Petey closed her eyes and remembered the feel of the creek on her bared toes and ankles.

When everyone was back in their half-houses, which still smelled of sugar sweet to welcome them all home, when everyone, even Hill, was fast asleep, she sneaked out onto Hill's tree limb and climbed onto his branch to sit. Up in the break in the tree limbs and leaves, she gazed at the stars and thought how there weren't so many as North Carolina stars, but the moon was as big and bright in Fort Worth as in Haywood County. The moon smiled down on her with its cool light that warmed her in Fort Worth just as it did in Haywood County. She really wasn't so far from home. The moon shone over both places the same, and she could shine in both places the same. Petey smiled. She went back into her half-house, to her lilac room, and snuggled into her sweet white iron bed. In a little while, the moon shone on her face and Petey closed her eyes, opened them. The moon was still there.

Chapter 11

Petey took the apple cakes from the oven, set them down, and wiped her hands on her apron. "Momma, they're done."

"Good. Go put up the closed sign. It's already past closing time."

Petey went to the door, turned the sign to the bakery to show "Closed" to any customers come too late. She looked out to the street. Coming up a cloud. Petey liked the rain, sometimes.

"Did you call Anna?" Momma asked. She put the cakes on the racks to cool.

"Yes. They're leaving for Paris early tomorrow." Petey turned from the window and began helping Momma clean up the bakery. Their bakery. Petey still liked the sound of those words.

"Well, good thing they get to go before she gets too big with that child." Momma smiled.

Petey nodded, wrapped up a pie Daddy asked to have for his poker party. He'd never played poker with a cigar in his mouth before until he'd began working at the bakery. He'd said he had to find some way to be a man, and playing poker with cigars in his mouth and cussing and maybe drinking a whisky made him feel manly, especially after he'd been decorating cakes all day, something he was good at, much to his surprise and embarrassment in front of his buddies. Momma would laugh; tell him, "No one would ever think you aren't anything but a big strong man, even when you're making little cute flower petals." Then she'd poke his arm, tease him, laugh again.

When the bakery was cleaned and everything put away, Petey and Momma took off their aprons to go into the washing machine. Their clean aprons for the next day hung on the rack, alongside Daddy's, Anna's, and even Hill's. Though Hill's mostly stayed hanging on the peg. He had better things to do, he said. Momma wouldn't let him come in anyway unless he took a long scrubbing shower from tip-to-toe and changed into clothes she kept in the bakery, ones that she would be sure didn't have animal hair, and no telling what all, on them. She said he must be sleeping with his animals.

Hill had a way with the animals. Thought like them. Understood them. He especially liked to save dogs no one thought could be helped. And Petey knew he did sleep with them. She'd come by early in the morning and had caught him curled up with them in the barn, his long hair in his face, and she was filled with love and tenderness for her brother. His bare feet twitched and his eyelids moved back and forth in his dreams. The wolf had watched her, its yellow eyes in protective warning.

The wolf Hill had found half-dead in the woods. And that wolf would hardly leave Hill's side and didn't let anyone pet him but Hill, and if the wolf was feeling generous, Petey. Sometimes Joey came to visit Hill, and Petey was filled with wonder over the big burly football player in the place of the little snotty-nosed blonde-headed kid who'd barely said a word and had always been such a good friend to Hill—his only real human friend that wasn't family.

Momma and Petey headed out to Petey's still good-enough used Subaru. Unless Momma had something planned and needed her car, Petey usually picked up Momma on her way in. She lived farther away than Momma did; her parents lived close to town. Petey smiled, remembering how Momma'd bought her first two used cars in Fort Worth, and then when they'd moved back to the mountains six years ago, one last used car, until finally, last week, Momma'd bought her first new car, a sparkling new 1982 Subaru Sedan she was so proud of. Daddy's 1966 Ford Country Squire had been traded in on a Ford truck he still had—he would always be a Ford man.

Momma took Daddy's pie and sat in the passenger side. They drove along talking here and there, sometimes thinking their own thoughts. She dropped off Momma at her house, and then Petey headed to her home, passing by the old place on the highway that still had the black barn. Someone else lived there she'd found out, a relative to the first owners. Didn't matter; she'd found her place three years ago, set back in the woods, in a little cove, with the creek running, and the wind falling over the ridgetops, cooling her sweetly in the summer.

She passed where Angela used to live before she moved to Oregon with her boyfriend who became a husband. They wrote each other, as they'd always done. In their visits, even while she was sick, Angela was still beautiful, would always be that way. The breast cancer didn't take that away from her. She was Lovely. During those days, sometimes in her letters, Petey had accidentally written "beast cancer" leaving out that R.

Petey turned up into her driveway, parked in her garage. She walked up her wooden stairs and went straight to the kitchen where she made herself a snack of cheese and pumpernickel bread to take to sit on the porch. She retrieved her pad and pen from the side table and started a letter:

> Dear Mary, how are you and David? The kids? I can't wait for your visit next month. It's a perfect time to come with everything blooming out and smelling sweet. Momma's bakery is doing well. I guess I should say our bakery, but I still think of it as Momma's. Anna and Stephen's child will arrive in six months. They're going to Paris and then they'll settle in with that baby. Anna said she is looking forward to being a momma now that she has her travel bug satisfied. Stephen says he's been ready to settle in for a family since day one. They tease and toss around. He says it took him five years to get her to be officially engaged, another five to get her to marry him, and finally, three years to make a complete family. Stephen asked when I'll get married. I don't reckon I ever will. I like knowing I can do what I want when I want to. Ole Barry Burke comes round sometimes asking me to marry him, but I just laugh and say no. I'm a bride of this mountain. He says he won't give up. Well, let him keep on trying if he wants to, maybe one day I'll give it a second thought. Hurry up time so it can hurry up and be time for your visit!
>
> Got to go now. Love, Petey.

Petey put the letter into an envelope, licked it, and addressed it to Fort Worth. She ate her snack. The creek sang to her. The distant mountains rose up. The moon would soon shine on her face, just as it had in the flatland, and as it had and would forever more at her home, in her sweet sweet mountains.

Augusta Trobaugh

Resurrection

The whole summer, Papa can't think about anything except my big brother, Danny, and how he is starting high school in the fall and trying out for the football team. Papa's been waiting almost all Danny's life for this, and early on, he brings home a big box of frozen steaks from the Piggly-Wiggly store down in Louisville and tells Mama to cook one up for Danny—rare—every single night, so he can get beefed up for the tryouts. The rest of us go on having okra and tomatoes and butterbeans and fried chicken and corn bread, like always. But Danny has to eat a steak on top of everything else.

Mama fixes the steak every evening, just like Papa says for her to do, but she goes around wiping her face on her apron almost all the time. Maybe the smoke from all those steaks bothers her eyes. Or maybe she doesn't like to think of Danny playing football. Not one little bit.

Grandmama pays no attention to the football excitement, because she never cares about anything except her evangelist programs on television and getting her tomatoes put up before they go bad.

I'm only in sixth grade in the fall, so I don't have to worry about getting ready to play football. Not yet, anyway. And maybe not ever, because Papa says he doesn't hold out much hope for me. I'm kind of small for my age, and what I do best is stick my nose in a book. I'll probably grow up to be a sissy, like Papa says.

But I don't mind, because I couldn't eat a whole steak every night to save my life, and I'd sure hate to be the cause of Mama's eyes hurting her all the time.

So no one pays much attention to me that summer, and that's O.K. I suppose. Mostly, I just like to be by myself anyway, but the only thing I do mind is that I don't get to go to the library a single time, because it's all the way down in Louisville. Nineteen miles and too far to walk.

So that whole summer, Mama cooks and wipes her eyes, Danny eats and eats, Papa slaps him on the shoulder—*hard*—all the time and says "That's my boy!" I read every book I have three or four times, and Grandmama sits all day long in front of the TV, hollering at the preachers and clutching her pocketbook in her lap. She's trying to make up her mind about which one of the evangelists she's going to send her social security check to, and even though Papa says to Mama in a loud voice that it wouldn't hurt for Grandmama to buy a loaf of bread or a pound of hamburger once in awhile, Grandmama doesn't pay attention to anything he says. She doesn't even speak to him. Ever. Or Mama or Danny either.

I'm the only one she ever says anything to, and it's always the same thing: "Boy, have you found Jesus yet?"

"No, ma'am." That's what I always answer, but what I really want to say is, "Why? Is Jesus *lost* or something?"

But I don't.

Of course.

Because I know what she really means is this: have I found Jesus and gotten myself *born again* at the Baptist church we go to over in Zebina, and the answer to that is always no.

From the picture of Jesus I've seen hanging in the hallway between the two Sunday School rooms, He's not someone I'm really interested in trying to find. Looks too pale and sissy-like. Just like me.

But when Grandmama asks me that same question late in August, it gets me to thinking about the church and the baptismal pool and the old robing house at the edge of the creek, and I don't have a thing left to read, and there's nothing else to do anyway. Besides, it's one place I can go where there's no one talking about football or asking me if I've found Jesus.

So maybe—just maybe—I could pretend to look for Him after all, because it would be fun to prowl through the woods behind the church and walk a long way down along the creek, so I would be like Stanley looking for Dr. Livingstone, only it'll be Jesus I find. And not that pale, sad-looking man in the Sunday School picture, but someone big and strong—like the giant in the Brawny Paper Towel commercial, and when I find Him, I'll get Him to make Papa leave Danny alone and my Mama stop crying, and maybe even go ahead and take my Grandmama to Heaven. Right away.

The next morning, I get up before daylight and put on my clothes and tip-toe into the kitchen to make some sandwiches to take, because I mean to stay away all day long. But Grandmama is already up, even that early, sitting in the dark living room with the blue-white light from the television set flickering over her face and the granny square afghan that's folded across the back of the couch. I try to sneak past, but without even taking her eyes off the television set, she yells at me, "You found Jesus yet, boy?"

"No, ma'am," I say and rush into the kitchen, throw together the sandwiches, wrap them in waxed paper, and stuff them into my shirt—and the whole time, she's firing words at me about *sin!* and *hell!* and *redemption!* and *grace!*

She's still yelling when I push open the screen door on the back porch—hard—and run past the bloody steak bones piled in the top of the trashcan.

It's a long walk, but there's something nice-scary and mysterious about the road in the soft light, especially in places where the kudzu is like big, green-elephant clumps on the fences or climbs up into the very tops of dead trees, so that already I am Stanley looking for Dr. Livingstone, walking among a herd of grazing kudzu-elephants while kudzu-great apes huddle silently in the tops of the trees.

I walk for a long time.

The sun is up and very hot, and gnats are singing in my ears when I finally come to the end of the road, where the church stands, square and white-washed on the hill, and with the cemetery nudging up behind it.

Just beyond all those silent stones and fresh-cut grass is what folks around here call the Todey plot. The Todeys are mean-dog folks who live just over the creek. They don't mingle with anybody except other Todeys and don't even send their children to school. Ever. But nobody messes around with the Todeys, and even the truant officer won't go over there because they'd just as soon shoot you as look at you. Everybody knows that.

A long time ago, there used to be a lot of trouble about the Todeys sneaking into the church cemetery at night and burying their dead in other folks' family plots. Of course, no one knew anything about it until they went to have a grave dug and would find a surprise-Todey already buried there.

That caused a lot of trouble, because they couldn't just throw the remains over in the bushes, so finally, they took to planting them on the other side of a thicket. And not in the church cemetery.

I asked Mama one time why Todeys couldn't bury their people in the cemetery, like everybody else did, and she said it was because the church cemetery was a holy place and the Todeys were certainly not holy people. And besides, they didn't own any of the plots, but just piled their passed-away folks into places where only good, up-standing Christians were supposed to go. She wouldn't say more, but Grandmama muttered about in-breeding and such as that. I had to look it up in the dictionary to find out what it meant. But I wasn't surprised. Everybody knew all about the Todeys anyway.

But a few years ago, when old Miss Allie Jenkins passed away, the Todeys bought a piece of her land—right next to the cemetery—off her son, who lives in Atlanta and didn't know any better, and they moved all their dead folks from where they'd been buried behind the thicket and into what everybody now calls the Todey plot. And more. They put up a chain link fence with rolls of barbed wire on top and a gate with a real padlock and painted the fence and the barbed wire a dazzling white—*Of all things!* Mama said when she saw that. Then they went to one of those concrete yard-statue places on the other side of Thomson and came back with their pickup truck loaded down with concrete angels—ten or twelve of them—and a big, old, six-foot-tall statue of Mary—Jesus' Mama.

They set all those statues up in the dark of night, because even the Todeys wouldn't have dared to put them up during the daytime, when someone cleaning graves in the real cemetery might have seen them. And on another night they put down bright green squares of fake grass on the ground in between all the graves.

But the worst thing of all was that once they got all that carpeting and the angel statues and the big concrete Mary in place, they painted yellow hair on all the statues and too-bright, neon-blue eyes without any eyelids on them and coal-black eyebrows and big, thick eyelashes. And red paint for rouge on their cheeks. So there they all stood, moldy-white and yellow and blue and black and red against the dark shade of the cedar trees, and that painted-up concrete Mary had one thick hand pressed to her chest, like she had indigestion or something and the other hand was held out so it looked like she was waiting for somebody to give her some Tums. That's what Papa said. But Mama said there wasn't a thing funny about it, that the only thing to do is ignore the whole thing. Pretend it isn't even there.

That's sure pretty hard to do. Still, I try, for Mama's sake, even though that morning she is in the house far behind me. So I turn my face away from the Todey plot and go down the hill toward the old baptismal pool. It was what they used before the church got that clear-plastic see-through baptizing tub that's installed behind the altar. At the old pool, icy-cold water pours out of an iron pipe stuck in the side of the hill, spills into the pool, and runs out the other end through a little space in the rocks. Then it flows under what's called a robing house and into a shallow branch that empties into a bog just this side of Brushy Creek. The robing house stands up on stilt-legs and it isn't an honest-to-goodness house of course, but just a one-room shack where people who get baptized could change into dry clothes afterward without having to walk all the way back up the hill with their wet clothes clinging to them. It has a tin roof that afternoon rain sounds nice on and big windows with no screens and is always cool, even on the hottest day. No one uses it any more. Except for me. I like to pretend that it's my house and mine alone, and that I have all the books I could ever read in it. And a dog that loves me.

When I get down to the bottom of the hill, I take a long, iron-cold drink of water from the pipe. Then I go into the robing house and put the sandwiches in the corner and stretch out on my stomach to rest awhile before I go off in those hot woods to look for the Brawny-Paper-Towel-man/Dr. Livingstone-Jesus.

I look down through the cracks between the planks at the shallow water rippling easily over white sand and the little pebbles down at the bottom that have gotten round and smooth from the water running over them for more years than anyone can remember. I can see tadpoles and salamanders in the branch and hear a far-away splash from the creek, where the otters are playing. Birds are chirping a little, and the squirrels are really going at it something fierce, running around and fussing in the tree tops because they know I'm in the robing house, and they want to tell each other all about it.

I lie there watching tadpoles and thinking about maybe staying there all day and all night long, and maybe never going back home. But I'm too afraid to sleep there all alone in the dark, so I know that in the late afternoon, I'll have to go back to where Danny chews and swallows and Papa watches every big bite of red meat that goes into his mouth and Mama wipes her eyes and Grandmama wears dirty pink bedroom shoes and holds onto the remote control so nobody can change channels or turn down the sound.

I watch through the crack in the floor and see three little tadpoles facing into the current and twitching their tails hard to keep from being swept away downstream. I know how they feel.

But in the next moment, something blocks my view, and it takes me a few seconds to realize I'm looking down through the crack right at the top of someone's head. Someone small enough to stand under the robing house.

"Hey!" I jump up, run down the wooden steps, and peer under the house.

It's a little boy—hardly more than a baby, just good walking age and still not too steady on his feet—starting to wade into the branch under the robing house, and with his arms held out to balance himself, but when he steps into that shallow, ice-cold water and his toes sink into the smooth white sand, he stops and looks over his shoulder at me with a very surprised look on his face.

"It's cold," I say. He smiles and gazes at me very comfortably, just as if he knows me. But I'm sure I've never seen him before. He's brown as a berry, like he's been out in the sunshine for the whole summer long, and has mahogany-colored hair and it all thick and curly and a solid body that seems to grow out of the earth like a stout little tree. Eyes that are big and round and the color of good soil in bottomland.

I look around, to see if his Mama or Papa is somewhere nearby, because nobody—not even the Todeys—would let a toddling baby go off alone like that. Besides, he sure doesn't look like any of the Todey children. They're all tow-heads and have watery eyes and weak chins. This little boy is dark and strong-chinned and solid.

"Who are you?" I ask.

He gazes at me, and one of his hands almost comes up, as if to wave at me. Then it drops back by his side. He is wearing only a pair of blue shorts, and he's so little, he still has a poking-out stomach, like babies have. And a smell about him like warm sunshine against a new fencepost.

"Who are you?" I ask again, squatting down. "Where's your Mama and Papa?" He pauses for a few seconds and then bends over and starts picking up smooth, round pebbles from the bottom of the branch.

"Where's your folks?" I try again, but he just keeps picking up pebbles.

I waddle under the robing house, ducking my head and watching out for the terrible black spiders that live there. And wasp-nests too.

When I reach him, he has so many pebbles in his hands that every time he tries to pick up another one, he drops some. But he just keeps on doing it anyway.

"Come on with me," I say. "I'll help you find your folks." Because maybe he belongs to someone visiting somewhere near or some family that's come to clean up their plots in the cemetery—although I didn't see anyone when I came through.

He turns and comes right to me, holding out all the smooth pebbles he's gathered. I hold out my hands and he gives them all to me, smiling as big as if he's just given me something very wonderful.

"Pebbles," I say, looking at the glistening white and gray and yellow stones and then back at him.

He blinks.

"Peb—bles." I break the word down so maybe he can say it. But he just smiles at me and lifts up his eyebrows, as if what I'm saying sounds pretty funny.

"What's your name?" I ask, but he just puts his hands on top of his head and sways a little from side to side, pursing his mouth and watching me.

"I guess you're too young to talk," I say unnecessarily, and he nods, as if I have just discovered some amusing secret.

"Come on with me then," I say again. "I'll help you find your folks." I drop the pebbles back in the branch and hold out my hand to him, but he makes no move to take it. I remember the sandwiches.

"Hey! You hungry?" I ask, and without waiting for an answer, I scurry from under the robing house, run up the steps, and grab one of the sandwiches.

When I come back, he's gone. Just that fast.

"Where'd you go?" I yell. My empty shout echoes back to me from the dark trees.

"Where'd you go?" I yell again, because the deep creek is so near, and he's so small and doesn't know anything. I dart out from under the robing house and run down to the creek and look all around and then I run back past the robing house and halfway back up the hill toward the cemetery, sending a whole cloud of tiny, brilliant green grasshoppers bounding away in all directions in the tall grass, my breath catching against my ribs and something inside hurting so bad, it's almost like having a serpent's tooth stuck in me.

But I can't find him.

I run back down the hill, and all of a sudden, there he is—under the robing house right where I left him, waiting in exactly the same place, with his feet in the branch.

I crawl back under the house. With my breath catching against my ribs, I unwrap the waxed paper so that the perfume of peanut butter drifts out. I tear the sandwich in two and hold a piece out to him.

He makes no move to take it, but he starts to smile and then to laugh, and finally, he laughs so hard, his eyes water.

"What's so funny?" I ask, looking at the sandwich to see if there's something wrong with it.

He looks down at his feet and laughs again, a deep, belly-wrenching sound.

I look down.

Hundred of tadpoles are wriggling around his toes in the clear cold water, so many tadpoles, they look like a fat, gray bouquet of wriggling flowers, all pushing each other and struggling to get to his toes.

"Tadpoles," I say, almost singing the word and starting to laugh myself, because I've never seen so many of them in one place before and none of them afraid at all.

He stands in the branch for a long time, while we laugh at the squirming mass of tadpoles around his feet.

But at last, he comes out, and a few of the tadpoles wriggle themselves up onto the sand at the edge of the branch.

I give him his half of the sandwich, and he takes it as if he doesn't know what to do with it. He smells of it and looks at me.

"It's good," I say, biting into my half. "M-m-m!" I add, rolling my eyes and smiling.

He bites into his, and the dark eyebrows shoot straight up.

"M-m-m!" he mimics me, rolling his eyes.

We eat and say *M-m-m-m!* and roll our eyes and laugh.

When we finish, he looks at the peanut-butter stuck to his fingers and then reaches up and wipes it off into his hair.

I lead him to the baptismal pool and wash his hands under the flowing water and wet the tail of my shirt so I can wipe the peanut butter off his face. I make a cup of my hands and give him a drink of water, and his mouth is warm against my palms. There's still peanut butter in his hair, but I can't do much of anything about that.

"Now listen," I say. "We have to find out who you belong to." The way he draws his eyebrows together and looks at me so hard, you'd think he could understand what I'm saying.

"Maybe we ought to take you to my house and get my Papa to help us find your Mama and Papa," I say. But the thought of taking him to my house makes my stomach lurch in alarm. It wouldn't really be much different than catching one of those little brown otters and taking him away from the creek. Put him in a cardboard box out on the back porch, with all the spare tractor parts and old feed bags and Grandmama's canning jars and the steak bones.

"Or maybe we could find them ourselves," I suggest. "Of course, the only place near enough for you to have come from is the Todeys," I say. "Your Mama and Papa visiting over there?"

He smiles and tilts his head.

So that's what we have to do, then. It's the only way. So I take his hand and we start up the hill toward the cemetery, because I have in mind that if we double back up to the crossroads, we can cross the creek at the wooden bridge and go over to the Todey place. See if any of them knows anything about a lost little boy.

Don't you ever go anywhere near the Todey place, I can hear Mama's voice just as clear as day, but there's nowhere else near enough for this little boy to have walked to the church.

So go to the Todeys, I must. No matter what Mama says.

As we pass through the cemetery, he spots all those garish angels and the concrete Mary standing in the Todey plot. He points to them.

"Yes," I say. "They're pretty ugly, aren't they?"

He doesn't answer me, but as we pass on and start up the road, he keeps looking back over his shoulder. Finally, I pick him up and carry him.

We go all the way back to the crossroads and turn left, to follow a road that leads down to the wooden bridge over the creek. He leans a little in my arms and looks down into the black water.

"That's the creek," I say. "You don't *ever* want to try and wade in that. It's too deep."

I start up the hill on the other side, walking in the sun-dried ruts that were made the last time it rained good and hard. Carved into the baked clay are all kinds of slip-and-slide marks made by big truck tires. The Todey truck, I am sure, since no one else I know of ever comes this way. And even the trees and the bushes look different here—dry and brown and with more brambles.

He must sense it too—the change in things once you're over the creek, I mean—because his arms tighten around my neck.

"It's OK," I say. "I won't let anything happen to you,.."

Finally, I gain the top of the hill and look down into a big chinaberry thicket standing in the middle of the wild grasses that grow all around in what was once a field of corn. But the corn is long gone and the yellow-silver weeds go almost as far as the eye can see. In the middle of the Chinaberry thicket, part of a rusted tin roof shows through the dark green leaves.

The Todey house.

I walk down very slowly, and then I stop and put the little boy down, pushing on his shoulders until he sits snug up against an old tree at the very edge of the thicket. "You stay here," I tell him. "And don't you make a single sound, you hear?"

For good measure, I press my finger against his mouth and say "Sh-h-h!"

The deep, sober eyes question for only a moment before I see obedience flicker through them.

I walk up to a rusty chicken-wire fence that goes all the way around the tilted house, and suddenly, a big pack of dogs—all of them a dirty yellow color—come tearing out from under the porch, yowling and snarling. Slowly, I walk along the fence until I come to an iron gate.

"Mister Todey?" I call. It's a high, girl-sounding shriek.

"Mister Todey?" I call again, even higher pitched.

A yellowed curtain at the front window moves. The barking dogs come right up to the gate, and one big mongrel curls back his upper lip and shows me an array of sharp, yellow teeth.

"MISTER TODEY!!"

The front door opens and Mr. Todey comes out. Behind him, in the dark room, two other hollow-eyed men who don't even blink when the screen door closes in their faces.

"Whutchuwont?" he asks, and then he yells, "SHUT UP! YOU DOGS!" in a voice that almost knocks me off my feet. The dogs shrink in unison and slink back under the porch, the big mongrel glancing at me once more over his shoulder and showing me his teeth. Mr. Todey is like a faded leather string, all thin and with yellow skin and yellow teeth.

"I SAID WHATCHUWONT?" he yells.

"Please, sir," I start, even though I know I'm not supposed to say sir to any of the Todeys. "You all got anybody visiting you that's lost a little boy?"

"Little boy?"

"Just a toddling baby, sir," I add.

Mr. Todey scratches his stubble on his chin.

"Got nobody visiting," he finally says. Then, "Where's this little boy at?"

"He's . . . he's at my house," I lie. "My Papa sent me over here to see if you all's got any visitors he could belong to."

"Got nobody visiting, I told you," he repeats.

"Well, thank you then," I say, taking a relieved breath and turning to go, but just then, two Todey boys about my age—only *big*—come around the side of the house. They are younger versions of Mr. Todey. Yellow hair, yellow skin, yellow teeth.

"He bothering you, Papa?" one of them asks.

"Maybe," Mr. Todey answers, and I feel the hair coming up on the back of my neck.

"You want us to run him off for you, Papa?" the other one asks.

There is a long, long pause, and my heart thuds hard against my chest, and my feet feel like they're already running.

Mr. Todey's mouth twitches a couple of times and then slowly webs out into a terrible grin.

"Do whatcha like," he says so low I can hardly hear him, and then I know the words, and they explode in my ears, like a starter pistol.

I lunge away from the fence and around the side of the Chinaberry thicket, the high grass swishing against my legs and I hear the gate slamming behind me and I run harder and faster than I have ever run in my whole life toward where I left the little boy. From a distance, I see his head pop up out of the tall grass and then go back down again, like a baby deer that's hiding because its Mama said that's what it should do.

Closer and closer I come to him, with my breath tearing through my chest and the terrifying sounds of running feet behind me. He sees me coming, stands up, and steps out into the clearing, holding up his arms to me.

I don't stop for a moment when I grab him, but just snatch him right off his feet and tuck him under my arm like you do a football and keep running.

Down the pitted hill, stumbling and clutching for a hold in the dried ruts and across the bridge, my feet sounding a loud tattoo on the sun-warmed wood and then up and across the flank of another hill and over the edge of a ravine and sliding down and down in old pinestraw until I manage to grab a sapling and stop the slide.

I don't move a muscle, listening for the footsteps behind me, and my breath tears through me like a tornado. The child doesn't make a single sound, so I loosen my grip on him and let him rest against the side of the ravine.

I listen for a long time, but no one is following us. I'm sure of it. The Todeys would never follow anyone over the bridge.

And at that very moment, I know what a real football player must feel like after he runs into the end zone with that ball tucked under his arm, and the referee throws up his arms in a victory sign and the air is filled with the white-hot sizzle-sound from hundreds of clapping hands.

"Boy! Would my Papa have been proud to see how fast I ran just now," I say. But while I am smiling and imagining Papa clapping me on the back and saying, "Way to go, son!" I look at the child, who has his eyes screwed shut and is shaking all over.

"Did I scare you?" I ask. "I sure didn't mean to. Just that the Todeys are awful mean folks, and we had to get out of there fast. You understand?"

Silence and a couple of hiccoughs.

I pull him to me and snuggle him against my chest. He is willing and pliant and burrows against me.

"I'll bet you're missing your Mama, aren't you?"

Because after all, he's only a baby and all alone. Except for me.

He pushes away from me and gets to his feet. I study him hard.

"You think you can show me where your Mama is?" Maybe this is the way to get him to help me find his folks, asking him something very specific, like *Show me where your Mama is.*

He nods and takes my hand. I stand up and let him lead me down into the bottom of the ravine and up the other side, going ever so slowly and following his clumsy baby-steps.

When we come out of the woods, we're back where we started, about midway between the robing house and the cemetery, and he doesn't even hesitate but leads me up the hill and in among the white stones until we come to the barbed-wire fence around the Todey plot.

He holds his arms up to me, and I pick him up. He points toward the fence.

"What do you want?" I ask. "I thought you were going to show me where your Mama is."

I move closer to the fence, the way he is leaning. He puts his small brown hand through the links in the white fence and touches his fingers to the clumsy, outstretched hand of the concrete Mary.

The Todey boys burst out of the woods beside the robing house, screaming filthy things, sounds that just don't register at first. I don't know when I start running, but I do and feel the child's body sway in my arms against the sudden movement, and right away I can tell that the Todey boys are going to catch up with us.

Fast.

I head straight into the woods on the other side of the road and suddenly see a big, stout tree-branch on the ground and I drop the child, grab up the branch, and spin around to face the Todeys.

They stop, faces bright yellow-red and eyes glowing.

Do whatcha like, their Papa said.

They glance at each other, smile, and start moving apart ever so slowly. I wave the branch back and forth and watch them so hard that I don't realize what is happening until the child walks around the side of me and toddles toward the Todeys.

"NO!" I shriek, and he looks up at me as if he is surprised. He blinks slowly one time and then moves determinedly toward them.

"You better let him come," one of the Todey boys growls. "Else we'll do something terrible to you."

"NO!" I scream, dropping the branch and running after him.

The fist comes out of nowhere, crashing into my nose. Cartilage bends, bone creaks, a tear duct explodes and the earth itself tilts up hard and smacks me right in the mouth. Dead leaves and bits of old pine needles on my tongue.

So that I watch through blood and the crossed fallen branches of some long-ago tree as the Todeys lead the little boy away, each one holding one of his hands so that his arms are spread as if in flight.

I am alive but not alive for a long time, and when I start trying to get up, the ground tilts and whirls every which way, hitting me in the shoulder one time and the chin the next. Something's gone wrong with time, because there's nothing but solid darkness all around me.

No sun. No moon. No stars. Just dark.

On hands and knees, I crawl until I find the side of the road and then I get to my feet and start running toward home, clawing dried blood from my swollen eyelid and drooling through a big lip and giant nose that are no part of me, merely some kind of terrible, cold, hog-fat stuck to my face and my breath is a swinging jagged piece of glass inside me.

I don't know how long it takes me to get home, but all of a sudden, there is the house in front of me. I come stumbling up the back steps and hear Papa yelling, "Eat the damned steak!"

I burst into the kitchen, letting the door slam behind me hard. Papa yells, "Dammit, boy! Where you been? And how many times I got to tell you about letting that door slam?" Mama's stirring the iced tea.

From the living room, Grandmama yells at the evangelist on television: "Tell 'em how they'll burn in hell!"

"Help me," I gasp. "There's a little boy . . . "

They all turn look at me. No one moves. No one says a thing. Danny sits at the table with a big piece of blood-red meat on the fork halfway to his mouth. Mama stops stirring the iced tea. Papa's eyebrows stick together in a dark V.

Mama comes toward me.

"My Lord!" she says. "What on earth!"

"Help me!" I gasp. "There's a little boy . . . "

Suddenly, the ever-present roar of the TV is gone, and from the dark living room, Grandmama shrieks, "You found Jesus, didn't you boy!"

An explosion in me, then—louder and stronger and far more hurtful than any Todey could have given me from a fist.

"YES!" I yell. "But the Todeys got him!"

I don't know where the word *YES!* comes from. All I know is that everyone is silent and very, very still. The only thing that moves is the terrible red juice dripping from the piece of steak on Danny's fork.

I bolt out of the back door and start back down the road to the church, knowing this was more than what it was. I would save Him. I would save Him! Even if the Todeys killed me for it!

I am suddenly strong and not hurt any longer, and I run headlong into the deepest twilight, my breathing smooth and knees pumping, past the Kudzu-elephants, now a deeper dark against the dark sky and my feet on a familiar road still warm from the hot August-day sun that now has slipped down past the horizon, and nothing left of day except the faintest whitewash behind the trees. Running and running but not tiring. Knowing I could run forever, if I had to.

As I get farther down the road, I see that the leaves on the trees are glowing like tiny quarter-moons, because of a brilliant-gold light that's nestled in the next hollow. At the church. Or another sun rising or setting or the church itself burning with a glow that grows ahead of me.

No! No! Even the Todeys wouldn't hurt Jesus, and Him just a little fellow. And even the Todeys wouldn't set the church on fire and maybe with Him in it!

But the light grows with every step I run and me not knowing what I will find.

Maybe the smooth, brown skin now blistering and erupting, and the shiny hair shriveled and crimped in the fire.

No!

Then hard-thumping heart glowing with a strange light all its own, when I know for sure it isn't a fire at all making the glow.

It's beyond fire. And everything is more than what it is, because when I pass the Todey plot, I see the concrete Mary statue—only no longer concrete, but a marble Mary, beautiful, standing just beyond where the white-painted fence of the Todey plot used to be but the fence is gone. A pearl-bright, gleaming Mary, washed clean of the yellow hair and the neon-blue eyes and the rouge and the black-streaked eyelashes. A Mary as graceful as music.

Delicate curve of slender fingers and gentle eyes lit from within.

I stand, with a strange and terrible storm of wind and rain passing through my chest, and I wonder if maybe I'm dead. Maybe the Todeys killed me and my body is lying in the woods and whatever is more than my body is wandering around a churchyard cemetery at night. Like a ghost.

But then I hear HIM laugh again, and I tear myself away from the questions and the wondering and the statue, because I am like the tadpoles—drawn to Him. Unable to resist Him. I race through the cemetery, dodging among the silent white stones and toward the impossible light that's not coming from the church, but beyond it—the robing house.

I come stumbling down the ragged hill, closer and closer to the light. Light, but not heat. And suddenly I can see Him, in silhouette at the very bottom of the hill, see Him in the dazzling light. Standing in the bog under the robing house with all that more-than-light coming out of Him, somehow.

He looks at me, smiles, and holds out His hand for me to see something in it. I move forward and see that two smooth, Todey-yellow pebbles resting quietly in His palm.

Cool air, then, against my flaming face, and without my lifting so much as a finger, I too become a rounded pebble in the cool, white sand. From beneath the water, I watch Him lean down, curls shining and dark eyes glowing, and I see the smile of delight as His small, brown hand comes down and lifts me into the light.

Sarah Addison Allen

In My Dreams

Fly By Night

I watched my house from the second story bedroom at Great Aunt Sophie's. I could see that the lights were on in my living room. A shadow passed by the windows there, and the curtains moved like fingertips had brushed them.

My mom was slowly walking around our house next door, in and out of each room, like she was looking for someone. The kitchen light went on once, then flicked back off.

"Louise!" Great Aunt Sophie called from the next room, and my elbows jerked off the window sill where I was kneeling. "Go to sleep."

There was no door, just a doorway, between Great Aunt Sophie's bedroom and the one I was sleeping in that night. As I knelt at the open window, pretending I was in bed asleep, I could hear her turning the pages of her book, the low mumble of the radio station out of Asheville that still played big band music, and sometimes I even heard the rattle of ice cubes as she poured iced tea into a hard plastic cup from the thermos she brought up from the kitchen. They had the easy, sleepy echo of sounds repeated night after night. Great Aunt Sophie herself was like that. She was worn in the best possible way, like the way your oldest shoes fit, the shoes that wouldn't slip when you ran on dewy grass and gave you traction when climbing hickory trees.

I ignored Great Aunt Sophie with the hope that she was just checking to see if I was asleep. If I didn't say anything, she would surely believe that I was. I turned back to the window I was kneeling in front of and continued to watch my house. The night outside was the thick black of a new moon, and lightning bugs ticked away in backyards as far as I could see. My bedroom next door was dark, but suddenly light spilled faintly into the room, as if the switch in the bedroom across the hall from mine had been turned on. The light covered my doorway and outlined the toy horses I'd placed on my window sill that very morning.

"Louise," Great Aunt Sophie called. "Don't make me say it again."

I should have known that she knew. She knew everything. She knew things nobody else knew.

I got up and walked to the doorway separating the two bedrooms. Her room had side-by-side twin beds, both covered with pink, quilted polyester bedspreads. She slept in the one on the left, farthest from the door and nearest to the open window. The bedroom I was staying in had one full bed with a knotty pine headboard pushed against the wall. The mattress was an old featherbed, and it felt a lot like sleeping on a nest of pine needles. I knew this because I fell out of a pine tree once and landed in a pile of needles, breath gone, thinking I was dead, and I looked up to see Great Aunt Sophie in her straw hat. I thought that was a horrible way to go, lying in resiny needles with Great Aunt Sophie's frown the last thing I would see. She told me to go home because she was in no mood for my antics and she hadn't raked that pile of pine needles just for me to jump in. I thought she had no respect for the dying, so I went home to tell my mother, who didn't believe me because I was breathing again.

Great Aunt Sophie and her husband Harry used to sleep in the featherbed room, but Great Aunt Sophie moved into the room with the pink twin beds after Harry died. My mom told my dad this once, as if trying to explain away some of Great Aunt Sophie's peculiarities. I didn't like the thought of sleeping in the featherbed room. I had never met my great-uncle and I didn't know if it was possible to be haunted by someone you had never known, but I didn't want to risk it.

"Go to sleep," Great Aunt Sophie said, laying her open book page-down on her chest and folding her fingers over it tightly, hiding the picture on the cover.

"It won't come. I tried."

"Then get yourself into bed. Sleep can't come into your head if you're sitting up at that window."

I walked into her room. There were places in Great Aunt Sophie's house where certain scents pooled. As you walked in the front door, you smelled Blue Grass perfume right away. Great Aunt Sophie kept the spritzer in a table drawer beside the door and always sprayed her gloves once before going to church. Then there was that place on her staircase, about three steps up, that for no reason smelled like lavender, as if just moments before a beautiful lady had walked up the stairs ahead of you. And in the twin bed room, it smelled of yellowy paperback romance novels and Rosemilk lotion, the kind they advertised during *The Lawrence Welk Show*.

I sat on the edge of the twin bed next to her. She had taken the thin pink bedspread off her bed and it was folded neatly at the bottom of the bed I was sitting on. She was on top of her sheets in deference to the cloying summertime heat, and her sunbrowned bare feet were crossed at the ankles. She had reddish-orange polish on her toenails and caked around her cuticles and skin, like she'd had trouble aiming the brush. For as long as I knew her, she'd always painted her nails this way, and I had no choice but to believe she did it on purpose.

"Mom can't sleep, either. I was watching her. She's walking around the house."

"It's understandable, Louise. Let her walk and tire herself out. Then she'll sleep. You'll see her tomorrow," she said, as if tomorrow weren't so far away.

Great Aunt Sophie was as practical as a pin. She intimidated me sometimes with her perfect rightness. She never had any children. I never asked why, but sometimes I thought it was because she didn't like kids. She didn't have much patience with me. Her husband Harry died when she was in her forties, and she never remarried. My dad had once said he could never imagine Great Aunt Sophie married. My mom told him that there were certain hurts that Sophie chose not to show, but that didn't mean they weren't there.

"Do you ever miss Harry?" I asked her, just to keep her talking so I could stay longer in her room.

Great Aunt Sophie looked straight ahead, not at me, as if seeing long ago things I couldn't see, maybe even the ghost in the next room. "Of course I do."

"After so long?"

"Yes," she said shortly, closing up her secrets. "You shouldn't be asking me these questions. You should be a-*sleep*."

"I miss my dad," I finally said. I had been afraid to say it all day, afraid that I was the only one.

Great Aunt Sophie paused, then nodded, just once. "I know you do."

I was surprised. Mom and Great Aunt Sophie had acted so normally that day. They smiled and accepted condolences as easily as they would have accepted a compliment, graciously and without fuss. I didn't understand. I didn't feel normal. It hadn't been a normal day for me. "Do you miss him, too?" I asked, because Great Aunt Sophie and my dad didn't get along and I was afraid that she was glad now that he was gone. They were friendly enough, I suppose, but Great Aunt Sophie couldn't put the fear of God in him with just a look like she could with most people and I think that annoyed her.

"Your daddy was a dreamer. He could dance, and that was in his favor." She slanted her eyes my way. "Never marry a man who can't dance, Louise."

Knowing how to dance was important to Great Aunt Sophie. Sometimes, when she took her bicycle out of the garage, she would do a little two-step with it if she was in a good mood. She loved her bicycle. I could remember seeing her once, dressed in her Sunday-go-to-meeting finest, pedaling past our house on her way to church. Then I remember seeing the back of her dress fly up right in front of old Harvey Williams, who had opted to walk to church that morning with his wife Annie because he was having one of his good days. From then until the day he died, he referred to that incident as his Sunday morning revelation. When my mom wanted to vex Great Aunt Sophie, she would bring this up.

I scratched at a circle of poison ivy on my leg, just above my knee. It had been hard to sit still at the funeral service that morning and not scratch. I had tried to think of everything I could remember about the last time I saw my dad to take my mind off the itch. I was in my nightgown in the kitchen, waiting for my Lucky Charms. He had his steel lunch box. He checked the refrigerator again to see if he had forgotten his thermos of orange juice. I could remember things he usually said: *Goodbye. I love you. Where's my orange juice?* But I couldn't remember if he said those things that morning or, if he did, in what order.

"Louise, stop scratching that or it will never get better," Great Aunt Sophie told me.

I did as she said. "I want to be home."

"Your mama needs to be alone tonight. You're a yard away. It's silly to miss a person who's only a yard away."

I opened my mouth and thought about that for a minute, knowing Great Aunt Sophie didn't suffer talking off the top of your head. "But it's okay to miss the people far off, right?"

Great Aunt Sophie nodded twice. "That's when you should miss them."

I'd never seen Great Aunt Sophie show an emotion stronger than indignation, and that one was her favorite. But I knew she loved me, just as I knew she loved my mom. She raised my mom from the time my mom was ten, when her mother died. My grandmother was Great Aunt Sophie's sister and she married a "no-good sailor man" that Great Aunt Sophie didn't like so much she never even said his name. He was still living, somewhere. No one ever mentioned where.

Sometimes it seemed like she was still raising my mom. She participated actively in everything my mom did, except for when she married my dad. Defiantly, they went to South Carolina and eloped. My dad used to say it took the summer Mom discovered she was pregnant with me for Great Aunt Sophie to finally give her blessing. That was a grand summer, he'd said. Warm weather and the promise of only good things to come.

It surprised me that Great Aunt Sophie wasn't hovering around Mom now, giving her a break from thinking, tonight of all nights. But Great Aunt Sophie had talked to my mom only once since we got home, and that was to say goodnight. She didn't even offer food. Great Aunt Sophie *always* offered food. Everyone knew that. In times of distress she could whip up green bean casseroles, broccoli cornbread and peanut butter pies, then be at the doorstep of the bereaved before most folks in the factory town of Clementine, North Carolina, even knew there had been a tragedy.

I didn't know whose idea it was for me to stay with Great Aunt Sophie that night. If I had been sure Mom was responsible, I might have been able to talk her out of it. But if it had been Great Aunt Sophie's idea, I knew arguing with her would be like throwing a stone up to try to hurt the sky. She was that vast, that unshakable. She thundered only when she wanted to. So I didn't say a thing as Sophie took a pair of pajamas out of my dresser and took my hand to lead me across our yard into hers after we all got home that afternoon.

She gave me cream of tomato soup which she had made from her own tomatoes, and then she melted some shredded cheddar cheese on saltine crackers in the oven. While I ate at her kitchen table, which was covered with a printed oilcloth, she took her garden shears and went outside. That night I discovered that she'd picked some Shasta Daisies and put them in a vase in the featherbed room for me.

I tried to scoot slowly, invisibly, to the top of the twin bed, so Great Aunt Sophie wouldn't see what I was doing and order me back to the *ghost* room. "Why doesn't everybody go to heaven, Aunt Sophie?" I asked, as I put my head on the pillow.

"God decides that, not me," she said, though I knew she had her own ideas on the subject.

I stared at the textured ceiling. "Do you think my dad's in heaven?"

My dad knew of heaven. He didn't go to church, but I think he understood the idea.

The winter before, on a cold, still Appalachian night in December, he had come in from somewhere, I don't remember where, and he was smiling. He smelled like the cold and cigarette smoke when he picked me up and carried me outside without even giving me time to put on my coat. My mom only smiled at him the way she always did, as if she loved him so much she couldn't speak.

The snow was frozen and it had hushed the neighborhood. It was so quiet that each step he took in the hard snow sounded like the pop of a paper bag full of air. Once we were in the front yard, he put me down, then pointed up. I followed his finger to the millions of bright stars overhead. There were so many of them it looked like there was no night, just stars, packed like an audience trying to get a better view of us.

"Look at that, Louise," he said in awe. "God, will you look at that. There you go."

There you go.

"Is that where he went?"

Great Aunt Sophie was silent for a good many moments. She reached over and took a bookmark off the table to her right. She marked the place in her book and set it aside. "I've pondered this now," she finally said. "And I believe your daddy's in heaven. Dreaming and dancing are heavenly things. Your daddy would fit right in."

"Your Harry's in heaven, I guess," I said.

"Yes, he is." She took a quick, deep, decision-making breath. "Do you want to know why I took that door away, Louise?" She pointed to the doorway separating the rooms. "It's because I can lie here and look into that room and see where he lived. My memories are in there, but my life is in here. That's the way it is, Louise. You can look at them, but you can't live them."

"I want to be home." I tried to keep my voice straight so Great Aunt Sophie wouldn't know I was crying. She didn't like for people to cry. It made her fidget. She all but left the room last week when Lorelei Horton tearfully told the Sunday school committee that her son was finally coming home from Vietnam.

I woke up just after two in the morning and static was coming from Great Aunt Sophie's clock radio. The big band station out of Asheville signed off at two and resumed broadcasting at six. I was still in the bed next to Great Aunt Sophie. She had covered me with the scratchy bedspread. I looked over to her and saw that she was asleep, breathing through her mouth. The static didn't seem to bother her.

I got out of bed, half-asleep, and went to the featherbed ghost room, my need to make sure my house was still there greater than my fear of being haunted. I knelt at the window again and stared at my house. Every single light was on now, even the front and back porch lights. It looked like the sun had fallen into the house and was shining out of every opening the hot yellow light could find. Even the basement light was on. I could see the shine crawling out of the one window in the bricks at the bottom of the house. That was my dad's wonder room. He made stuff there, fixed stuff, too. He fixed Great Aunt Sophie's coffee percolator once, which I thought was very nice of him.

I rested my chin in my hands. The static from the radio was becoming familiar now and it was lulling me back to sleep. But that's when I noticed something on the roof of my house. I lifted my head and stared hard, trying to make out what it was.

The figure moved from between the dormer windows at the front of the house, to the edge of the back of the house. She wore a white nightgown I could see in the darkness. She sort of danced around the rooftop for a while, like she testing her balance. I didn't understand her presence on my rooftop. Before this night, I'd never had the perspective of looking out over my house. I wondered if she had visited before, or if tonight was special.

The lights from the house illuminated her figure like stage lights. She went to the edge of the roof and held her arms out wide like she was going to fly.

I remember thinking, *She can do it. She can fly.*

Then I heard a sound over the static, like a voice rising above applause. The angel standing on my roof was crying. It was the unhappiest sound I'd ever heard. The hurt in it pricked my skin like someone had pinched me, and tears came to my eyes.

She doesn't want to fly.

Then she lifted her hands up to the sky as if asking for help from God. She put her hands on top of her head and tucked her chin to her chest. Was she praying?

God, help me not fly.

I heard some movement in the next room, like maybe Great Aunt Sophie had gotten out of bed and gone to her window. Then I think maybe she said, "Good Lord in heaven, no."

I closed my eyes and felt the warm from the light from my house. I hoped the angel would stay, that she wouldn't fly away since the thought was agonizing her so. I remember hearing Great Aunt Sophie saying softly, over and over, "Don't do it, don't do it, don't do it."

But I couldn't help it. I had to go to sleep.

When I woke up again, it was morning and the air was wet with the scent of cut grass and gasoline. Someone was mowing somewhere in the neighborhood. I was on the floor below the window and Great Aunt Sophie's pink polyester bedspread was again covering me. I sat up and looked around. I could hear voices coming from outside so I crawled to the window and looked out. Great Aunt Sophie was down in her rose garden, and my mom was hanging her favorite green and white striped bed sheets on the clothesline in our backyard. They were talking to each other, calling back and forth like they did almost every sunny day when there was outdoor work to be done.

"Mom!" I yelled.

Both she and Great Aunt Sophie turned at the sound of my voice. Mom smiled up at me. "Come over here and give me a hug, sweetie girl," she called.

And I was out of the house in nothing flat.

I ran right past Great Aunt Sophie and over to my mother. As I hugged her, I grabbed her shirt tight in my fists as if she would fly away if I let go, as if I'd caught her just in time. She bent down and kissed the top of my head. She was fine, the way all Southern ladies were fine, as if there were no hurts great enough to break them. But I knew there were, and I held her tighter.

Great Aunt Sophie watched us, her hand shielding her eyes from the sun. She stood there for a long time. Finally, she lowered her hand and picked up her basket of roses. She walked back to her house and her ghost there, and Mom and I held hands and walked slowly together to our house to greet ours.

Nothing Disastrous

It was the spring Great Aunt Sophie was caught without her Coca-Colas. That's how she remembered things, in terms of events that were importantly disastrous to her and only her. One morning in late April the whole town woke up to two inches of ice and, inconveniently, it was Great Aunt Sophie's grocery day. She stocked up on her weekly supply of Coca-Colas every Wednesday. Within forty-eight hours everyone in town was referring to it as the spring Sophie got caught without her Coca-Colas because the power might have gone out but the telephone lines were blessedly spared. Reverend Joe finally got his car out and took her to the grocery store. That's when Great Aunt Sophie decided that being a Yankee, even a single one, wasn't such a sin and maybe he did have a right to be in the pulpit.

That spring was also the one-year anniversary of my mom losing her breasts to cancer. But that wasn't disaster enough for Great Aunt Sophie. She said, "Your Mama's alive and well now and there's nothing disastrous about that."

The ice storm passed and May that year was divine and warm. Mom started wearing summer dresses again. Her counselor had told her she would go through a mourning period, missing her breasts. And she quietly did.

The spring that Great Aunt Sophie was caught without her Coca-Colas, the one year anniversary of my mom losing her breasts, was also when Reverend Joe finally brought his wife down from Connecticut.

Her name was Fala and she had beautiful dark hair that wasn't quite brown, but not quite red either. And it was always so shiny. The light through the stained glass made it look like she had glitter in her hair. I liked to watch her. She sat alone on the very first pew every Sunday.

I think she was afraid of us. She asked us to repeat ourselves like we were speaking a new language she was trying to learn. I think she tried to be a good preacher's wife, but Great Aunt Sophie complained that the parsonage's telephone line was always busy because Fala called her family every seven minutes. I thought that was extraordinary. I'd never known anyone who called somebody every seven minutes. My babysitter talked for at least a half an hour before calling someone else when she watched me on the evenings Mom had to work. At the homecoming picnic the first Sunday in July, I decided to ask Fala about it.

She looked a little confused when I asked her, so I repeated myself, more slowly this time.

"I understood you," she said. She had walked away from the church picnic to smoke under the hickory tree near the road and I had followed her. "I talk to my family a lot, but not every seven minutes." She flicked the ashes off her cigarette with an agitated movement. She smiled at me, a little thinly. "I think your great-aunt was just trying to make a point."

"Oh," I said. She finished her cigarette but made no move to return to the picnic. Instead, she fished out another and lit it. I leaned against the trunk of the tree figuring she would tell me to leave if she didn't want me there. "How do you get your hair to do that?" I said after a stretch of silence. "It's so shiny."

Her hand went to her hair and she stroked it as if comforting herself. "Cream rinse. My sister sends me down a supply of it every couple of months. It's from a salon we used to go to in Hartford."

"My hair won't do anything but braid," I said.

Fala reached over and touched my hair. "It's dry," she said. "You need some cream rinse. I'll bring you a bottle of mine next week. You can tell me how it works." Then, out of the blue, she asked me, "Your mother had breast cancer, didn't she?"

I nodded.

"My grandmother had breast cancer, too." No one in town ever said that word *breast*, at least not twice during the same conversation. As far as the town was concerned, my mother had an affliction. But it seemed to me that whether or not it was an affliction didn't matter because it was still in her breasts. But here Fala was saying it out loud like she was saying *cabbage* or *antelope*. She took another drag off the cigarette and looked out across the field. "I was named after my grandmother. Fala means 'crow.'"

She said that as if it really pleased her and I thought if my name meant crow, I wouldn't be too happy about it. Neither would Great Aunt Sophie. She didn't like crows. She was always shooing them out of her yard, running out her back door, waving her arms and fussing. We lived next door to her so the crows would fly over to us until she went back inside and then they flew back.

"I'll come by. How about tomorrow? When will your mom be home?"

"Usually about five-thirty except on Thursday and then she works at night."

"I'll come after dinner," she said with a nod. She dropped her cigarette and stepped on it. "We should get back. Some of the church ladies are giving me that look."

Fala came by at seven-thirty the next evening and gave me a yellow bottle of cream rinse which I promptly used. It stung my eyes. She was still in the kitchen, talking to my mom, when I went to bed.

She was over at our house a lot the next few weeks. Then Reverend Joe, larger than life and as big as our doorway, started showing up.

It was hard to eavesdrop because the kitchen opened into the dining room and there was no place to hide close enough to hear. Sometimes I would sit outside on the back porch steps in the evening and throw rocks from the driveway into the yard to try to quiet the cicadas so I could catch words coming from the kitchen. Reverend Joe and Fala talked a lot. When Mom talked, she talked very low like she knew I was trying to listen. I had to stop eavesdropping after Robert Junior, who mowed our grass in the summer, complained about the rocks in our yard flying up and hitting him in the head.

I finally asked my mom about these sessions when we were at the grocery store. I tried to slide into the conversation by remarking over the cantaloupes, "Reverend Joe and Fala are over at our house a lot."

"Friends talk." She put some oranges in the cart and walked ahead of me.

"But why you? I mean, there are lots of other people in this town."

"Would you share all your secrets with your Great Aunt Sophie?" she asked over her shoulder.

She had a point. "No way. What do they talk about, Reverend Joe and Fala?"

"Fala's grandmother always wanted her to marry a preacher," Mom said, putting a package of bacon into our cart, which she told me I couldn't push if I ran into her heels one more time.

"The grandmother she was named after?"

"Uh-huh," Mom said, looking at the ground beef.

"She had breast cancer, right?"

Mom looked up at me. "How did you know that?"

"Fala told me."

"Oh. Yes, her grandmother had cancer. And her grandmother wanted her to marry a preacher so Fala promised her. That's why she's here."

"Was Reverend Joe the only preacher she could marry?"

Mom laughed at that and I was glad because I loved her laugh. It caused these little lines around her eyes as if she was so happy she had to squint. She was so beautiful. She had started wearing make-up like she used to and by this time she had stopped remarking every time she passed a mirror that she was as flat as a boy. "No, honey. Reverend Joe is originally from Hartford and he went up there to visit some family last year. It was right after Fala's grandmother died. Reverend Joe and Fala knew each other in school and they renewed their acquaintance. He proposed and she accepted." Mom had this way of explaining things that always made them make sense. I missed that when she wasn't around.

"They're over at our house a lot," I managed to work in again. "Great Aunt Sophie says visitation means visiting lots of people, not just one."

"Aunt Sophie's being persnickety, honey." We moved to the cereal aisle and I darted off. "Don't tell her I said that!" Mom called after me.

The sessions with Fala and Reverend Joe lasted through the summer, sometimes stopping for a few weeks, sometimes happening every other day. The last session was on the day before Halloween, and it was with Fala. I remember because Fala brought the costumes she was making for some of the Sunday school kids and Mom helped her sew. A few weeks later Reverend Joe and Fala went up to Hartford to spend Thanksgiving with their families. Only Reverend Joe came back.

Reverend Joe and Fala divorced in the spring of the next year and the ladies at church clucked with sympathy. Two months later Reverend Joe started seeing my mom. I remember the night he took up half the couch as he sat waiting for my mom to get ready for their first date. He told me my mother was the most serene and compassionate person he had ever known. I told my mom this the next day but she just smiled as she did the dishes. It was the two-year anniversary of my mom losing her breasts, the spring great-aunt Sophie ran over her iris bed with her lawn mower.

I asked Great Aunt Sophie what she thought about the divorce. It was pretty big news. It was even in the newspaper. Fala had floated into our lives, left conditioner at several people's houses, made some people envious, some mad, left cigarette butts in the church courtyard, and only ever talked to my mother. I thought she was fun and mysterious, like someone on summer break from school who had come down to visit with us like the Jessup twins from Illinois.

Great Aunt Sophie sat in her iris bed wearing her big straw visiting hat and black and white gardening gloves. "Fala's much better off than my poor irises," she said to me, poking the ground with a trowel. "Everyone is alive and well and, in all probability, happy." She looked at me, shaking her head as if I should understand this by now. "There's nothing disastrous about that."

Lazarus

I was ten when my mother remarried. When I got out of bed the day of the wedding, I was not happy. I was in an early morning state of confusion that didn't often happen on Saturdays because I was usually allowed to sleep in. But by eight o'clock there had to have been at least twelve women in the house already, and they were clucking like a yard full of guinea hens. No one could find my mother's wedding shoes. Shelly Gaddy, my mother's maid of honor, was the one who had jarred me awake that morning. She came into my room, looked under my bed, looked in my closet, then finally looked under my covers. Why in the world she thought I was sleeping with my mother's wedding shoes, I don't know.

They were low-heeled white patent leather pumps that had aged yellow and my mom had worn them when she married my dad. She didn't even know she still had the shoes until I told her about them. A couple of months before, she and some of her friends had been sitting around the kitchen table, lamenting. Apparently, they couldn't find the right shoes to go with the wedding dress Mom had bought with her employee discount at Staler's department store. The dress was so creamy it was almost yellow. It was long and silky with a layer of lace overlapping the dress which Mom said she liked because, ever since her breast cancer, she didn't particularly care to wear form-fitting things. I'd walked in and said, "What about those old yellow shoes in your closet, Mom?"

"I don't have any yellow shoes, honey," she'd responded.

"Yes you do."

"No, I don't."

So I'd turned around and went to her room and pulled them out of her closet. I carried them to the kitchen and said, "See?"

Her friends gave a unanimous gasp and Shelly had said, "They're perfect!"

Mom had taken one shoe out of the box and weighed it in her hand. She'd smiled at me and said softly, "Thank you, Louise."

She'd discussed it with her husband-to-be, Reverend Joe, and he'd said he didn't mind her wearing them at all, that it would be a nice tribute to the memory of my father.

I had cold cereal that morning while the wedding party in the house scurried around trying to figure out what to do about the missing shoes. Great Aunt Sophie came in through the kitchen door at exactly ten o'clock, looked around skeptically, then demanded to know what was going on. She had worked too hard for anything to go wrong with that particular day. She was wearing her straw visiting hat, which she always wore when she came over to our house. I thought that was pretty silly since we were family. And we lived right next door.

"I can't find my shoes, Aunt Sophie," Mom said, leaning against the kitchen counter with an ice pack on her head. She had been looking in the lower kitchen cabinets and had banged her head when coming out. I wondered why anyone thought her shoes would be in the kitchen cabinets in the first place. Even if by chance someone had put them there, that's not the kind of place you would forget.

"Your shoes?" Great Aunt Sophie said, frowning. She turned to me. "Louise, do you know where your mother's shoes are?" She asked this as if I were naturally the primary suspect and no one had had sense enough to confront me yet.

"No!" I said. "I would have said something before now if I did."

"Well, don't get testy," she said. She eyeballed me critically. "What are you still doing in your nightgown?"

"The ceremony isn't until four," I reminded her and she squinted at me.

"She's still trying to wake up, Aunt Sophie," Mom said. "We didn't mean to, but we woke her up looking for my shoes. She was up late last night."

"They were on the back porch the last time I saw them," I offered, feeling a little guilty that I was being contrary on my mother's wedding day.

"The back porch! Yes! That's where they were last night. I cleaned them and left them out there to air and dry."

"Well they aren't there now," Great Aunt Sophie observed doomfully, going to the back door and looking out through the screen. "Do you think someone took them?"

Mom took the ice pack off her head and turned to Great Aunt Sophie. "But who would take my wedding shoes?"

No one could answer that question so the next two hours were spent on the phone calling everyone in town trying to ascertain if any would-be shoe thieves were lurking about.

At noon, my best friend Sue meandered down the street to my house. She came by to ask if someone really did steal my mother's wedding shoes. By that time, most of the town knew. Several offers of substitutes had come in, but my mom had her heart set on her own— the ones that had vanished.

"Let's go walking," I said to Sue. "It's crazy here."

"Are you excited about being in the wedding?" Sue asked me as we headed down the street. We had been on the phone several times the week before and she was forever changing what she was going to wear. The last I heard it was her green dress with the daisies on it. I was prepared to be surprised, though. I had no choice in what I was going to wear, but I liked the dress anyway. It was icy pink and so shiny that if you turned the right way and held still, you could see things reflected on it, distorted, like when you blur your eyes looking at Christmas tree lights.

"Yeah, I think so," I said. It was so hot that sweat was making the back of my knees slick. "Mom sure is. Oh, and she wants me to be sure to thank your mom again for letting me spend the night with you tonight. Otherwise I would have to stay with Great Aunt Sophie."

"And my mom said to tell your mom that she's sorry she doesn't have any shoes she can borrow. My mom's feet are bigger than Bigfoot's," Sue said, rolling her eyes. I laughed. Sue was going to be as tall as her mother. She was already a head taller than me.

We came to Mrs. Yardley's old overgrown field at the end of our street. It was one of our favorite stomping grounds. There was a big rock in the back corner that we liked to climb on. In the spring we'd sit on it and make crowns out of dandelions, in the fall we'd pile the top with fallen leaves and make a leaf slide, in the winter we'd never stay long, but in the summer we'd stay all day and sun ourselves like lizards.

We entered the field and the weeds topped my knees. We stopped short when we saw a black lump jump up from the wild onion and Queen Anne's lace not far from us, then disappear.

"Whoa," I said. "Was that a dog?"

"I think so. But what's it doing?" Sue asked quietly.

"I don't know."

"Louise, come back here right now," Sue hissed as I walked toward where the dog had last jumped up. I didn't pay any attention to her and, apparently fueled by my bravado, Sue followed me at a distance.

There was some movement and rustling a few feet away, so I quietly approached the noise. When I got there and looked down I found a skinny black Lab on his back, chewing on something he was blissfully holding between his two front paws. He was making content cooing and grunting noises and was occasionally rubbing his back on the ground by squirming his body around.

"Is something wrong with it?" Sue asked as she came up behind me.

At the sound of her voice, the dog realized he had an audience and immediately jumped up. Sue screamed and ran to the rock and jumped onto it, stomach first. She shimmied her legs wildly until they were safely underneath her and not sticking out in the air where a vicious mad dog could bite them.

But Sue's legs were the last thing on the dog's mind. He had taken off in the opposite direction. When Sue finally stopped screaming, the dog stopped at the edge of the field. I stood there, looking from one to the other. Then I looked down and saw what the dog had been chewing on. One of my mother's wedding shoes.

I picked it up. "Sue!" I yelled, waving the shoe. "Look!"

"What is it?" she called back. "Did it kill a rabbit? A cat? Oh God, Louise, run! It's coming back! Run!" I turned to see the dog trotting back to me, wagging his tail, his long tongue dripping drool out of the side of his mouth. He apparently saw that I had discovered his toy and was coming back to take credit for it.

He approached me and made some half-hearted jumps at the shoe, which I was holding up and away from him.

"Watch out!" Sue screamed and the dog backed away.

"Stop it," I called to her. "You're scaring him."

"Whoop-tee-do! He's scaring me, too!" she shot back.

"Come here, boy," I called to him and he came to me as trusting as you please. I patted his head and he leaned against my legs. He was so skinny I could feel his ribs. He had gray around his muzzle and one eye was caked with some dried yellow stuff. He was in sorry shape, but as happy as a plum. I decided I would love him even though he smelled worse than those rotten banana peels Great Aunt Sophie always put around her rose bushes in the spring.

"It's okay, Sue," I said to her. "He's harmless. He's a stray. I think he needs something to eat." Then I remembered the shoe. "And look! It's one of my mother's shoes. I think he's the one who took them."

Sue slid off the rock. "Your mom's going to be maaaaad," she said, as if trying to make the dog tremble at the thought of my mother's wrath. But my mother had no wrath. Now Great Aunt Sophie—well, that's another story.

We found the other shoe nearby and then we ran out of the field. We were going to save the day. I just knew it.

Mom had almost decided on another pair when we burst into the house, Sue with one shoe, me with the other, and the dog with nothing but an eagerness to be in on the excitement. We found my mom in her bedroom, modeling a pair of shoes someone had brought her.

We proudly presented Mom with her wedding shoes. One was in good shape. The other had some pretty bad chew marks on it.

"Where did you find them?" Shelly asked me as she took them from Mom and gave them a thorough inspection, making a disgusted face when dirt and drool stuck to her fingers.

"Over in Mrs. Yardley's field. The dog had them."

"What dog?" Mom asked as she took off the shoes she'd been trying on. She was wearing her red cotton robe and as she bent over it fell open a little and I could see the beginnings of the two long scars on her chest.

Maybe the smell finally clued her in. She looked up. That's when she noticed the dog in her room and took a startled step back. "Louise, get the dog out of my bedroom. Get him out of the house," she said calmly, not taking her eyes off of him.

"But Mom, can I keep him?" I said, going over to him and petting him protectively. "You know he didn't mean to eat your shoes. Look at him. He doesn't belong to anyone. Can I have him? I'll take good care of him. Please? I've never had a dog before."

"Take him outside and give him something to eat," Mom said, shaking her head. "We'll discuss this later."

"If I ask Reverend Joe and he says it's okay, can I keep him?" I asked, referring to Reverend Joe for the first time in a parental capacity. This seemed to please Mom but she stood there, still looking at the dog, probably thinking about this possibly being her and her husband-to-be's first joint venture.

"All right. Just get him out of here."

"Can I go over to the parsonage right now and ask him?" I persisted. We were in the process of moving into the parsonage where Reverend Joe lived, though not even half of our stuff was over there yet. "Please?"

"Okay, go on. But be back here by two *or else*."

Great Aunt Sophie entered the bedroom at that moment and the dog came up to greet her. "What is this?" she screeched, throwing her hands in the air and backing up against the wall. Then she saw I was there and everything seemed to make sense. "Louise, you get this mongrel out of this house immediately! This is your mother's wedding day! Are you purposely trying to upset her?"

"No ma'am," I said as Sue and I and the dog ran out.

We ran most of the way to the parsonage. We went into the house without knocking because the last time I knocked Reverend Joe told me it was my house and you never knocked to come into your own home.

Reverend Joe's family had come down from Connecticut for the wedding and they were staying at the parsonage. I forgot that, or I wouldn't have come storming in because I knew Mom wouldn't like for them to think I was rude. Reverend Joe's mother was sitting alone at the dining room table with a cup of coffee. She smiled at us, unruffled, as we entered. She was a small woman, dressed entirely in floral that day, right down to the plastic flowers at the tips of each high-heeled shoe.

"Hello girls," she said. "Are you excited about today?"

"Yes ma'am," I answered. "Look. I found a dog and I'm going to ask Reverend Joe if I can keep it."

"That's sweet, dear. Where did you find him?"

"In a field. He stole Mom's wedding shoes and was chewing on them."

"On her wedding shoes?" Reverend Joe's mother looked distressed. Apparently, no one had thought to fill her in on this news. "Goodness. I should call her."

As she got up, Sue and I ran to the kitchen. Reverend Joe wasn't there so we ran out the kitchen door. Reverend Joe was standing next to his father, by his father's car. I thought they were probably talking about tires because that's all Reverend Joe's father talked about when we had lunch with them the day before. He was very proud of how well the tires on his new car traveled.

"Reverend Joe!" I yelled from the porch.

He looked up at me and frowned. "Louise?" He said, walking over to us. "What's wrong? Is it your mother?"

"No." I shook my head and tried to catch my breath as I walked down the steps. "It's a dog. I found a dog and I wanted to ask you if I could keep him. When we move in here, I mean."

Reverend Joe watched the dog come slowly down the steps after me and collapse onto its side in the grass, panting and flopping its tail in a tired greeting. "Looks like a stray," he said.

"Yes. We found him in a field and he likes me. Can we keep him? I've never had a dog." I figured if I kept using that line, I'd get more sympathy points. As if all kids should have dogs and I'd been deprived of a significant childhood staple because I'd never had one. "Mom says it's okay with her if it's okay with you."

He smiled in that same way Mom had smiled. Like it was a family thing. "Let's get him some water," Reverend Joe said. "Pop? Will you get out the water hose?"

So it was settled. I officially had my first dog. Reverend Joe found an old pie tin and we had to fill it up four times before the dog had enough water. Then Reverend Joe's mom made him a meal of leftovers.

The dog liked Reverend Joe. It was hard not to. Reverend Joe was a huge man, tall, overweight, divorced once and a freely admitting sinner with good intentions. He commented that the dog was very dirty, so Sue and I and Reverend Joe found ourselves giving him an outside bath. The dog jumped around trying to catch the water from the water hose, so bathing him was like trying to shoot a moving object. All three of us ended up as wet as the dog.

When we were finished, Sue said she had to go home to get ready for the wedding. She later told me her mom got mad at her because she had to wash her hair again.

I stood with Reverend Joe outside. I was late already but I didn't care. We were both dripping, standing in the warm sun, watching the dog. The dog smelled around the back yard for a while, periodically shaking himself. Finally he decided on a place to sleep and collapsed. But then, looking discontent, he stood back up, walked a few steps to the left, and plopped back down. The first place he had picked was in the shade of the chokecherry tree. The second was in the sun.

Reverend Joe laughed. "Sundog."

"Is that what you want to call him?" I asked.

He put his arm around my shoulders and squeezed. "No. But how about Lazarus?"

Reverend Joe's parents were sitting on the back porch swing, watching us. His mother was smiling. I couldn't be sure, but I think she had tears in her eyes. Or maybe it was just the pollen.

Great Aunt Sophie was always complaining about the pollen.

A preacher from Jonestown performed the ceremony because Reverend Joe couldn't officiate at his own wedding. Most of the town of Clementine was there and had to have a good look at Mom's shoes as she came down the aisle. Great Aunt Sophie had improvised with masking tape almost the same color as the shoes and you could hardly tell that they had been chewed on. I was anxious for the reception to start because Lazarus was outside the church, waiting.

After the ceremony, Great Aunt Sophie parked herself beside me as Mom and Reverend Joe danced the first dance at the reception in the fellowship hall below the chapel. "Are you happy, Louise?" she asked me.

"Yes ma'am," I answered, taking a swipe of icing off the wedding cake I was standing beside, knowing it would make her mad. She was positively possessive about the presentation of the food at the reception. The sausage balls, which she normally only made at Christmas, were in a perfect pyramid. And her butter mints were neatly separated into groups of yellow, pink and pale green, with none of the colors touching.

"Good." She paused. "Your mama's been through a lot, but she's happy now. You know that, right?"

"Yes ma'am." I was still kind of mad at her for making Lazarus stay outside. I argued with her, but she said the dog didn't have the sense God gave a little green apple and she wasn't about to have him hanging around all her carefully prepared food.

Great Aunt Sophie watched Mom and Reverend Joe dance for a while. "Never marry a man who can't dance, Louise," she said quietly as she walked away. Great Aunt Sophie loved to dance, but never with anybody. She'd dance across her kitchen floor sometimes when she cooked. I saw this many times in the days before the wedding when I watched her and her friends fix the food for the reception. Her friends would laugh and clap as Great Aunt Sophie danced with an invisible partner around her kitchen table.

The reception lasted well into the evening. I finally got to slip outside with Sue and we ran laughing across the church courtyard with Lazarus at our heels. We played keep-away with a stick and Lazarus barked and barked. Finally, out of breath, I collapsed back onto the dewy grass. Sue was catching fireflies and letting them go. I could hear the music coming from the fellowship hall as I looked up at the stars.

The moon glowed like half-hearted sunlight above me. My world slowly drew up into a noisy, shimmering bubble and floated above the earth for a while.

The Wayfarer

On Friday afternoon after school, the day of my grandfather Charlie's arrival, my best friend Sue and I sat under the chokecherry tree in the back yard and watched Robert Junior, who was in high school, chop wood. He was chopping a lot of it. Reverend Joe had announced that he wanted to always have a fire burning in the fireplace that winter. I didn't understand why. We had a furnace. Reverend Joe had given up trying to chop the wood himself earlier that week after scratching his leg with the ax. Mom told him a one-legged preacher was the last thing this town needed, so he hired Robert Junior.

"Have you ever met your grandfather?" Sue asked me. Sue thought my family was fascinating. Until Reverend Joe married my mom, we were girls, all of us. Me, Mom, Great Aunt Sophie, Great Aunt Anna who died five years ago, and Great Aunt Anna's daughters who drove over from Tennessee every August for the church homecoming. Sue resented her brothers, all six of them, for not being girls.

"Nope," I answered. "My mom was only ten when her mother died. Mom was sent here to live with Great Aunt Sophie then."

"Didn't her dad want her?"

"I don't know." What I did know was that when my grandmother took off to marry my grandfather, Sophie and Anna got really mad because they didn't like him. But when they heard that their sister had died, Great Aunt Sophie wanted Mom to come here to Clementine, North Carolina, to live. I suppose my grandfather didn't argue too much. Mom said it's been forever since she's seen him. She keeps the eleven letters he's written her, though. I've seen them. That's where Reverend Joe got his address. It was Reverend Joe who invited him, and it had taken weeks for my mom and Great Aunt Sophie to get over the shock and forgive him. And I still wasn't sure Great Aunt Sophie had.

"Are you excited about seeing him?"

"I guess. I don't know. Everyone else seems a little..." I shrugged. I watched Robert Junior lift the ax and swing it down on a log, splitting it cleanly in half. He wasn't wearing a shirt. "Everyone else seems afraid, I guess."

"Afraid of your grandfather?" Sue turned to me, her eyes wide and mischievous. "Why? Did he do something bad? Was he in jail? Did he kill your grandmother?"

Robert Junior looked over at us and I was embarrassed. "No! Stop it. My grandmother died of cancer. My grandfather was a fisherman up north. I guess he was on the ocean a lot and couldn't take care of my mom."

"Then why is everyone afraid? Is he mean?"

"No." I thought about it for a minute. "He's unexpected."

That evening Reverend Joe tried to build a fire. I was sitting on the couch doing my math homework in a loose, goofy, too-girlish dress my mother made me wear. She had bought it at Staler's department store with her employee discount, which was her excuse to dress me in frilly things I hated. Sue wanted to be there that evening to meet Charlie, but Mom said no. Mom wanted Great Aunt Sophie to be there, but Sophie said never in a million years.

Reverend Joe proved to be an interesting distraction and I watched behind my textbook as he fumbled through his attempt to create and maintain a fire. The first time he burned his fingers with the matches because he couldn't find a place to light the paper, even through the gaps in the grate, because he used heavy wood that flattened everything beneath it. The second time he used too much newspaper and the outside papers burned then flickered out, leaving the tightly bunched papers in the middle untouched. The third and final time he successfully trapped a fire and made it burn in one place, but then the big blackened log on top rolled off and onto the brick hearth. In the time it took for him to freeze, then make a panicked dash for the fire tongs, the flames had burned down all the kindling.

He finally declared that this particular November evening in the southern Appalachians was not nearly as cold as the ones Charlie was accustomed to way up north, and he would probably want to go straight to bed anyway. Reverend Joe shrugged on his coat and left for the airport.

My mother came out of the kitchen. She stood there in the arch separating the living room from the dining room for a few seconds, long enough to hear the car door shut, then she moved quietly to the fireplace.

She cleaned out Reverend Joe's mistakes with the ash shovel and pail he had proudly bought that day at the hardware store, and in minutes a fire burned so hot I could feel it from across the room. It made shadows move and roll on the wall behind me.

My mother amazed me. She knew exactly how much paper to wad, how much kindling to stack and just the right size log to top it all off. And she seemed completely unaware that she had mastered an enviable skill. She reminded me of how Great Aunt Sophie always seemed to know exactly how much a pinch or a handful of any given condiment measured without ever checking. It was hard to believe I was related to these women. I wondered if I would ever do anything enviable.

My mother clopped another log into the fireplace, sending sparks crinkling. Turning around, she said with a nod, "That should do it." Anticipating my remark she said, "Your stepfather has never spent a winter in Maine. I spent most of my childhood there. Joe can teach you math. I can teach you how to build a fire." She smiled as she left the room, leaving me to wonder about the part of her childhood that didn't take place in Clementine, North Carolina. The part I didn't know, the part she would never tell me.

It didn't take long for me and my dog Lazarus to gravitate to the fire. Drugged by the hissing whirl, I stretched out in front of the hearth and put my head on Laz's stomach. He didn't seem to mind his pillow status; he only opened his eyes for a moment to make sure it was a familiar head.

I dozed off soon after, lulled by Laz's breathing. I was occasionally aware of my mother stepping over us to place another log in the fire, but when I heard the front door open, even half-asleep, I could tell that my grandfather had arrived. It wasn't because he banged his boots on the hallway floor in any peculiar manner—my mother had trained us all to do that. No, I knew because he moved differently. He *swished*.

He slowly walked into the living room and I stared at him. He stopped, not yet spotting me, and swung his heavy dark blue cape over one shoulder with more grace than a man of his size is ever reckoned to have. The movement revealed most of his large, compact body and his two thick arms doughed to thick red hands. He leaned heavily on a walking stick as he unfastened the throat clasp of his cape and Reverend Joe appeared from behind him to take it. The gesture wasn't meant to be grand, but it was to me anyway. I'd never in my life known anyone who wore a cape.

"Where's my Margaret?" he said in a flaky voice like he was talking into the wind. Lazarus lifted his head.

"She's probably in the kitchen," Reverend Joe said, walking past him with a hard leather suitcase in his hand. "I'll get her."

Left in the living room with him, I had no idea what to do. Should I move or talk? Would I startle him? I panicked when he began to walk to the fireplace. Would he step on me? Would he trip over me and into the fire? I couldn't imagine trying to explain a situation like that to my mother.

He stopped, however, right at the place where Lazarus and I began. I stared at his scuffed black boots with the small silver buckles at the ankles for a moment, long enough to ascertain that he wasn't going to kick me, then I cautiously looked up to his face. His hair was dark blond like my mother's, only thinner.

His face, as he looked into the fire, was a red weather-beaten color, nearly the same as his hands. The balls of his cheeks were glossy. He stared into the fire like something he hadn't seen in a long, long time.

Lazarus, after some half-hearted scrutiny, decided there was no immediate danger and dropped his head back down to the floor with a thud. Charlie looked down and immediately stepped back with an exclamation that sounded something like, "Iche!"

I didn't move.

"I thought you were a dog," he said.

I opened my mouth and discovered I had nothing to say. Finally, I answered, "No."

"You're Louise, aren't you?"

"Uh-huh."

"I'm your granddad, Charlie."

My mother walked into the room. He turned around and they studied each other very carefully, like they wanted to make sure they were the right people before this reunion went any further. Very hesitantly Charlie held out his heavy arms because, it seemed, he didn't know what else to do.

My mom hugged him and cried for a long time. She was very quiet about it, her head tucked into his shoulder. It struck me as strange, my mother crying to her father. It was as if everything that had troubled her mind since she was ten came out at once now that her daddy was there. Her *daddy*. Her mother was gone, and Great Aunt Sophie was okay, but never a person you could cry to.

Reverend Joe stood near the couch and watched them. I didn't want to move and disturb them but my neck was cramping and I wanted to get up. I started to sit up but Reverend Joe shook his head adamantly, so I was stuck on Lazarus's stomach.

My mother finally stepped away and wiped her eyes with her fingertips. "I'll go get the tea. You sit." She took a step and leaned over me. "Louise, get up. Your grandfather is here," she whispered, as if I had no idea what was going on just a foot in front of me.

It wasn't but a short time later that I think I loved my grandfather for the first time—the only time, really, because I didn't know it then but I would never see him again. All he did was hand me his walking stick. Without stopping his conversation with my mother about his fifth ex-wife Terry, without even looking at me, he handed me his walking stick. I had been staring at it, wishing for a closer look. He acknowledged my presence with that gesture. Without ever saying a word, he told me he knew I was there.

There was a beautiful masthead lady carved in the wood. She was buxom to the point of mythical proportions and had long hair that swirled around her torso coyly. Her expression was sad, though. Sort of homesick. For a long time I sat on the arm of the couch with my hand on the top of the walking stick where it was worn from lots of leaning, and gazed into the fire.

"That fair lady was Charlotte Naomi," Charlie finally told me. "I sailed her for thirty-two years. Wrecked on the rocks at Pemaquid, though, and shook that lighthouse good." He laughed and set down his tea. The tiny cup had looked ridiculous in his large hand, anyway. "And that," he nodded, "that, is very nearly a difficult thing to do."

My mother suddenly stood and walked over to the fireplace. I watched as she shooed Lazarus out of the way and pushed a log onto the low flames.

"Look here," Charlie said, drawing my attention back to him. He pushed up the right sleeve of his thinning black sweater and revealed another Charlotte Naomi tattooed in green-black ink on his inner forearm. But she looked only penciled in. His walking stick was real and round and sad.

When my mother didn't sit back down, one by one, we went to join her by the fire. I stood by Charlie and offered him his stick back. He shook his head and instead rested a heavy hand on my shoulder.

All four of us stared silently for a while. My mother then said quietly, "Mama used to say that you can always tell a wayfarer by how he stands to the fire, that the first thing he does when he sees a fire is walk up real close to it because he knows he'll eventually leave again to the sea, and he wants to remember the warm."

Charlie glanced at my mother, but then focused back on the fire.

He left Sunday afternoon. Reverend Joe had to go to church that morning, but Mom and I got to stay home with Charlie. He made blueberry pancakes for us for breakfast.

Great Aunt Sophie knew the moment he was gone. She called my mother nine minutes after Reverend Joe and Charlie left—the exact time it took from our driveway to her house, which they had to pass on their way to the interstate, which led to the airport in Asheville. I was helping Mom fix dinner when the phone rang.

"Hello?" my mother said. "Oh, hello Aunt Sophie. I was expecting you to call." Mom winked at me as if to say she knew what Sophie was up to. She was in a good mood. "Oh, really?" she said, looking surprised. "All right, here she is." Mom held the phone out to me. "Aunt Sophie wants to talk to you."

"Me?"

"Yes."

"Why does she want to talk to me?"

"I don't know, Louise." She shook the receiver. "Why don't you ask her?"

Mom took the knife from me and began peeling the potatoes I had started. She was much faster at it. "Hello?"

"Hello, Louise."

"Is something wrong, Aunt Sophie?"

"No, nothing's wrong," she said shortly. "Does something have to be wrong for me to call you?"

"No ma'am, but you usually talk with Mom, not me."

"Well, I want to talk to you," she said decidedly, even though it still sounded a little odd. "Is your mama in the same room with you?"

"Yes, she's right here. She's peeling potatoes." Mom looked like she was trying not to laugh.

"Oh." Great Aunt Sophie paused. "Well, Louise, why don't you stop by my house on your way home from school tomorrow? I'll make you some of your favorite cookies."

"Great! Thanks, Aunt Sophie. Can Sue come, too?"

"That will be fine. I'll see you tomorrow, then."

"Okay. Bye!" I hung up the phone and walked back to the kitchen sink, amazed. "Aunt Sophie is going to make me some cookies. I'm stopping by her house tomorrow after school. Is that all right?"

Mom threw her head back and laughed at the ceiling. "She's shameless!"

"What are you talking about?"

Mom wiped at the tears in her eyes. "Aunt Sophie didn't like that I'd known she was going to call me as soon as Dad left. So, determined to prove me wrong, she didn't ask me a thing about him. But she's going to give you the third degree about him tomorrow, Louise. I'm giving you fair warning."

I shrugged. It didn't matter to me. I was getting cookies.

Sue and I stopped by Great Aunt Sophie's house on our way home, as promised. Sue had been looking forward to it ever since I told her that morning in homeroom. Great Aunt Sophie was stubborn and vocal, but she cooked like nobody's business. Her house was the first house on the right, the second street off of Main. It was a well-known house for two reasons: the constant smell of cooking coming from it which seemed to make evening walkers pass by her house more often than the others, and her beautiful roses which, in a good year in these mountains, lasted until the end of October. When that happened, she would stick the roses in a carved pumpkin, like a vase. Mom and I used to live beside her, before we moved into the parsonage with Reverend Joe, and sometimes I dream about my old house.

Great Aunt Sophie let us in and led us to her kitchen where, sure enough, there on the oilcloth-covered table was a big plate with a stack of cookies on it. The cookies on top were just out of the oven, the chocolate just warm enough to feel on your lips, like a quick kiss from someone not sure how to say I love you.

Sue and I sat down and immediately started in on the cookies. Aunt Sophie poured us glasses of milk. "Thanks, Aunt Sophie," I said.

And Sue repeated, "Yeah, thanks, Aunt Sophie!"

Sophie poured herself a cup of coffee and came to sit at the table with us. "So, Louise, did your grandfather have a nice visit?" She took one of the cookies for herself. She broke it in half but didn't eat it.

"I think so. Mom made some special dishes and he ate a lot. He asked about you. He didn't know that Great Aunt Anna had died and he said he was sorry about that. Why didn't you ever come over?"

"I was busy," she said dismissively. "Did you like your grandfather?"

"Yes ma'am. He told me about his adventures on the sea. I wanted him to tell me more but sometimes Mom wanted me to leave him alone. I think he and Mom talked a lot when I wasn't there. Reverend Joe stacked wood against the garage all weekend."

"What did he look like?" She sipped her coffee then set the cup down and twirled it in a slow circle.

I took a moment to swallow some milk. "Didn't you ever see him, Aunt Sophie?"

"A long time ago, dear. He was just a young man, as handsome as all get-out, when he married my sister. He moved her up north, away from her family and all she knew, and I never saw her again."

"Well he's old now." I couldn't believe I said that to her. I felt my face grow warm. "I mean, not old, but old*er*. He's big, but not fat. And I'm almost as tall as he is. He's got Mom's blond hair."

"Your grandmother had blond hair, too. Your mother is more like her," Great Aunt Sophie said defensively.

"And he walks with a cane."

I had told Sue everything I could remember about his visit, which is why she said, "Tell her about the cane, Louise." She crushed another cookie, whole, into her mouth. With the way we were eating you'd think we'd never had cookies in our whole lives. We were twelve. We should have known better. But we didn't know whether to try to stay kids as long as we could, or go barreling into adulthood. We were kind of like Reverend Joe when the traffic light turned yellow on Main Street. He never knew what to do. He'd go from brake to gas, brake, gas, brake, gas. He'd usually end up stopping right in the middle of the intersection and have to go forward anyway because there wasn't any choice then.

I nodded and turned to Great Aunt Sophie. "He has this beautiful cane, Aunt Sophie. It's got a masthead lady carved into it. She's beautiful and she looks so sad. Her name is Charlotte Naomi and he's got a tattoo on his arm of her, too. Charlotte Naomi is the name of his ship, the one he wrecked. That's how he hurt his leg. He sailed her for thirty-two years. Did you know that all boats are called 'she,' Aunt Sophie?"

Great Aunt Sophie wasn't looking at me anymore. She was silent for a good many minutes. Sue and I looked at each other curiously as we continued to stuff ourselves.

"Aunt Sophie?" I finally said again.

She looked startled. "Yes, girls." She pushed herself away from the table and started to fuss around in her kitchen cabinets. Her fingers were clumsy in her haste, slipping and letting the cabinet doors close with a bang. "Here, let me get you some bags and you can take the cookies home." Then we were dismissed.

When I got home, my mother came into the living room the moment I walked in. I ruefully handed her the bag of cookies and told her I couldn't eat dinner because I was full. I was more than full. I was sick. She reached into the bag and took one. "So, what did Aunt Sophie say?" she asked as she bit into the cookie with an expectant, almost girlish look on her face.

"Nothing much." I shrugged, just wanting to lie down. "I told her what he looked like and about his cane. Then I told her about the Charlotte Naomi and she got all quiet and sent me and Sue home."

Mom had the cookie almost to her mouth for another bite, but then she lowered her hand as a hushed look fell across her face. She slowly sat down on the edge of the couch and shook her head. "She didn't know," she said quietly.

"Didn't know what?"

"About the ship." She paused then looked up at me and smiled. "My mother's name was Charlotte Naomi," she explained. "My dad loved my mom. That's always been a hard thing for Aunt Sophie to accept."

"Oh," I said. "I'm going upstairs now, Mom." I felt awful. I never wanted to see another cookie as long as I lived. I was getting too old. In my younger days, I thought, I could wolf down cookies with the best of them. I felt defeated.

"Okay," my mom replied, distracted, as she dropped her half-eaten cookie back into the brown paper lunch bag. She carefully folded the top of the bag and set it in her lap. She smoothed her hands over it gently, as if to wipe away any creases. Then, sighing, she reached for the phone.

God's Honest Truth at the Fashionette

Vivian opened the door and propped a broken piece of cinder block in front of it. The day was warm and breezy. She hated to look out the window and see that there was such grand weather going on and she couldn't be out in it. She kept the door open as much as possible. She stood in the doorway and watched the traffic pass. A pickup truck pulled into the parking lot.

She waved as an older couple got out of the pickup. Sometimes Vivian would see them driving in town. Ginger sat close to James in the cab of the truck, not all the way over on the other side. Sometimes Vivian wondered why. Did Ginger still love her husband that much? Or was it just habit?

"That must be Ginger and James," Harriet said from her chair, where Vivian had left her when she went to open the door.

"Right on time." Which is to say an hour early, Vivian added to herself, for her own benefit. She knew these people. She knew their habits. They came to her, to her place, and she hosted them.

"Sophie should be here any minute. I'm surprised she's not here already," Harriet said as Vivian picked up her comb and resumed brushing through Harriet's wet hair. "I can't wait to hear what she has to say about Lorelei Horton's new car."

"Time to get pretty!" Ginger said as she walked in, her arms stretched wide like she was receiving applause from an audience. "Harriet," she said, breathlessly, like she had a secret to tell. "Have you seen Lorelei's new car?"

Harriet laughed and jiggled her wet hair out of place. "Yes. Yes, I have."

"Has Sophie?" Ginger asked, vaguely disappointed that she'd been the bearer of old news.

"I have no doubt," Harriet said as she shook her head. Vivian had to put both hands on her neck to still her. Harriet was a fidgeter, as anxious and impatient as a toddler sitting in the chair.

"That color," James said as he walked in behind Ginger, shaking his keys in his hand like dice, "is not found occurring naturally in the

151

known universe."

"Are you referring to my hair or Lorelei's new car?" Harriet asked him.

"I'll get back to you on that one as soon as Vivian is finished with you." He winked and pocketed the keys.

"You are a wicked man," Harriet laughed.

"Yes, he's dreadful," Ginger agreed simply. Ginger was tiny, barely over five-two and, in his heyday, James was well over six feet. They didn't look like they fit, yet no one could imagine one without the other. "But I've been married to him for fifty-eight years and I'm used to it."

James sat down in one of the cracked plastic waiting chairs lining the long front window with FASHIONETTE written on it in white shoe polish. "This is the thanks I get for bringing you to gossip with your hair cronies every Tuesday."

"Don't be silly," Ginger said, sitting next to him with a flourish. "You enjoy it every bit as much as we do." She patted his knee at the face he made. "Go on, tell them. Tell them what you heard."

"What did you hear, James?" Harriet asked from under the veil of her wet hair as Vivian combed it forward.

James settled himself comfortably in his chair. "My cousin Roy over in Jonestown told me that Lorelei had bought herself one of those dancing hula girls that you put on the dashboard for her new car."

"You don't mean it!" Harriet said, parting her hair so she could look at James.

"That's what he said."

"Lord, that woman thinks she's sixteen," Harriet said.

"Where is Sophie? She's always here before we are," Ginger said, looking pointedly to her right as if Sophie was going to pop out of the bathroom.

There was a concerned pause.

"Didn't you pass her out on the highway?" Vivian asked.

"No."

"Why she insists on riding that bicycle all the time, I have no idea," Harriet said, nervously twirling her garnet pinky ring under the yellow plastic covering her from neck to knee. Where was Sophie? Harriet had offered to drive her to the Fashionette that very morning, like she did every Tuesday. Old and stubborn, Harriet thought. One sneaks up on you just as fast as the other. Didn't Sophie see how dangerous it was, riding that bike at her age? Too independent for her own good, Harriet thought. Sophie never wanted help. She never needed help.

Harriet had to learn early how to ask. Her husband, God rest his soul, was a no-good son of a gun. She married him when she was eighteen. But when he came home from the war, she hardly recognized him. And when she thought of him now, she couldn't picture him without a drink in his hand, his fingers blurring into the glass like it was an extension of him. Most of the time he even slept with the glass, in the living room chair, and over time she found she preferred him there rather than in the bedroom with her.

There was never enough money. Harriet took a job at the factory, back when it was small and only made parachutes, to support herself and the children. Whatever her husband managed to make went toward his liquor. She'd known Sophie for ages, ever since Sophie's husband let Harriet have credit at the gas station he owned when things got tight.

Harriet still worked at the factory three days a week. Social Security wasn't enough to live on and the factory didn't have retirement. She wondered what it was going to be like when she was finally too old to work. Would she know when it was time or would she be one of those poor old souls who tried to do everything for themselves and ending up breaking a hip in the garden or in the dairy section of the grocery store? It hurt her deep in her heart to think of being a burden to her children. They were the sweetest things known to man, but not in any real position to support her. She asked so much of them anyway. They mowed her lawn and had her car serviced. Her youngest had her over for lunch after church every Sunday and her oldest brought her dinner from the diner every Thursday, turkey pot pie night.

Being old never seemed to bother Sophie. She did it easily. Harriet liked that about her. Being old on your own, knowing you could do it. For heaven's sake, she even rode her bike out on the highway. Sophie did it because she knew she could. But what would it mean if something happened to her on her way to the Fashionette?

One down, Harriet thought. That's what it would mean.

"I don't have a clue how those things stay on the dashboard," James was saying. "Some sort of glue, I guess. But why would Lorelei risk hurting the interior of her new car like that? Those hula dancers can really move."

"And how do you know that, James?" Vivian teased as she began to snip the ends of Harriet's hair with short, quick movements. She barely had to look at what she was doing.

"He thinks he's a man of the world," Ginger said. It was an unwritten rule at the Fashionette that men entered at their own risk. Teasing James was a big part of Tuesday afternoons at the Fashionette.

"I've been to Korea," James said.

Ginger patted his knee again. "There aren't hula dancers in Korea, dear."

James grinned. "How do you know?"

Vivian smiled and surreptitiously glanced at the digital clock over on Beth's side of the Fashionette. Sophie was late.

Vivian didn't like that Sophie wasn't on time. Harriet, Ginger, and Sophie made appointments together so that they could spend all afternoon at the Fashionette. Sophie was usually the first to arrive because she had to leave so early to get here. She bicycled instead of driving a car. She had refused to learn how to drive after her husband died, or so Vivian was told. This happened before Vivian even knew Sophie.

Vivian didn't consider herself a spring chicken, but at fifty-seven she was younger than most all her clients. Her only employee, Beth, quietly doing a teenager's perm in the chair across the small room, brought in most of the younger clientele.

Vivian had moved the Fashionette out onto Clementine Highway because it was the only place she could afford. It was nice enough, but Clementine Highway was much busier than it used to be, ever since the factory on down the highway expanded. Vivian worried about traffic holding back her regulars, especially Sophie, riding that bike. She rode down the side of the highway like nobody's business, which she always said was true, anyway.

Vivian looked outside at the beautiful day. The rolling green mountains looked like kids playing under a green blanket. Vivian couldn't remember the last time she was on a bicycle. Her boys used to have bicycles. She remembered that much. What did she do with those bikes? She had no idea. Travis was three and Barry was four when they died, along with their father, when that train hit their truck. God, how long ago was that? She thought. More than thirty years? Sometimes, even when she tried really hard, she couldn't conjure up their faces. She sometimes thought of her boys' fat cheeks, crusty with breakfast, and the veins in her husband's hands. But that was it, memories going by like traffic passing.

She had the Fashionette and it was her life now. It had moved to six different locations since she'd opened it thirty years ago, but her regulars followed her. Harriet and Sophie, who'd been cohorts since she'd known them, had brought cake and casseroles to her when her family died. It was the one thing they didn't talk about when they all got together at the Fashionette, although Vivian thought she wouldn't mind so much now.

Ginger and James came into her life after she opened the Fashionette in its first location on Main Street, back when the leases weren't so high in downtown Clementine.

She pinched her eyebrows together and tuned back in to the conversation. She hoped Sophie was all right. One thing she would never forget in all her living days was that losing people was hard. Deathly hard.

"I've seen the car," Beth was saying from across the room. She was putting the solution on the young girl's hair she was perming. "Lorelei parked at the grocery store and no one would park next to her."

"I wouldn't park next to her," Harriet said, her hands fidgeting under the yellow plastic, twirling her pinky ring again. "That paint looks contagious."

"James parked right next to her in front of the Dairy Queen yesterday," Ginger said.

"I was looking for the hula dancer."

Ginger shook her head. "Devil man."

James looked innocently at Harriet, who was now having her hair curled with hot rollers. "Don't look at me," Harriet warned. "I think she's right."

Beth smiled as she set the timer for Tracy Lyn's perm. The young woman was silent, like most of her clients were. They either didn't have much to say or, like Beth, they enjoyed listening to the conversation over on the older ladies' side.

Beth could have gotten herself a booth of her own at Clipper's in Jonestown. But she was closer to home working for Vivian. That son of hers was always getting in trouble. Lord, he was only thirteen. Sometimes Beth was tempted to ask the Tuesday afternoon club about how they raised their children, about what to do. But they had their own little world over there and she rarely interrupted unless she had something pertaining to the conversation at hand.

Beth owed Vivian for hiring her while she was still in beauty school over in Jonestown. She needed the money after her husband Kenny left her. Vivian said she understood. Being a woman is rough, she said. You need a job, you need a conscience and, when it comes to men, you need accouterments. Beth had to look up the word later. It meant to outfit as in the military. Beth supposed you had to steel yourself when it came to men.

She liked it at the Fashionette. She liked that her younger clients were well behaved and sometimes talked politely about school and their fresh lives, and she liked to listen to the keen-minded ladies. Her own mother had Alzheimer's. Beth had to finally put her in a nursing home last year. Her son was getting worse by the day and Beth just couldn't take care of them both. It broke her heart harder than when Kenny left, to put her mother in the home. She hated seeing her fade away and wanted to stop it somehow, but she couldn't. The harder she tried, the worse it got. It was like sweeping back the sea.

Where was Miss Sophie? Beth wondered. She'd never been this late. Come to think of it, Beth couldn't remember her *ever* being late. Could she have forgotten? Beth glanced at the wall phone near the bathroom. Maybe she could sneak a call to Miss Sophie's house and remind her. Her mother's symptoms started with forgetfulness. Good Lord in heaven, she hoped it wasn't that. She eyed the phone again.

"Where did Lorelei get the car?" Harriet was asking.

"At a dealership in Charlotte," James answered, recognizing a man question when he heard one. "No one in this part of North Carolina would have the gall to sell something like that."

"I can't wait until she comes for her Thursday morning wash and set so I can see this car for myself," Vivian said.

"You won't believe it," Ginger shook her head. "You just won't believe your eyes. That *color.*"

"Where did she get the hula dancer?" Harriet asked.

James shot a look at Ginger. "Korea?" He offered.

Ginger popped his knee. She loved James with all her heart and soul, in a fanatical kind of way. She thought every day of losing him and loved him even more in hopes that it would make him stay. She was the only one of her friends whose husband was still alive and she felt privileged, like she'd done something right to deserve this. Like she was somehow different from Sophie and Harriet in an enviable way.

Their children didn't visit anymore—they didn't like her, and she knew it. James was hurt by that, so she tried to make up for it. She was always with him, close to him in the truck, laughing with him on Tuesdays at the Fashionette, going to choir practice with him even though she couldn't carry a tune and Helen the organist didn't like her.

Ginger didn't know how to be independent. Sometimes she would wonder what it would be like, living without James. She tried to imagine the sympathetic glances she'd get, the calls and offers to be driven places. It was almost unbearable. *Almost* because of one person. Sophie knew how to be independent. Ginger both loved and hated it about her. In the name of all that was holy, she hoped Sophie was all right. She was the one who showed her that living was possible after loving a man so much. She was proof that it was possible to get on without driving.

Ginger discreetly glanced at James' wristwatch. She never wore one herself. They had been at the Fashionette for half an hour and Sophie still hadn't shown herself.

You can do it, Sophie. You can do anything. Maybe, Ginger thought, independence isn't something you can find or lose. Maybe, for good or bad, you either have it or you don't. If that was the case, Ginger thought it would just be easier to die when James did.

"Do you think Lorelei is color blind?" Vivian was asking.

"No, I think she knows exactly what color her car is and she's getting a kick out of everyone talking about her," Harriet said.

"Well, you ladies are doing a good job of it, that's for sure," James said.

"Oh, don't you even try that." Ginger smiled at him. "You're one of us."

Traffic outside whizzed by on Clementine Highway. The timer for Tracy Lyn's perm ticked away steadily. A light wind blew in and Vivian and Harriet, closest to the door, felt the breeze on their legs. Everyone looked around uncomfortably. Harriet spun her ring nervously. Ginger tried to think of something to say. James noticed for the first time that FASHIONETTE was spelled with two T's, not one. Time slowed, movements became sluggish, the tick of the timer lingered longer after each tick, breathing became lazy.

Then, like the burst of a bubble, Sophie stomped in saying, "Doggone it!"

"Sophie!" Harriet exclaimed, startling everyone more than Sophie did in the first place. She almost hopped out of the chair before Vivian stopped her. "Where on earth have you been?"

Sophie proceeded to take a tissue out of her wicker purse. She patted her forehead. Her face was flushed, and her curly silver hair was pushed flat against her head on one side, sticking out like fire flames on the other. "My bicycle had a flat halfway down the highway. Had to push it the rest of the way here."

"Didn't anyone stop to help you?" Ginger asked, perched on the edge of her seat. She reached out and took James' hand.

"Of course," Sophie said impatiently. "One of which was Lorelei Horton in that fluorescent monstrosity she calls a car. But I didn't need help. I've got the patch kit right here in my purse and as soon as I've cooled down I'll fix it. Lord, but it's hot out there." She looked across the room. "Hey there, Beth. How are you?"

Beth was leaning against the counter but stood up straight when Sophie unexpectedly spoke to her. "Not bad, Miss Sophie."

"Since you're waiting on that little girl right there, would you mind getting me a glass of water?"

"Of course I will," Beth said.

Sophie sat down next to Ginger. She patted the sides of her hair, then sighed and let her hands flop to her lap. Everyone was staring at her. Sophie looked at each of them. "I'm an old woman," she finally said, shaking her head. "I don't remember getting old and that's God's honest truth. But here I am, and I'm an old woman."

Vivian walked over and turned on the air conditioner. She pushed the broken piece of cinder block away from the door with her foot. With one more look and one final breath of the beautiful day, she closed the door, shutting out the sound of the highway.

I'll See You in My Dreams

Great Aunt Sophie liked tight, no-fuss perms that sat close to her head, the curls as round as Christmas peppermints. It used to be that she could easily pedal over to the Fashionette for such a coif. But she retired her bicycle about three years ago. Her doctor said it was time. Of course, her doctor started saying it was time fifteen years ago. It just took that long for her to finally agree with him.

I have a standing engagement with Great Aunt Sophie and, when it's time for a perm, I leave early from work and drive her to the Fashionette, past the factory out on Clementine Highway. When she was able, she used to go for a wash and set every week, now she settles for a perm every couple of months. I pick her up at her house, and the first thing she always says to me is, "So, do you like working at *Staler's*? Did you have a good day?"

And I always answer, "It's all right. A job, I guess," leaving her to guess who actually buys those designer briefs and the boxers with chili peppers on them. She's bound to know the men if I tell her.

I sell men's underwear at *Staler's* department store. I have the dubious distinction of knowing what almost every man in town wears underneath. Sometimes, walking down Main Street, I imagine I'm getting sheepish looks from the men, especially the older ones. Like I know their secret.

It was a fairly bold move for a factory town store like *Staler's* to put a woman in charge of men's underwear, but I guess they figured it was good plan when they found out that more women buy men's underwear for their men than the men do for themselves. There was actually a study done somewhere. Great Aunt Sophie doesn't believe me when I tell her this.

"What kind of person would go up to a stranger and ask her if she buys her man his underwear?" Great Aunt Sophie says. Apparently she has no problem with asking me, though. She called me up last Sunday and said she'd just been to *Staler's* with her friend Harriet, who still drives. She said she saw this ridiculous pair of men's orange boxer shorts with big green dinosaurs on them that glow in the dark. "Tell me who buys those, Louise," she said to me. "Tell me who actually buys that sort of thing."

I wanted to know what she and Harriet were doing wandering around in the men's underwear department at *Staler's* when she knows neither Mom nor I work there on Sundays.

Sophie asks me to come in when I take her home from the Fashionette. It's a feverish late September day. It's the kind of hot that sticks to the sides of the mountains, like the colors in this particular Appalachian autumn. As soon as we walk to the kitchen, she opens the back door to let the breeze come in and stands there for a moment, looking out as if she sees someone. Then she turns around and begins to fuss around the kitchen, her feet whispering against the linoleum.

Her kitchen smells like a combination of apples turning soft and the scent of fine linen napkins that have been locked away too long in cabinet drawers. The smell makes me feel good, like when I was young and Great Aunt Sophie wasn't quite as old. But then it silently reprimands me for not coming to visit as often as I should. Shame on you, Louise, it says.

"So tell me how you are," Great Aunt Sophie says, going to the faded green pie safe in the corner and gingerly bringing out an apple pie. Maybe her stiff, knobby fingers are up to no good again. She doesn't seem to trust them to carry the pie over to the counter. She cuts a piece right there and takes it to the microwave. This is all done before she's even taken off her sweater, or exchanged her going-out eyeglasses for her at-home eyeglasses.

"I'm fine, Aunt Sophie," I say, sitting at the heavy wooden kitchen table covered with a finely-kept, flowered oilcloth, which she's had for as far back as my memory stretches. There's a huge bowl of apples on the table, waiting for her to do what she does to apples in the fall— can, bake, fry, stew, candy, dry, dip in caramel, marinate in sugar to pour over friendship bread. She keeps promising not to touch another apple recipe until the apples decide to peel themselves. But Sophie's not that patient.

She puts the piece of freshly microwaved pie in front of me. Warm curls rise up from it. "Smell that, Louise," she says to me as she hands me a fork. "That's what my heaven's going to smell like. Apple pie. Hot apple pie . . . and leather shoes, new ones. The dancing kind."

I take a bite because I know she won't move until I start eating. Just as soon as the fork reaches my mouth, she turns and goes to the kitchen drawer to do her eyeglasses exchange. She leans against the counter and rubs her eyes tiredly, at length, before she puts on her at-home eyeglasses.

She sighs and pushes herself away from the counter then she takes off her sweater and ties a blue apron around her waist. "So tell me, how's that best friend of yours, the one you knew in school? Sue? I haven't seen her in a while."

"She's fine, too. I saw her just yesterday. She's pregnant," I say as Great Aunt Sophie turns on the portable radio in her kitchen window. A big band tune comes out softly.

"Pregnant again?" she asks over her shoulder as she starts making coffee in her new automatic drip. The air whooshes into the sealed coffee jar as she opens it. "How many will this make?"

"Just three." I take another bite of her pie. "Her husband wants a boy this time."

"Humph," Great Aunt Sophie says. "Like he can control that."

I smile. Some things I just know I inherited from Great Aunt Sophie and no one else. "That's what I say. She won't listen. She's in love."

"You're a good girl, Louise. Have I ever told you that? You are. You need to find a nice man and have children. I'm not going to be around forever to tell you this, so you better hurry up." Her automatic drip gurgles and she sways a little to the music as she brings a cup down from the cabinet.

I watch her. Great Aunt Sophie isn't the kind of person you would ever think of as a dancer, but she loves to dance. Not that she ever dances with anyone, but I know that if she's having one of her good days, she'll sometimes dance to her refrigerator and back when she cooks. And when she used to bring her bicycle out of her garage, she would sometimes dance with it all the way to the road.

"I'm sure I'll find a nice man some day, Aunt Sophie."

"Yes, yes. I suppose so. You're only twenty-five. I'd like to see the day, that's all." She pours a cup of coffee and comes to sit beside me at the table.

"Twenty-four," I remind her, thinking that ever since I had that Yes-I'm-old-enough-to-have-coffee conversation with her several years ago, she always seems to make me older than I am whenever coffee is involved, even though she never gives me any. I'm old enough to sell men's underwear. I wonder what she would say if I tell her that.

"I got married when I was twenty. I told you that once, didn't I?" She has the creamy eggshell-thin coffee cup in both of her hands as she takes a sip.

"No ma'am. I don't recall that you did."

"My Harry. He was a good old soul. I had a dream about him." She pauses then laughs. She sets her cup down and leans back in her chair as she puts a hand to her cheek. "When was that?" She shakes her head. "Ha! I can't even remember. Maybe it was as close as last night."

"You had a dream about Harry?" I never knew my great-uncle. He died long before I was born.

"I dreamed I was sixteen again and my hair was long and blond." She pats the sides of her newly permed hair. It's the purest silver you've ever seen, like a new nickel, and it smells something powerful. It makes my nose tingle when the breeze from the open doorway blows the smell my way.

I look at Great Aunt Sophie carefully. "Your hair was long and blond?"

She smiles, a tad mischievously. "Long, maybe. But not blond. But that's what dreams are about sometimes, aren't they? How you want things to be." She nods to the plate in front of me. "Do you like the pie? Harriet's apples weren't great this year."

"The pie is wonderful," I assure her.

"Did I ever tell you how I met my Harry?" she suddenly asks, but distantly, like she's asking someone else in the kitchen, someone behind her in the doorway.

"I don't think so," I say.

"Don't be silly." She's definitely talking to me now. I recognize that tone. "I know I told you a long time ago. When you were little. Remember these things, Louise. They're important."

It's an art, I realize. Guilt is an art. And Great Aunt Sophie is a master artist. When are you getting married? Why don't you stop by and see me? Didn't you ever listen to me when you were little? I would never backtalk Great Aunt Sophie, but the answers are always there: In time, I do, and no. Sophie orbited my world when I was little, large and looming like a full July moon. I used to watch her carefully—the best way to avoid her was to always know where she was—but I never listened to her much. I should have known I was going to be tested later.

"Yes ma'am," I promise her.

"All right, so listen up. There were three girls in our family— Anna, the oldest, me in the middle, and your grandmother Charlotte, the youngest," Great Aunt Sophie begins, counting off each sister on a different crooked finger. "Anna married when she was seventeen to a boy over the state line in Tennessee. She had been married about two years when her first child came along. Mama and Daddy packed me and Charlotte up and sent us on a train to help her out with the baby.

"Mama sent me with secret instructions to have an eye out for every little detail so I could tell her when I got home. Anna married into a family with money, you see. When Charlotte and I got there, the house was as big as any place I had ever seen. But everyone lived there. The whole family. Ma and Pa Coleman, Anna and her husband, another son and his wife, and two daughters, not to mention a couple of housekeepers. It seemed to me that they needed all that space because nobody was ever going to leave. And the family just kept growing. Charlotte and I were put in the same room, the only room they had left, I think.

"It turns out Anna already had a woman to help with the baby, Evangeline, so Charlotte and I weren't really needed. But Anna was happy to have us there and we spent a lot of time together. It was just like when we were girls. Anna was close to twenty then, I was sixteen and Charlotte was going on fifteen. We spent hours just walking around the orchard on the estate. Sometimes we'd go into town and people would remark on what pretty girls we were."

Sophie smiles at the memory. But then she shakes her head. "I always thought your grandmother was the prettiest of us three. I told you she had this beautiful head of golden hair, remember?"

"I remember," I say.

"Somehow, the brown eyes we were all born with seemed to look better on her. Now, Anna was tall and stately and fit right in with money. I was somewhere in the middle, but there we were in this little town in Tennessee and suddenly I was a beauty. There were several dances in town and we were never wanting for a partner. Anna let us borrow her lipstick. Oh, those days, Louise," she sighs. "Someday, when you're old enough, you're going to look back on your life and remember things that, even though you didn't know it then, will make you know who you are now."

"I'm not so young," I have to say.

To that she just laughs. "Anyway, after we had stayed long enough, Mama and Daddy called for us to come back North Carolina. We were upset something terrible. We'd had the time of our lives. But then I remember Anna coming into the room and telling us that there was another dance that very night in town and we were all going to go. Of course that made everything all right because then we would get to say goodbye to everyone. We had been there almost three months. The whole summer.

"I was wearing my best blue dress that night and my hair was pulled back with a ribbon. There was this boy, you see, that I thought I fancied and I wanted to look nice for him." She laughs lightly, amused at herself. "What was his name? I can't even remember. He always smelled like cloves because he chewed them to help this toothache he had."

"It wasn't Harry?"

"Nooo," she says with elongated emphasis. "That night, someone new, someone I had never met before, asked me to dance. That was Harry. Oh, this is horrible to admit, but I didn't want to dance with him. He was handsome enough, I suppose. His clothes were clean and starched, but old, I could tell. I had become a little high and mighty, spending all that time in that big house, living with one of the most respected families for miles around. But I didn't have a good excuse not to dance with him, and I had to be polite. So we danced. And, Louise, it was like time stood still."

Aunt Sophie holds her hands out and, with effort, makes them freeze for a moment, as if it's very important to her that I understand what she means. "He was such an incredible dancer. Never marry a man who can't dance, Louise. Never do it. He was much taller than me but he moved like grace. Fast dances, slow dances, whatever the band played. His hands felt rough even though he barely touched me. I learned he lived on a farm with his family. He was nineteen and the oldest of eleven. We talked and talked and laughed and laughed. He told me he had come to all the dances I came to, but never had the nerve to ask me until then. That made my heart flip. I was having the best night of my life, and I can say that with confidence, Louise, because I'm old. You can't say that now so don't even try."

"Yes ma'am," I say, but I think about it anyway.

"We danced five dances in a row, then the band leader said goodnight and the band played *I'll See You in My Dreams*. Harry took my hand and put something in it. It was a button, the little bone button I had lost off my sweater the first time I went into town with Anna and Charlotte. He said it was the first time he saw me. He worked afternoons at the local filling station and he said I walked right by him like a queen in a parade and my button fell right off. He was too shy to run after me, so he kept it in his pocket. He said he liked to take it out and think of me. That's when he said he loved me. I didn't know what to say. I started crying right then and there because I loved him, too. That's the way things happened back then."

She pauses to have a sip of coffee and it seems like she's going to stop right there. So I have to ask, "What happened next?"

She shrugs. "I left the next morning. I was so sad I couldn't say a word. And Mama always used to say I was awful to live with for the next few months. But then the next spring, Mama, Daddy, Charlotte and I went to church one Sunday and who should be there but Harry!"

"Here?" I say, smiling at her as I lick my finger and press it against my plate to pick up the last few crumbs from the pie crust.

"Yes, here. I couldn't believe it myself. He was staying at the boarding house that used to be on Carberry Avenue, where the Burger King is now, and old Mr. Johnson had hired him at his filling station. I couldn't go up and talk to him, of course, but Daddy went up and shook hands with him then introduced the rest of us. Charlotte knew who he was but I pinched her arm to stop her from saying anything. She said I left a bruise that lasted weeks."

"He came all the way up here just to be near you?" I shake my head. Of all the people I know, Great Aunt Sophie is the last person I would have suspected of harboring a romantic past.

"Yesiree. He sold all he had, saved up for months, and came to Clementine, North Carolina because he loved me. He called on me a few days later and we started courting. We had to wait nearly three years before we married. He had to save up for a house. Daddy approved of him because he was such a hard worker, and always so polite. Daddy bought a car, his first, and Harry always knew what to do for it. He could fix anything. Old Mr. Johnson eventually let Harry buy him out. Of course, when Harry died, I sold the station to Harlen Duckett. It's a good thing I never learned to drive, Louise. There's too many memories in the smell of a gas station."

She squints then looks down into her coffee cup. "Harry died two days after our twenty-first wedding anniversary. Did I ever tell you that? Life is like living in a house and death is like walking out the door. It's that simple. Harry walked out the door to go to work, and two hours later I got the call. It was a Thursday afternoon. But you want to know something? He loved more in his forty-four years than most people do in a lifetime. He did a lot of things well, Louise, but the thing he did the best was love me. How many people can say that?"

She picks up her cup and takes another sip. "Not many, I think."

I push my plate away and rest my chin in the palm of my hand, studying her. "Didn't you ever want any children?"

"I wasn't able," she says quietly and my heart breaks right then and there, so quickly I don't know what has happened at first. I didn't see it coming. No one ever told me. I always assumed it was because Sophie didn't like kids much—their unpredictability, the patience it took to deal with them. She was always exasperated with me when I was younger. I sit up and look at her, startled, sad, ashamed of myself for asking such a question.

She smiles at my silence. "Harry wanted them, but he said he didn't care so long as he had me. The year after he died, your grandmother Charlotte, who had moved to Maine with that no-good sailor man she married, died. She had one daughter, your mama. She came to live with me, then, and I consider her mine. She was my saving grace, I guess. And she gave me you, of course. So you liked the apple pie, did you?"

"It was wonderful," I say softly.

"Would you like another piece?"

"No, thank you."

"I'll pack up a piece for your mama," she decides with a nod. "You can take it over to her later."

"Okay."

She sighs and leans back in her chair. "Life has been mostly good, all in all."

I smile at her.

She laughs and reaches over to pat my hand. "Remember these things. I'm not going to be around forever." She suddenly looks over at the kitchen door. "Will you look at that! September's not even gone and October is already trying to come in!" I turn to see that the breeze has blown in some dry fallen leaves from her back yard, scattering them across the kitchen floor as if someone had walked in, but then turned and left before we could see him.

Sophie gets up and takes her broom from the broom closet, waving me back down in my attempt to help her.

"So what was your dream about?" I turn in my seat and ask her as she sweeps. "The dream about Harry."

She stops to think. Her breath is a little short already. "I dreamed we were dancing."

She's standing in the kitchen doorway, leaning on her broom, with the sun behind her. I can only see her silhouette, like an echo of her. Like a memory. Like a dream.

"You're a good girl, Louise," she says, walking out the door and disappearing.

Then the only thing left is a door full of sunshine.

Phyllis Schieber

The Manicurist

Special Excerpt from
THE MANICURIST
A Novel
Now Available in Trade Paperback and Ebook

Chapter One

First meetings could be so telling. Tessa knew this as well, if not better, than most. She was almost always accurate, tallying her small conquests according to conscience. After all, some conclusions, especially about people, were simply obvious. So when Tessa looked up from her work station in response to the woman's question about whether or not she needed an appointment for a plain manicure, and felt a stirring that was as inviting as it was alarming, she was prepared for something, though what she could not say. Before Tessa could say anything, the woman, just as cheerfully as she had the first time, asked her question again.

"Do I need an appointment for a plain manicure?"

The woman was in her sixties, perhaps younger, or maybe older. Tortoise shell glasses hung around her neck on a braided silver chain. Strands of dark hair, sharply streaked with grey, escaped from a loose bun that was pierced with elaborately painted black enamel hair pins. She was plump, which probably explained the skirt with the elasticized waist, and she immediately endeared herself to Tessa for no other reason than she seemed so comfortable with her appearance.

"Yes," Tessa said. She stood for no apparent reason. "Usually, especially on a Saturday. The receptionist, Kara, will be able to help you."

"But today is Thursday." The woman eyed Tessa's black slacks, black sweater and black flats, a combination that imitated what all the other workers were wearing. "Are you the manicurist?"

The collision of feelings that Tessa had first experienced made her suspicious, and she reminded herself that as a general rule, it was always best to honor instinct before emotion.

"Yes. I am," Tessa said, slightly flustered. "I'm the manicurist." Her pale cheeks felt hot, and she shook her head as though this could help her regain some composure. She wondered how this woman had managed to elude Kara. Anna Marie, the manager of Escape, a day spa, referred to Kara as St. Peter, insisting that no one could get by without some interrogation. "What I meant to say is that we don't encourage walk-ins, but it's been a slow day, and I just happen to have a cancellation. And, well, you're here."

The woman smiled so genuinely that Tessa smiled also and stooped to help her with the mesh shopping bag that kept toppling over.

"Thank you," she said. "That's very kind of you. Very kind." She offered her hand and said, "I'm Fran Hill."

Tessa casually ignored Fran's hand and set the mesh shopping bag against the wall. It was brimming over with fresh produce. She smelled garlic, onions and parsley, and something else she could not quite make out in a blend so compelling that her stomach growled.

"Excuse me," she said, deliberately patting her belly with both hands as a way to discourage any further contact. "I'm Tessa Jordan. So do you want a manicure?"

"Yes. I definitely need a manicure today." She tried to make it seem as if she had never offered her hand in the first place and fiddled with the waistband of her skirt. "Have you had your lunch, Tessa Jordan?"

"Well, no. Not yet."

Fran sat and rummaged through the bag, mumbling softly to herself, but in a way that invited eavesdropping. "One of these days I'm going to finally clean this bag out. Just dump everything. Way too much stuff." Finally, she pulled a Barbie thermos from the depths of the bag and set it on Tessa's table.

"Wait a moment. Just a second," Fran said. "Here now." She produced a cloth napkin and a soup spoon. "Try this." She unscrewed the lid of the thermos and inhaled deeply as the aroma was released.

"It does smell wonderful, doesn't it? Eat right from the thermos. I have gallons of the stuff at home. Whenever I'm in a tizzy, I seem to make soup. Too much soup, always too much. I have to give it away, so I can make more."

Hesitantly, Tessa took the spoon from Fran. Tessa had been witness to some strange things in the salon, but Fran and her soup were unprecedented. There seemed to be no way to politely discourage this woman from imposing her soup on strangers.

"Go on," Fran said. "I promise you it isn't poisonous. Once you get to know me you'll understand my need to feed everyone."

Once I get to know her? Tessa swallowed and tried to discreetly sniff the soup. "But isn't this your lunch?"

"Oh goodness, no. I've already had my lunch."

"Weren't you bringing it somewhere?"

"Yes, certainly, I was," Fran said in a tone that suggested Tessa had asked a really funny question.

"Well, it does smell wonderful, and I am hungry." She held the spoon to her lips, and was about to take her first mouthful. Then she looked at Fran again, more carefully this time, and said, "Have we met before?"

"No," Fran said. "I don't believe we have. Go on now, have some soup."

The soup was quite unlike anything Tessa had ever eaten. The stock was flecked with bits of yellow corn and something else that wasn't bacon but gave the broth a smoky flavor. Tessa bit hungrily into chunks of chicken and fat lima beans.

While Tessa ate, Fran studied the nail polish display. She held each bottle up to the light, squinted and then examined the label on the bottom, and said the names aloud. *Keys To My Karma, Bubble Bath, Spring Bloom, I'm Not Really a Waitress.* She seemed more interested in the names than in the colors. Fran waited quietly, a bottle palmed in her hand, for Tessa to finish. When the last drop had been scraped from the thermos, Tessa wiped the spoon with the napkin and screwed the lid back on.

"Did you have something in mind?" Tessa asked.

"Excuse me?"

"A color," Tessa said. "Did you have a color in mind?"

Fran plucked a bottle of pale lilac polish from the display. "I like this, Peach Daiquiri," she said, handing the bottle to Tessa. "You don't think it's too young for me, do you?"

Tessa set the bottle down and considered not only the question, but the woman who asked it. Tessa worried she would be unable to defend herself against Fran's intentions. Although Tessa was usually able to avert the onslaught of feeling that touch could deliver, Fran's will seemed very strong. It did not take much of either intelligence or vision to see that she had arrived with a purpose. Tessa stalled before beginning the manicure. She spent more time than necessary setting up her area and fussing with her tools. Fran watched these rituals without complaint. She had positioned the bottle of polish close to Tessa on the padded rest. Fran's hands remained on the table, anticipating Tessa's ministrations with patience. When Tessa saw this, she felt as if Fran had transformed the work station into an altar, a place where her jagged cuticles and careworn hands would be sanctified.

"Too young?" Tessa said. Her own hands felt unsteady. "I wouldn't worry about that if I were you. Nail polish is supposed to be playful."

Fran smiled. "I suppose it's an odd question anyway coming from someone who uses a Barbie thermos."

"Yes, I suppose so." Tessa laughed and took Fran's hands, relieved by the absence of turbulence that could only be interpreted as a good sign. "Besides, I've always liked Barbie. I think she's unfairly criticized."

"I wholeheartedly agree," Fran said.

Tessa dipped a Q-Tip into a dish of warmed cream and slathered the pink concoction around the tired edges of each of Fran's nails. She rubbed the cream in well and examined each nail carefully, scowling at the cuticles.

"I prefer to just push the cuticles back, but I might have to trim some of these hanging pieces."

"Do what you have to do," Fran said.

Tessa took an orange stick and began to gently push back at the cuticles. Then she selected a pair of clippers from her tray and deftly trimmed the stray pieces of skin. She excused herself and returned with a heated washcloth. She pressed the palms of her own hands together as if in prayer.

"Like this, please," she said.

Fran obeyed. Tessa wrapped the warm cloth around Fran's hands and patted gently. After a few moments, Tessa removed the cloth and dropped it into a bin. She drew a deep breath and reached for Fran's left hand. First, Tessa massaged each finger and then moved to include Fran's entire hand. It was a large hand that immediately made Tessa suspect that Fran was comfortable with delicate work. It was Tessa's experience that people with small hands had notions about their own talents that far surpassed reality. The feel of Fran's hand was both solid and flexible. It suggested the sort of courage that was easily masked as perseverance. But Tessa knew better. This was a strong woman, and though Tessa usually tried to disregard what she felt when attending clients, her thumb pressed hard on the center of Fran's palm, probing for details.

"Are you looking for something?" Fran asked.

Tessa dropped Fran's hands.

"Oh, please," Fran said. She reached across the table and held Tessa by the wrist. "I'm sorry. I didn't mean to startle you. Continue. Please."

Tessa was suddenly very tired. It had been some time since she had felt so overwhelmed by simple contact.

"Are you all right?" Fran said.

"I'm fine," Tessa said. She felt confused, not at all herself. "I'm sorry."

"Don't be, please. It's all right."

"I know a bit of palmistry," Tessa said. "It's interesting in my line of work. To know palmistry, I mean."

"Of course," Fran said. "It must make the work more meaningful."

"It can."

"And it's so convenient. What you do and all. So lucky for you to have your skills so closely intertwined," Fran said.

"Yes, I guess it is lucky," Tessa said. "Though I don't really consider myself skilled in palmistry. I took it up as a hobby."

She was talking too much even though she was eager to change the subject, or to stay on it. She wasn't sure at all. All her wires had been crossed somehow, and the good feelings she had toward Fran were less generous now.

"I love to pry," Fran said. "Especially if I could go unnoticed."

She had said this as though they were confidants, and it chafed at Tessa's nerves. She was exasperated all over again.

"I wasn't prying."

"Yes, of course," Fran said quickly, trying to be conciliatory. She offered Tessa both hands at once, but Tessa tapped them, dismissing them. "How did you learn palmistry?"

"I guess you do love to pry," Tessa smiled. "And you're quite good at it."

"Tell me about myself," Fran said.

"I just did," Tessa said more pointedly than she had intended.

But she was curious about this woman, and reached for Fran's left hand, holding it in both her own. Fran's thumb was firmly jointed. She was, as Tessa had expected, a woman of rare will. Tessa assessed the length of Fran's fingers, noting that the third finger was unusually long.

"Do you paint?" Tessa asked.

"I used to. Oils," Fran said. "Miniatures. I don't anymore."

"I thought you might have some experience with delicate work."

"Most people assume I'm clumsy."

Tessa nodded and then scrutinized Fran's nails. They were shell-shaped and finely hued, but sorely neglected. She massaged Fran's hands again, one at a time, but this time without any reserve. She tugged at each finger, waiting for Fran to speak, knowing she would.

"Are you self-taught?" Fran finally asked.

Tessa ignored the question and continued to tug. "Do you prefer square or round?"

"You decide for me."

Tessa picked up the scissors and made one single cut across each nail, leaving each square. Then she selected a file and began to work, filing directly across the flat edge of the nail in one constant direction. Fran closed her eyes and seemed to be sleeping. She even kept her eyes closed when Tessa followed through all the same steps with the left hand. Neither of them spoke. Tessa first buffed, and then applied nail strengthener, and a base coat. Finally, Tessa unscrewed the bottle of polish and applied the first coat, using three strokes on each nail. One at the center of the nail, and then one stroke on either side. She applied a second coat, and still no word passed between them. Fran's eyes remained closed, giving Tessa full access to scrutinize every detail while maintaining a careful distance. She had few friends, mostly because the exchange of confidences that was eventually expected was not something Tessa easily shared. Yet now, in spite of Tessa's typical wariness, she wanted some assurance that she would see Fran again.

"You'll need at least twenty minutes to dry," Tessa said. Fran's eyes remained closed, but Tessa knew how to open them. "My mother taught me about palmistry. She felt it would be useful."

Fran's eyes flew open. Now, she stared at Tessa's face, but said nothing. Nothing at all.

"Do you like your nails?" Tessa asked almost too cheerfully. "The color is good for you."

"Yes, they're lovely," Fran said. She gave them a perfunctory glance. "Very shiny and all, but I can't wait twenty minutes. I simply can't wait that long. I really have to be going."

Tessa calmly watched as Fran soaked one cotton ball after another in nail polish remover and rapidly wiped the polish from each fingernail.

"There now," she said when she was done. "That's better." She blew on her damp nails and waved her hands about a bit. "I hope you're not angry."

"Not at all," Tessa said, though she was a bit stunned. She shrugged. "They're your nails and your money."

Fran stood and rummaged in her purse. She withdrew a five-dollar bill and placed it under the bottle of polish.

"Thank you," Tessa said. "That's very generous. And thank you for the soup."

Fran screwed the lid back on the Barbie thermos and dropped it into her satchel. She took a bobby pin off one of the nearby trays and secured a wayward strand of hair. The whole time, she kept her eyes on Tessa. Fran groped around in her coat pocket and withdrew a piece of tattered red ribbon.

"I found this. I want you to have it."

Tessa made no move to accept the offering.

"Take it," Fran said. "I understand it's good luck to find something red. I was told that you should never walk by anything red that you see on the street. You can wear it as an amulet if you like. It's supposed to protect you from enemies."

Tessa's mother, Ursula, had believed in amulets, curses and charms, yet nothing had been able to save her.

"I don't have any enemies," Tessa said. She kept her voice calm even though her heart was racing. "At least none that I know of."

Nodding ever so slightly, Fran dropped the piece of red ribbon on Tessa's work station. Fran was out the door before Tessa could find the courage to even ask what had brought her to the salon since it was evident she had not come to have her nails done. Tessa picked up the ribbon and ran out of the shop after Fran.

"Mrs. Hill!" Tessa called after her. "Take your ribbon!"

But Fran was already more than halfway down the street. If she heard Tessa, Fran chose not to answer. Tessa just watched from the doorway. It was hard to imagine what she was in such a hurry to get to, and Tessa felt almost envious about whatever gave Fran such a sense of urgency. Tessa strained for a last glimpse of Fran, but she was nowhere to be seen. Then, just as Tessa was about to turn away, she saw Fran, crossing the street against the light. The mesh shopping bag was dangling off her arm. One hand was held aloft to slow oncoming traffic, the other hand was pressed against her forehead as a visor to block out any glare as she scanned the ground for new treasures. And Tessa felt oddly relieved, as if what had been lost was now found.

Chapter Two

Soon after Tessa's seventh birthday, her mother took her on an adventure. At least, that's what Ursula called it, *an adventure*. She must have planned it carefully, which was unusual for her. Dennis, Tessa's father, was out of town on business, and Ursula's mother Lucy, who lived with them, was fast asleep when Ursula carried Tessa away in the middle of the night. Tessa remembered waking in the back seat of their car. Her mother had been cautious, belting her in carefully and tucking the blanket around her on all sides even though it was a warm night.

For the first few moments after waking, Tessa said nothing, trying to get a sense of where they might be going and taking in her mother's mood. Ursula had an unlit cigarette dangling from her mouth and was listening to an Oldie's station. She was wearing a sleeveless lime-green dress, and her elbow rested on the open window. Her arms were firm and tanned, and she seemed happy as she hummed along to the music. The next time she looked in the rear view mirror, she saw that Tessa's eyes were open.

"You up, angel?" Ursula said. Tessa sat up and nodded. Ursula told her not to worry. "We're going on an adventure."

What Tessa did not know, could not have known, was that their so-called adventure was precipitated by her father's desperate threat to file for sole custody of Tessa and to have Ursula permanently hospitalized unless she promised to take her medication consistently.

Ursula could not have known that it was an empty threat. Dennis would never have followed through even though he feared the worst, the very worst. He loved Ursula too much, and yet not enough.

But that morning, Ursula was free. It was the summer, and everything was green and lazy. Ursula soon pulled over at a roadside diner. Before they got out of the car, Ursula helped Tessa change out of her pajamas and into shorts and a tee shirt. Ursula pulled everything, including socks and sneakers, from a big straw bag that was on the front seat. "I even brought your toothbrush and a tube of toothpaste. You can wash up in the bathroom before we have breakfast." She tousled Tessa's hair. "And Daddy says I'm not responsible."

Inside the diner, Ursula drank lots of black coffee and finally smoked her cigarette, taking one deep drag after another. She looked beautiful. Her hair was pushed out of her face and held back in a ponytail. Several of Tessa's fancy bobby pins kept the loose hairs in place. Ursula must have grabbed a handful of the pins for Tessa and stuck them along the sides of her own head for safekeeping. After they ate, Ursula lifted Tessa onto the hood of their car and combed her fine hair, arranging the pins in neat rows on each side of her head, congratulating herself out loud for thinking of everything. "I can handle this. I'm fine. I have everything under control."

For the first time since she woke, Tessa was afraid. Her mother's eyes were too bright, and her voice was too high.

Ursula recognized Tessa's apprehension and reassured her saying, "I'm fine. I just had one cup of coffee too many." Then she kissed Tessa once on each cheek. "We're going to see a friend of mine. She's from the center where I go for my appointments. She's nice. You'll like her. I promise, Tess." *Appointments.* That was the name they used for Ursula's visits to the psychiatrist. *Appointments.*

Minutes later they were off, driving up the New York State Thruway, passing villages and towns with names that Ursula said aloud, drawing out the syllables with exaggerated emphasis and making Tessa giggle. She was sitting up front now, and she kept checking the speedometer, just the way her father had taught her to do. *If Mommy goes above fifty, you scream. Fifty-five is the absolute limit, Tess. Thirty-five on the local streets. Got it?* Tessa breathed more easily when she saw they were cruising along at a safe speed.

Ursula knew what Tessa was doing, and she laughed and said, "You shouldn't spy on your mother like that."

But Ursula showed Tessa where to look on the map, and pretty soon they came up on the sign they were waiting for. Kingston. Route 28. Before long, they exited at Fleischmans, and Ursula followed some handwritten directions until she spotted the large, run-down house dotted with rickety fire escapes and said, "There it is!"

She seemed amazed that she had actually found the place. Mrs. Margaret's was a boarding house run by a stern local woman of the same name. Most of the guests were older women who escaped the sweltering heat of New York summers by buying a few weeks at Mrs. Margaret's. The accommodations were sparse, but there was plenty of company, and the mornings and evenings were cool and redolent with the scent of lilacs.

There were daisies growing along the dirt driveway, and a litter of new kittens trailed their mother. A large, white-haired woman came jauntily down the front steps, held out her arms to Ursula, and drew her into an embrace. "My dear, Ursula, I hoped you were really coming. And this must be your Tessa," she said in a voice so heavily accented that Tessa thought the woman must be playing. Effortlessly, especially for her size and her age, the woman crouched down to make herself eye level with Tessa and shook hands with her. "I'm Amelia. Come. Everyone's getting ready to prepare for lunch. We have our cooked meal in the afternoon, just like when we were in Europe." She slapped her other hand over Tessa's, and pulled her against her sturdy body. "Come. We can get to know each other while we cook."

Ursula and Tessa followed Amelia into the huge kitchen.

There must have been ten women inside, all wearing aprons and chatting as they sliced and chopped and diced. There were multiple burners, and steam rose from the pots, while oil sizzled and hissed from frying pans.

"It's a communal kitchen," Amelia explained. "Some of us share the cooking, but others make their own meals each day. I made some borscht yesterday. We'll have it cold with boiled potatoes. We just have to fry the chicken cutlets. You can bread them, Tessa. I'll show you how. I made the cucumber salad early this morning with cukes and dill fresh from the garden."

Ursula was fumbling in her purse, looking for a cigarette, which she found and rolled between her thumb and forefinger. With her free hand, she tapped Tessa on the shoulder and said, "Mind if I step out for a smoke?"

Tessa shook her head, just a bit uncertainly.

"You help Amelia," Ursula said. "I'll be right back."

"Shouldn't we call Daddy and Grandma?" Tessa said. "They might be worried."

Ursula's voice had an edge when she answered, and she rolled the cigarette faster between her suddenly tense fingers.

"You just worry about yourself," she said.

Amelia put her hands on Tessa's shoulders and steered her in the direction of the sink where Tessa was instructed to wash her hands before she was placed at the big butcher block in the center of the busy kitchen. The other women were delighted to see a little girl, and they huddled around Tessa as if she were an exotic bird. One woman brought a stool over so Tessa could reach the butcher block more easily. Another woman draped an apron around Tessa's neck and folded the starched fabric over several times at the waist, winding the strings around three times before finally tying them in a big bow.

"My best apron," the woman said proudly.

"Thank you," Tessa said shyly.

All the attention was overwhelming. It was not long before Tessa forgot all about her father and her grandmother. She even forgot about her mother. The women had her buttering noodles, folding dough for *pierogen*, and frosting a cake. They called out warnings to watch her fingers and to keep the stool steady. Tessa nibbled on bread hot from the oven, savored bites of paprika laden goulash, chewed mouthfuls of freshly grated cabbage slaw and sipped refreshing berry soup with dollops of homemade whipped cream. Before it was time to sit down to their meal, Tessa was sated.

She kept looking out the window for the swirls of smoke that she knew came from her mother's cigarette. Ursula did not come back inside for a long while. Finally, Tessa saw Amelia step outside. The smoke disappeared, and Ursula followed Amelia back into the kitchen. It might just have been Tessa's imagination, but the kitchen grew quiet as soon as Ursula came back in. At first, the women eyed Ursula suspiciously, gauging her ability to care for their new little charge. And Ursula, who understood and appreciated their concern, smiled widely and genuinely at all of them before grasping a steaming potato dumpling between thumb and forefinger and taking a big bite. "This is incredible," she said.

Immediately, the bustle resumed. Ursula and Tessa were ushered into the dining hall and seated while platters of food passed before them as if they were visiting royalty. The day passed in a haze of wonderful food and endless stories about the countries the women had left behind.

Ursula was different while they were there. By the next day, she hardly smoked at all, and she slept through the night. Perhaps it was the comfort of so many women gathered in one place, doing what women did best, taking care of each other, that made the difference. Perhaps it was all the good food and the clean air. Perhaps it was the absence of her history to haunt her. After night fell, Ursula and Tessa swam naked in the lake. They played with the kittens, whom Tessa named after the women she liked best--Amelia, Margaret, Dorothy, Sophie and Lily. She thought fleetingly about her father and her grandmother, but they seemed far away to her.

One night, after she had been bathed by one woman, powdered with scented talc by another, dressed and combed by still a third and, finally, read to by her own mother, Tessa fell into a deep and immediate sleep. But sometime in the middle of the night, she awoke.

Her father's voice was detached with controlled rage. "How could you, Ursula? It's no different from kidnapping."

Her grandmother was pleading with Ursula, trying to be conciliatory. "You should have phoned sooner. We were sick with worry, Ursula. You simply cannot stop taking your medication on your own and then just disappear."

When Tessa wandered in on them, rubbing her eyes, Dennis scooped her into his arms and pressed his face into her neck. "I'm sorry," Daddy," Tessa said. "I'm sorry you were worried."

Dennis could not hold back his tears. Lucy discreetly left the room.

Dennis went into the bedroom and took the blanket off the double bed that Ursula and Tessa had cozily shared with the kittens all week.

"I'm taking you home," he finally said.

Tessa cried. She wanted to stay. Her mother had been so calm and so happy all week. Tessa loved the kittens and Amelia and all the other women. And the food was so good, and so much fun to prepare.

"Let me stay, Daddy," she begged. "We're fine."

Ursula joined them in the bedroom and kept her eyes to the floor as she spoke. "I should have called. I'm sorry," she said. "I just didn't want it to end, the good feelings. I just didn't want them to end." And then Dennis pulled her so close that Tessa, between them now, could no longer tell where her mother's body began and her father's ended.

Chapter Three

Tessa waited for Fran to appear again, shopping bag in hand and wearing the same agreeable outfit. But Fran did not appear on Tuesday, nor did she materialize on either Friday or Saturday. By Sunday, Tessa was so confused by her own reaction that she decided to tell Walter about the strange woman who had come into the salon.

"I had the strangest client this week," she said. "She seemed to appear out of nowhere."

"Who was she?" he asked as though Tessa was deliberately withholding this significant piece of information.

As if on cue, Tessa sighed and said, "Never mind."

Walter narrowed his eyes and fixed his gaze on her with the sort of intentional restraint that comes from knowing someone well.

"You give up on me too easily, Tess."

She studied him with the sort of resoluteness she generally reserved for a particularly trying conversation with Regina.

"You need a haircut," she said.

"Ah," he said. "Diversion tactics. "Very clever. I'm impressed."

He ran his hand through his almost completely grey hair. He was still handsome, still drew attention from women, both young and old. And while Tessa loved him, more than she had ever loved him, his pragmatism often infuriated her. No matter what they argued about, it always came back to these two issues: Walter's predisposition for prudence and clarity, and Tessa's reckless disregard for both, compounded by a lingering melancholy that left him with the feeling that he was in some way responsible.

"Well, *that's* something," she said. "It's not that easy to impress you."

When she had first identified Walter as the object of her love, everything had seemed possible. The world seemed renewed. But eventually she realized that no one, not even Walter, could change her past.

"I'm listening," he said. "Impress me some more."

"The woman who came into the salon," Tessa said, measuring

each word so that he would not misunderstand. "She seemed to know me... although I know I never met her before."

"How is that possible?"

She knew exactly what he feared. Her premonitions had the potential to alter the shape of their lives. He worked too hard to stay within the lines to invite any opportunity for variance. Walter did not want to know the future before it was upon him.

He had no investment in Tessa's intuitiveness. Any time she told him something that she sensed, he accused her of violating people's privacy. His response was not surprising. She had been groomed to hide her perceptions from everyone. Ursula knew better than anyone that it was an affliction to be out of the ordinary. She warned Tessa to keep her gift under her hat, often scribbling notes to her with "QT" in boldly exaggerated letters. It was advice that Tessa took to heart. She never allowed her presentiments to enter the forefront unless they were persistent, like the time she was having coffee with Janine, a neighbor, and an image of a pool and a toddler, floating face down in the water, began to hover near Janine's head. Almost faint with apprehension, Tessa asked Janine if she was thinking of putting in a pool. Janine laughed and said that she thought about a lot of things, but that, no, they weren't planning on it anytime soon. When Tessa asked if Janine knew anyone who had a pool, she said, yes, her sister-in-law had a pool. She was watching Janine's kids that morning. One of them, Malcolm, was only two.

"Call her," Tessa had said, trying to hide her panic. "Call her right now. I think the gate is unlocked."

For whatever reason, Janine did not question Tessa's urgency. Perhaps Janine was one of the few who understood and valued all ways of knowing, or perhaps she saw the fear in Tessa's eyes and responded. As Janine dialed her sister-in-law's number and began to speak, the images that had been floating above her head began to twirl. Tessa wanted to reach for them and contain them as if doing so would guarantee Malcom's safety.

"Mary? Is Malcom with you? He's outside with Leo? I think the gate to the pool is open." Janine had looked at Tessa. "I don't know. I just had a feeling. Hurry, would you? I'll hold on." She'd pressed her phone against her chest and in a faltering voice said, "She's gone to check." Janine held the phone to her ear and said, "Yes? Mary? Thank goodness. Don't cry. It's okay. Is Malcolm okay? Leo? I'll be there.

Don't cry. It's okay."

Janine never asked Tessa how she knew though from now on Janine was mindful of Tessa in an almost reverential way. It seemed to Tessa that Janine could never do enough for her after that incident when all Tessa really wanted was to pretend that nothing out of the ordinary had happened. Of course, it was too late for that.

Later that evening, she had told Walter about the incident. He'd congratulated her and then said, "I thought you were going to put a stop to that."

Furious, Tessa asked him if he would have preferred that she let the little boy drown.

Walter had said, "Of course not," but they both knew he would have preferred that Tessa was not the one to divine the future.

It was a position to which he remained persistently loyal. Even now, the realization that Tessa felt something compelling about the strange woman worried Walter enough to make him take notice.

"How is anything possible?" she said.

She saw him bristle at this question. In some ways, Tessa knew, Walter was right to still distrust her. Though he insisted they were meant to be together, and that he had loved her from the start, she would never be certain if he would have loved her on his own, or if her crafty impositions on him had influenced their future.

"Who would know that better than you?" Walter said.

"No one, I guess," Tessa said. "No one understands the impossible better than I do. Is that the answer you're looking for?"

"I stopped looking for answers long ago," he said.

"Well," Tessa said, "maybe that was a mistake."

Tessa first saw Walter in a framed photograph on the piano in his parents' music room and immediately dreamed of seeing her own photograph included in the Jordan family gallery. Her own family gallery was scant and unsatisfying—a few snapshots of herself or her grandmother taken by friends at holiday gatherings with "Guess who?" scrawled in assorted unfamiliar handwriting. No one had ever bothered to date these pictures, making it even more difficult to place them. And while photographs of Tessa's smiling parents were displayed on the mantle in her grandmother's house, they seemed frozen in a time she could barely remember.

Mrs. Jordan, Kit to her friends, was Walter's mother, as well as the school nurse. When Tessa was a senior, she began to make constant trips to the infirmary. These visits had little to do with illness and more to do with the serious way Kit Jordan listened. Unlike Tessa's grandmother, Mrs. Jordan was always calm. Tessa complained of headaches and dizziness and was allowed to rest, sometimes with a cool compress on her forehead. Mrs. Jordan knew that Tessa's parents were dead before even checking a record. The rumors about Tessa's parents had almost mythical proportions in their village. And, as is the nature with all rumors, those about Tessa's parents were viciously exaggerated.

Tessa's losses had deeply touched Mrs. Jordan, and she offered the quiet, well-mannered girl a job babysitting her own Althea on Saturday nights. Althea protested that she didn't need a babysitter (after all, she was almost ten), but after meeting Tessa, Althea's objections stopped. They got along like friends, and Althea looked forward to their evenings together. Walter, Althea's older brother, was away in Chicago at law school, and Tessa began waiting for him to come home the moment she saw his photograph. She liked the way he seemed embarrassed by the camera's attention on him, yet still determined to have the last word. He had a sort of half-crooked smile that was disarmingly flirtatious—something that would allow her to later suggest it was he who had seduced her.

Tessa was seventeen then. She had been kissed by boys and had felt their excitement as they pushed against her, signaling their needs. But as soon as she saw the picture of Walter, she knew that everything up until then had been a rehearsal for her life with him. Walter would be hers. She thought only of him and waited. He would be everything to her. She would be everything to him. Everything. Together, they would have a perfect, normal family just like his. Her whole awful past would be vindicated by a blissful life with Walter Jordan and his flawless family.

Tessa knew exactly what Walter was worried about. It was always the same whenever anything occurred that referenced Tessa's insight. And even though he said very little on the subject of her mother, whatever he said, or didn't say, was always cautionary. He wasn't much of a talker, her Walter. Still, early in their marriage, he'd approached Lucy with his concerns. He wanted Tessa to thrust aside her preoccupation with Ursula's disappearance and focus on her own family. Walter told Lucy that he simply could not get through to Tessa.

Lucy made repeated calls to Tessa, obviously at Walter's prompting, urging her granddaughter to remember her poor mother's end. "And think of the baby," Lucy pleaded. "Think of Regina." Tessa promised although she knew that no one had the power to conceal something if it chose to reveal itself.

And here they were, all these years later, still trying to make sense of that which could not be explained.

Walter tried to bring the conversation back to the unidentified client.

"I'm just attempting to understand why someone would come into the salon pretending not to know you when she does."

"There was just something about that woman," Tessa said. "I can't let go of it. She knows something."

"About what? Did you feel threatened by her?"

Tessa thought about Fran's soup and was immediately hungry for it again.

"No, I felt surprisingly relieved."

"I'm sure it was nothing," he said. "Just coincidence."

"Probably," Tessa allowed. "Just coincidence."

Unconvinced by her tone, he persisted. "How could she know you? Did you recognize her?"

"No. I just had the feeling that she knew me. Almost as if she'd been watching me for a long while."

"It's very unlikely," he said.

"I'm sure you're right," she said. "Very unlikely."

They looked at each other and looked away. Tessa picked up the newspaper and turned the pages though she stared off into the distance.

"If this is about your mother, Tess, I want you to let it go. Can you promise me you'll let it go?"

There it was. Walter had uttered the unmentionable.

"I don't make promises. You should know that by now."

"Make an exception." His voice was steely. Even he heard it and flinched, but he was staunch in his request. "Just this once."

The first time she met Walter he was home for Thanksgiving, and he had brought his girlfriend Charmaine. Tessa immediately noticed Charmaine's dark, exotic looks. Her hair hung like black satin across her broad shoulders and down her strong back. She was tall and muscular; in short, a woman who commanded attention.

Tessa ignored Charmaine and focused on Walter. It was as though he already belonged to her. *I want you*, she thought over and over. She said his name forwards and backwards, *Walter, Walter, Retlaw, Retlaw*. She repeated to herself, *I want you. I want you. Walter, Walter, Retlaw, Retlaw*. Her mother had kept a book of spells and charms hidden, but Tessa knew all about it. Dennis forbade Ursula to poke around in that magic nonsense, but she did anyway. It was such a relief from everything else she heard inside her head.

So when Kit Jordan told Tessa that they would not need her Saturday or Sunday, Tessa knew she had to act quickly. Soon Walter would return to Chicago. On Friday morning, Tessa brushed her fine, light brown hair and applied some mascara. She dabbed some blush on her cheeks. Her lips were good, full and surprisingly pink. And her nose was straight and strong, as was her jaw line, a complement to her long neck. She stared at her image in the mirror. She was still so colorless, so pale, next to Charmaine.

The Jordan home was in the most expensive part of the village, facing the Hudson River and the Palisades. As she walked, hating the cold and especially the winter wind blowing off the river, Tessa went over and over what she would say to Walter. The sun was so bright that Tessa made her hand a visor, shielding her eyes from its glare.

When Walter opened the door, he seemed momentarily confused, trying to place her.

"Theresa isn't it?" he said. "Thea's nanny."

"Her babysitter. And it's Tessa, not Theresa." She hated herself for sounding so petulant. "It's not a very common name."

"I'm sorry. I'm not very good with names. Come in. Come in. It's freezing out."

He motioned her inside. She followed him, rubbing her arms through her coat.

"Everyone's out at the mall. Were they expecting you?"

"No. I wasn't expected." Tessa felt ridiculous. "I came to talk to you, Walter. I came to see you."

"Me?"

"May I hold your hands?" she asked.

"What for?" he said.

"Just for a moment."

"Are you going to read my palms?" His smile came and went as quickly as his next breath.

"That too," Tessa said with such conviction that Walter could think of nothing else to say.

He held out his hands, palms down, as most men often did, in what Tessa always saw as a final act of self-defense. Tessa took his hands and immediately turned them so his palms faced up. She rubbed each of her thumbs across the width of his smooth skin, jolted by what their touch roused. Her thumbs followed the same separate path across each upturned hand. First, she moved from his wrists slowly up towards the heel of his hand where she briefly lingered before cautiously exploring his Line of Life. She relaxed when she saw that it was both long and clear.

She closed her eyes to give her the courage she needed to venture across his Line of Heart. Yet even closed eyes could not divert the sudden pull she felt everywhere as she traced the course of her own future. He pulled back slightly, but she held on. She studied his palm. It was as she had expected. His Line of Heart seemed to spring from Saturn, just below the fleshy part of his middle finger, evidence that Walter could be self-centered. And there was more. His palms and fingers were slightly tapered. He would never be very good with money. Tessa found no surprises in Walter's hands. She had sensed all this about him the first time their hands grazed each other's in their cursory introduction. His imperfections did not concern her.

"Are you done?" Walter said.

"Yes," she said.

"Have your worst fears about me been confirmed?" he teased uneasily.

"Yes."

She could not yet tell him that palmistry was a ruse, a way to gain entry into the everyday world and quiet suspicions others might have about her. Palmistry merely verified what she already knew. Yet Tessa did not want to deceive Walter from the start, at least not completely.

"Sometimes I sense things about people," she said.

"I think they'll be back soon," he said nervously. "My mother, that is, and Charmaine and Thea."

"I sense things about you," she said, ignoring his warning.

"And I sense things about you," he said.

Walter, Walter, Retlaw, Retlaw.

It was as though he could hear Tessa's voice inside his head.

"Did you say something?" he asked.

Tessa shook her head.

"You're so pale," he said. "Do you feel well?"

"No. I'm fine. I'm always pale."

She worried that he was comparing her to Charmaine.

"Charmaine doesn't love you," Tessa said.

"I intend to marry Charmaine," he said, pulling himself up to his full height as if to defend himself against Tessa. "I've already told my mother. She's offered my grandmother's ring."

Tessa pretended she had not heard.

"I've never met anyone like you," he said.

"I know," she said so simply that it required no further response.

He touched her face, pausing briefly, before drawing back. In that fleeting, awkward moment, Tessa wondered if he was recalling Charmaine's exotically dark skin, her physical strength, and her self-confidence. Tessa knew she would have to rely on different attributes to win Walter.

"You lost both your parents in a car accident, didn't you?" he said.

"My father died in the accident. My mother disappeared," Tessa said. "I was told that she died some time later."

It was the first of many half-truths to come. She told herself it was different than lying. Looking back on that first time with Walter, Tessa wondered how different it might have been if she had told him the whole truth instead of a half-lie, half-truth—it didn't really matter which way she said it—not then and not later.

"Poor Tessa," he said.

"Yes," Tessa said. "Poor me."

"Maybe I've been too hasty about Charmaine."

"Maybe."

"Would you like to stay and have leftovers with us?"

"Yes," Tessa said. "I'd like that very much."

And there it was. The fairytale ending to the story Tessa had already written from start to finish. She had done nothing more than to allow Walter to play hero to her defenselessness. She had made herself vulnerable, allowed him to possess her. His family would embrace her, welcome her into the fold, and they would all live together, happily ever after. The ordinary existence she longed for was within reach at last.

Tessa and Walter had their own piano now; their own family photos as well, though none of them were of Walter's parents or sister.

It was as though they had never existed. There were photographs of Regina at every stage of her babyhood. Several of her as a sweet infant swaddled in a pink blanket; another of her at six months, yawning widely and wearing a headband with a daisy on one side. And, Tessa's favorite, Regina smiling up at her from Grandma Lucy's arms. Regina's toddler years were captured in photographs of her in various Halloween costumes from the inevitable lime green lizard to the irresistibly endearing ballerina, followed by pictures of them at the beach with Regina in inflatable orange water wings. Tessa loved the photo of the three of them on a hiking excursion. Regina, strapped to Tessa's chest, facing forward, her chubby legs dangling from the carrier. Walter, standing behind Tessa, hunched forward with his arms wrapped around the two of them, making them appear to be some sort of mythical three-headed creature. They look indescribably content.

In later pictures, Regina, scowling and semi-toothless, her curls spilling out of a Yankee baseball cap, arms crossed defiantly, dares the camera with her flashing blue eyes. The photographs of her as an emerging adolescent, playing the role of Sarah Brown in a school production of *Guys and Dolls,* gave hints of the beauty that she would soon become.

Interspersed among these were pictures of Tessa as a serious child, standing between her parents or clinging to Ursula's side, arms wrapped around her mother's waist. One of Tessa's favorite pictures was her parents' wedding photo. Ursula, incandescent in a short, white eyelet dress, gazing up into the joyful expression on Dennis's face. They look luminous together, like every other young couple on their wedding day. It was this more than anything else that Tessa had always loved about the photograph. There was nothing in the photograph that foretold the future that would dismantle their anything but ordinary lives.

But Tessa could never deny how their futures had unfolded, just as she could not pretend that pushing forward with Fran might catapult them all into a place where no one wanted to be. Walter's love and commitment had been tested many times, and Tessa had to wonder how many more trials he could endure. She supposed they were about to find out.

"I think I have made a lot of exceptions for you," she said, giving the photographs a cursory glance. "And what if it is about my mother?"

"What are you saying?"

"I'm not saying anything. I'm just suggesting that there is something about this woman that can't be ignored."

"What exceptions have you made?"

"What?" Tessa said.

"You said you've made exceptions for me. What exceptions have you made?"

"I don't know. Lots."

"Name one," Walter said.

"I haven't turned you into a frog."

Walter laughed. "Well," he said. "The only explanation for that is that you don't know how."

"Don't bet on it," she said.

"I'm not a betting man."

"Now, *that's* not true either."

"I just want to say one thing," Walter said. "What if this woman never comes back to the salon?"

"That's not possible," Tessa said.

"But what *if?*" he persisted.

"She'll be back. It's only a matter of when."

"I wish you would let this go," he said. "You could make yourself unavailable."

Tessa didn't answer.

"Tess?"

She shook her head, not with spite, but with resignation. There was no choice, and there were no words to make that any more understandable.

Walter stood, looked down at her while his hand moved over her head, smoothing her silky hair. He bent all the way over and kissed the top of her hair right where her part fell, exposing her scalp, and then left the room without looking at her or saying a word.

Once, a long time ago, Tessa had believed that Walter could change her life. She had believed that belonging to his perfect family would obliterate everything about her own flawed history. But the Jordans had never lived up to Tessa's expectations. On the contrary, they had betrayed her, leaving her with yet more loss to mourn. Photographs could be so deceptive, capturing a mere moment in time, not nearly substantial enough to invite assurances about the future.

Tessa walked over to the piano and looked at her parents' wedding picture. Impulsively, she picked it up and held it towards the sunlight, streaming in through the bay window. Perhaps there was something she had missed in her mother's eyes, her father's stance. But there was nothing. They were radiant, hopeful.

Gently, Tessa placed the photograph back on the piano. Something else was happening now. Tessa could feel the shift, the slight difference in the way everything felt. And it had everything and nothing to do with Fran.

About the Authors

Sarah Addison Allen is the New York Times bestselling author of GARDEN SPELLS, SUGAR QUEEN and THE PEACH KEEPERS (Ballantine Books)

Augusta Trobaugh is the acclaimed author of southern novels including SOPHIE AND THE RISING SUN, (Dutton) narrated by the late Rue McClanahan for audio and optioned for film.

Kathryn Magendie is the bestselling author of TENDER GRACES, also SECRET GRACES and SWEETIE, all for Bell Bridge Books.

Phyllis Schieber is the author of WILLING SPIRITS, (William Morrow) THE SINNER'S GUIDE TO CONFESSION, (Berkley Books) and a summer 2011 title from Bell Bridge Books, THE MANICURIST.

CPSIA information can be obtained at www.ICGtesting.com
Printed in the USA
LVOW06s2154060414

380579LV00003B/300/P